FAIR HELEN

ANDREW GREIG

A veritable account of
'Fair Helen of Kirkconnel Lea'
scrieved by Harry Langton

Quercus

First published in Great Britain in 2013 by Quercus Editions Ltd
This paperback edition published in 2014 by

Quercus
55 Baker Street
7th Floor, South Block
London
W1U 8EW

A CIP catalogue record for this book is available
from the British Library

PB ISBN 978 1 78206 673 6
EBOOK ISBN 978 1 78206 637 8

10 9 8 7 6 5 4 3 2 1

Printed and bound in Great Britain by Clays Ltd, St Ives plc

Typeset by Ellipsis Digital Limited, Glasgow

For Lesley.

*i.m. Gavin Wallace, who cared for our
literature and its makars.*

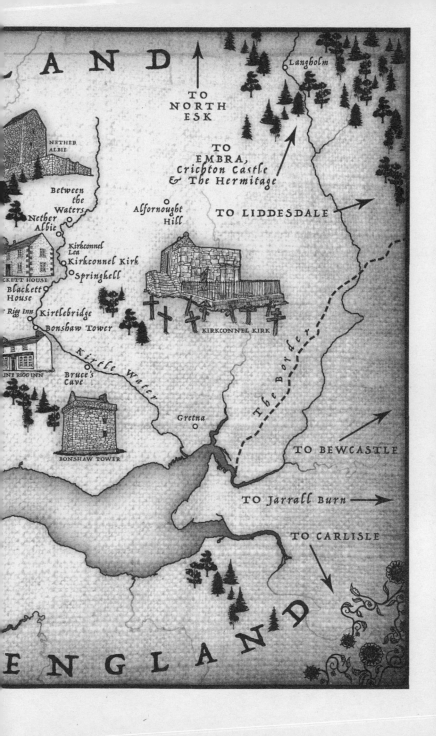

A glossary of Scots dialect words and their approximate English meanings is placed at the back of this book.

'I have gathered a garland of other men's flowers, and nothing is mine but the cord that binds them.'

Michel de Montaigne

Fair Helen of Kirkconnel Lea

O gin I were where Helen lies!
  Night and day on me she cries;
O that I were where Helen lies,
On fair Kirkconnel Lea.

Curst be the mind that thought the thought,
Curst be the hand that fired the shot,
When in my airms burd Helen dropt,
Wha died for sake of me.

I lighted down, my sword did draw,
I hacked him in pieces sma,
I hacked him in pieces sma,
For her that died for me.

O Helen fair, beyond compare!
I'll make a garland of thy hair,
To bind my heart for evermair,
Until the day I die.

O gin I were where Helen lies!
Night and day on me she cries;
And I am weary of the skies
Of fair Kirkconnel Lea.

'Ane doolie sessoun . . .'

These winter morns are bitter cold and the draughts unstoppable under the roof of Hawthornden. My breath puffs clouds as I scrape clear the garret window, ice slivers melt under yellowed fingernails.

Yet today I am snug as a bug on a dug. I have donned shirts, a shift, my disreputable jerkin, two nethergarments. A quilted bunnet sits cosy on my head. A hefty plaid borrowed from Drummond is happed round my shoulders, and falls clear to the floor. What remains of my right hand is warm in wool, as are my feet and scrawny thrapple.

Even the hot wine I fetched all the way up from the kitchens has remnants of warmth.

In my green days, when morns were cold and the world much awry, I would scurry about trying to keep warm and right it. I complained bitterly (if silently) at the injustice of it all. Now I shrug and don more clothing – resignation, or wisdom?

Having little time left for either, I sit amid so many layers and furs I am more bear than man. The weather – sleet driven out of the North. The past — ever-present. I look down at it from this high, enwrapped place, and note how readily my living breath fogs the view even as I contemplate how to begin.

Ane doolie sessoun to ane carefull dyte
Suld correspond and be equivalent . . .

Or as we say in present days, now the Kingdoms are united and the Court gone south, 'A dismal season to a woe-filled work should correspond and be equivalent.' Ah, Robert Henrysoun, what a falling off is here!

I lean forward to wipe the glass with the back of my good fist, before at last commencing the story that is not mine yet remains the only story of my life.

PEEL TOWER

I had not seen Adam Fleming since his mother's wedding. He had been silent and inward then, remote across the crowded hall. Tall, slim and agile, in his black cloak of grieving for his father, tallow hair cut straight across in the new Embra style, dagger in embroidered pouch, he had been every inch the young Borders gallant.

Now as I stepped onto the battlement of the peel tower, my dearest friend stood mouth agape with muddy britches, un-- matched slippers, his shirt stained and torn. Short sword stuck skew-whiff in his belt, he was bouncing and catching an old cork tennis ball as though his life depended on it.

And he was right, I concede now to the bleary pane, the scratching quill. It probably did.

He looked up at me. His eyes flickered over the laddie who had showed me up. He bounced the ball off the bale-fire cage, caught it, swayed a little. So it is true, I thought. Not yet noon and drink taken.

'It is Harry Langton, sir,' the boy said uncertainly.

'No doubt, no doubt.' Adam kept stotting and catching the ball. In our university days *tennez royale* had been all the rage, along with the speaking of French to mask our uncouth mother tongues. He had been effortlessly good with racquet, rapier and small pipes, while I was a dogged trier.

Plus ça change, I murmur to none, and huddle deeper within coarse blankets. This stern house is silent. It is hours till chapel service, which I attend for the sake of dinner if not my soul. No choice but to sit here and feel again, like a dirk slipped between the ribs, dismay as he cut me dead.

The sleekit laddie — Watt his name, and I regret his end — hesitated. Judging me hairmless, he turned and padded down the tower stair. I heard him *slap slap slap* on the worn sandstone, hesitate at the trip-step, then gone.

Stott stott stott of the tennis ball into the drunken hand of my bedraggled lost friend. I could smell stale wine across the distance between us. Still, he never fumbled the bouncing ball, even when he looked out absently over the valley, the Kirtle burn, the woods and braes of his small corner of the Borderlands.

He flicked the ball between his legs, caught it as it rebounded off the castellation, then hurled it far into the walled garden. He turned to me and his grey-green eyes were now bright, perhaps too bright.

'Harry,' he said quietly, and we embraced. 'Thank God you are here,' he murmured, breath hot in my ear. Hot, but not vinous. Only his stained shirt stank of claret. 'I need your help and counsel, old friend.'

4

Once he had said those words I could not have ridden back to the city, the courts, the college where we had once disputed fine points with words and argument, not the finer point of dagger and short sword. In any case, I was not quite the free man my friend imagined.

'So,' I said. 'You seek advice from the daft, or a loan from the penniless?'

'Still poor and honest, then?'

'Poor, at least,' I said.

He smiled, though I had spoken but careful truth. From the courtyard below a lassie's song rose. An axe thudded in the stables, kye moaned from Between the Waters. Doos flew in and out of the storey below, all grey flutter and reproach. The pale sun lit on our faces, the Kirtle water glittered, and for a moment the Borderlands lay at peace.

He slung his arm across my shoulder, the way he would when we were students, no more than boys, slipping into the Embra night, bound for mischief, or heading into the examination hall of the Town's College.

'I am in love,' he announced. 'And they mean to kill me.'

I addressed the less implausible first. 'Who is she?'

'Helen.' He turned his gaze away from the circling pigeons. 'Helen Irvine, of course.'

'Ah,' I said, trying to sound surprised. 'Fair Helen.'

And who else would he have set himself on but my childhood confidante, Cousin Helen? Even in the city I had heard the new flower of Annandale lit soul, heart, loins. And she was Irvine of Bonshaw's daughter, and the families were long at feud.

'So Will Irvine plots to kill you for fancying his daughter? Even by Borders standards that is high-handed.'

I was trying to calm his fervour, and my own.

Adam shrugged. 'Feud is like fire in a peat-bank. It smoulders, it burns, it sleeps again. Irvine could perhaps be persuaded to the match – despite my mother's remarriage, I am still heir to these small lands – were there not another asking for Helen.'

'Who?'

'Rob Bell.'

'Ah.'

In student days I had passed Robert Bell of Blackett House, striding down the crowded High Street past St Giles, sword set high in his belt, Flemish pistolet on a sling, swerving not a jot for anyone but Jamie Saxt. Upon his father's death amid a storm of daggers in a wynd in Gala, he had lately become the Bell heidsman. Folk said young Robert Bell had a future, though most hoped it short.

'Bell's not half the swordsman he thinks he is.' Adam grinned, looked carefree for a moment. 'He swings that long pistol like it was his cock, and we are meant to be impressed.'

'They say he shot one of the Farrer boys across the mart square in Moffat. I am impressed enough.'

'A coward's weapon, killing a man at a distance.'

'What would you do if he points his pistol at you, out of sword's range?'

'Duck, of course!'

After our laughter, a shout came faint from the far woods about Kirkconnel Lea. Blackett House, set high above the Kirtle water, was but another call away. From its watchtower on a calm day, a pistol shot would carry to Kirtlebridge, making one I cared for there start at her work. And if she in turn stood in her inn courtyard and loosed off a shot, the report would carry to the Irvines' stronghold at Bonshaw. (How small a stage our drama treads – Embra apart, one could ride to any of the principal locations, even the English border, within the hour. Aristotle would have approved.)

A horse whinnied in response, then silence but for the faint *wheesh* of wind and water that, like feud and memory, pour forth unceasing in the Borderlands.

'You smell like a coach-house drain,' I said. 'People say you are a sot, and not right in the head since your father died. You muck about with tennis balls. You can't be arsed to dress mannerly. You neither fight nor work nor study. What use—?'

He put his hand, long-fingered, scarred and weathered already, on mine.

'I think some among my family seek to kill me,' he said.

'In a shirt like that, I am not surprised.'

His dagger point lay at my throat. His eyes were watchfires lit.

'Dinna fuck wi' me, Langton.'

I looked him in the eye, wondering at the rumours I had heard of his state of mind these last eighteen months. I kept my voice steady as a man may with steel at his thrapple.

'Does Helen Irvine not love you even as she teases you?'

His head went down, his shoulders shook. Now he was not greiting but laughing, his moods shifting like an aircock.

'She claims she does, the flirt!' His arm about my shoulder. 'I have missed you as I have missed the better part of myself.'

Fortunately, he was already turning away. As we headed for the stairwell, he murmured in my ear what he was about this very evening, and my part in it. Then we clattered down the echoing stone, past Watt loitering ahint the portal, and we were laughing and chattering like lightsome young men, careless of present danger and future grief.

The chapel bell tolls, my stomach rumbles. My host William Drummond asks little of me but that I organize his library and correspondence, look over his Latin essays that seek to harmonize Crown, Church and the People (not likely at the moment), and offer some helpful though not overly critical responses to his English verses in the Petrarchan manner. He likes having this relic of lang syne living in his garret, so he and his friends may enjoy tales of lawless days that now appear romantic. But he does insist I attend household services, which are of the unheated, penitential sort.

I sit a minute longer by my morning's work, seeing again Adam Fleming, mouth agape as though munching empty air as I first stepped onto the peel-tower battlement.

We have made a start.

TRYST

Fair Helen, cousin Helen, Helen Irvine, Erwyn,* Irwin, Ervyn, Irving, of Bonshaw or Kirkconnel or Springkell – call her as you will, she did once live and breathe, and when she smiled the joy of the world declared itself at the in-by of her mouth.

She is long gone, yet still her step stirs dust along the whispering gallery. The folk tales and the ballad have many versions, the chaste, the bawdy and the sensational ('*He cuttit him in pieces sma*'), none of them sound and siccar. I, who was there at the margins, have come if not to set the record straight then at least to add my honest errors.

She was born plain Helen, daughter of Will Irvine of Bonshaw. She would die Fair Helen of Kirkconnel Lea. Her whole life extended twenty-one years wide by some five miles long, all it takes to get from Bonshaw to Kirkconnel.

In the days before her blooming, when we still shared much,

* *Erwyn* – a green margin, as in *Eire*. Indeed in my mind she is limned in green.

she told me of the first time she came to know herself living – our second birth in this world.

She said she was by the peat-stack ahint the barnkin wall, setting her nose to smells of field and burn and muir. She rubs her hands on the peats, enjoying the crumble and mush. She sniffs her palms. The lines are now brown as burns after heavy rain. She studies how they run down the wee braes and heuchs of her hands.

The burn below their house is the Kirtle. A kirtle is also what she pulls on after her smock then waits for her mother to lace up. The burns in her palm, the peat they burn in winter – how oddly things come together!

Doos clatter from the peel tower, and for the first time she kens herself.

She sits on in the yard, crumbling and rubbing the fields in her hands. A telling-off will come, for breaking up the peat, for getting her kirtle mucky, but for now everything is connected and siccar.

So she told me as we sat within Bruce's cave, cross-legged in the stone-smelling dimness, hearing the river crash by below, her thin child shoulder warm on mine.

Adam and I waited below Kirkconnel Brig. The arch over our heads rippled with reflected afterglow from the western sky. I was being bitten by things near-invisible, he was tight-strung in the gloaming, exultant in the way of those who are about to learn they are loved.

He had changed shirt and britches, run fingers through hair, dragged it down about his lugs then carefully adjusted it to show the lobes and the gold snake ring he had bought from a Romany in the Lawnmarket. Green half-cloak about his shoulders, dagger at his hips, he was quite the thing of the *ton*. Apart from the fact we wore heavy boots and were lurking under a bridge on the margin of his violent rival's lands, we might have been two young callants about to salute the salons and bawdy houses of Embra.

Mostly we were silent, for each had much to think about. On our way here, skulking like broken men as we followed the Kirtle water downstream from Nether Albie, pushing birch and elder aside, alert to bird cries, starting at roe moving in the woods, he had been whingeing. Of late Helen had insisted on secret trysting, and he did not like it.

'Do you think her honest?' he had demanded of me as we set out from the family compound, supposedly to check the kye safe-gathered in the in-by pastures. 'At Langholm mart a fort-night back, she was with her father and Bell, laughing! She gave me the high nod as though we were scarcely aquaint. She says she needs time to prevail upon her father, to end the blood-feud and help my family be reinstated. I do believe her!'

And who would not believe Helen's eyes so wide and candid? We strode the old Roman Way where puddles shook in the wind, scrolling up the sky. I wrapped my old cloak round me, said nothing.

'Then I think she is waiting to see the airt of the wind.'

I said nothing, knowing lovers to be touchy. When we were bairns I learned my fair cousin cheated, so innocently and so well, at our games of Dirk, Paper, Stane, or Parlour-Men. Through summers spent in Annandale among my mother's people, we had been close, maybe very close. It had gone hard each year when Lammastide came, and I went back to my life in the city.

'Can I trust her, Harry?'

Startled, I stepped into a puddle, looked down to see my boots muddied and the evening sky shattered.

'I would trust her mind to pursue whatever ends her heart was set on,' I replied carefully. 'What that is, you should ken better than I.'

'I swear her beauty is in her soul!' he exclaimed. 'She makes aa' this —' he gestured at the escarpment, the river, the distant Lea, the shallow wooded valley that was now his world — 'seem murky and dim.'

He had turned to me, arms out wide, as if helpless.

'I ken how that is,' I muttered.

Perhaps my voice betrayed me. He looked at me with some curiosity, then around about. This evening no one travelled the old road to Ecclefechan. We were in a dip, unseen. He darted onto a track, overgrown and faltering as hope itself, that wandered through the heuch then back to the burn, to bring us here to wait beneath the brig.

In my old age, eyes far gone from scrivening and scholaring, the moments that stay with me are as faded manuscript pulled into lamplight. Through long nights I peer into them, trying to decipher their meaning.

This is one of my favoured passages, where we stand in wait for fair Helen Irvine. The sky is turning sere and scarlet through the arch where he stands, head bowed. It outlines his long straight nose, that fine forehead. His eyes are hidden. Darkness silts up the valley, thickening over the Lea and the Long Barrow. Only the roof of Kirkconnel kirk above the trees catches the last light.

We are listening for a sound that is not river-run nor last bleats, or birds settling to roost. He paddles the toe of his boot in the stream in little sweeping curves, frowning with concentration.

There is pattern to what he does, but I cannot decipher it. I nudge and soundlessly enquire. He looks up, startled. Leans his lips to my ear, his breath warm as he whispers.

'My name in water – see how quickly it is lost.'

Once again his toe inscribes *Adam Fleming*. I whisper to him in turn.

'Write hers, and be lost together.'

His teeth flash in the gloaming under the brig. In that moment we are close again, the troubled, intoxicated lover and I. With his other boot he delicately toes *Helen Irvine*, then we stand side by side to watch it unravel and be gone.

'You are sic a daftie, friend,' I whisper.

He grins back, delighted. In the shadows he looks young again, playful as he was before his brother's then his father's death.

'But a sincere one, I think!'

Ah yes, sincerity. That is perhaps the difference. I have lived by truth of tale and translation, that serve another master.

So silently came she, we heard nothing. The late glow gilded her face as she smiled upon me.

'Cousin Harry,' she murmured, pressed her smooth cheek to mine. Then she cooried into him as though passing into his very core.

I looked down at the water that had borne their names away, and awaited my instructions. When she unclasped Adam, I could see she was indeed more than bonnie these days. She made all else seem a shuttered lantern.

'You will be lookout for us at our trysting, Harry?'

I nodded. There was no place for me where they were going. Their shoulders, hands and thighs leaned into each other, two saplings caught in prevailing gusts. Their fingers tangled already.

She kissed me again, looked briefly into my eyes. For a moment nothing had changed since we were bairns on these very banks. He gripped my shoulder, grinned.

'*Merci*,' he said. 'Gie the kestrel cry if needs be.'

It was our old signal to each other, when one stood below our lodgings, or needed assistance in a tavern brawl.

'Surely,' I said. 'Ca' canny.'

He laughed under his breath, took a quick look round, then followed her through the last green light into the trees, towards the kirk and Lea where the grass grew long.

I followed them downstream, then eased myself down against a great beech whose branches trailed heavy in the water, and tried to think of anything except what they were now about.

Let me hold her face and form before me in the lamp-troubled dark, 'Fair Helen', as the ballads cry her.

I see her best as I knew her first, as a child with me in the fields, so quick and canny. Her eyebrows were set straight and honey-dark above her eyes, and those the colour of sky right overhead. Close up, they had queer paler flecks in them like bits of scattered glass.

Among the corn we made our dens, and filled them with our make-believe, confessions and lichtsome games. We fossicked every Roman camp and abandoned tower, wandered far downstream to find her family's cave where they had once hid the Bruce a winter through. She pressed an ivy rope into my hand, seized another, then slid out of sight down the cliff, eyes shining, mouth agape in the thrill . . . Into how many sleepless nights has she descended so, to light my darkness!

Though younger than I, she was strong-willed and liked to win. At Dirk, Paper, Stane she would bring her hand from behind her back a moment after mine, adapt it in mid-air and laughing wrap her paper round my stone, or break my dirk with her stane. I did not hold it against her. It seemed already I loved some things more than winning.

One long afternoon, cooried in our den on Kirtle bank, she persuaded me to show her mine. I did and lay there as she stared.

She did not laugh but nodded thoughtfully, lips parted, faint lines knotting between her eyebrows, as though she were studying a featherless chick fallen from the nest.

I pulled my britches up. 'Now you,' I said.

In truth I was relieved when she ran giggling. When I caught her, she cried, 'It's nothing! Harry, there is next to nothing there!' And laughed so merrily.

When I sit in the corner of a howff, fuddled with ale or bad claret, and someone begins to sing the dolefu' ballad of 'Fair Helen of Kirkconnel Lea', forgive me if I smile awry.

I was in a dwam, they were expert, I had lived too many years in the city. An arm crooked round my throat, gloved hand clamped across my mouth. I was hoisted up and hit once in the face, twice in the belly. I slumped and was dropped. Seized by the hair, my face was lifted to what moonlight there was.

'It is not he.'

There were three. The man who had whispered I did not know. The one who stood looking down at me was Robert Bell. A third turned away and stood guard.

Bell hunkered down and stared at me. He had abandoned his Frenchified look, let his beard and black hair grow full. He looked every inch a Border bully in his pomp, hardened and skilled. The moonlight glinted off the Flemish pistol at his hip, the dagger in his fist. My life had been too short. I would be another body found in the woods.

'It is Fleming's bum chum,' he said quietly. 'I had heard he was back.'

What madness possessed me then I do not know. With my death towering over me, I made the kestrel cry. It rang sharp and clear before a fist knocked me sideways. The first man put his hand to his sword, looked to his master.

Would I could say courage came to me at my last.

'I am unarmed,' I whimpered.

'More fool you.'

'I am a priest now. I am here only to see my mother's people.'

Neither of these was strictly true. The man in the shadows spoke in a muffled voice.

'It is o'er late now.'

Robert Bell lifted me by the throat as if I were a scrap of prey and stared into my soul and I into his. Then he drew back and hit me full in the face.

For some years my crooked nose brought, I liked to think, a certain distinction to my features. Now in old age it just adds to my battered and agley appearance, and it aches when the snell winds blow.

I came back to the taste of blood, thickening in my throat. I rolled on my side, coughed and spat it out. Ribs and belly ached with each breath and movement. They must have given me some parting kicks before disappearing into the night. But I lived. I had not thought to. (Only later would it come clear why I had been spared, and at whose direction. Or perhaps Rob Bell had looked into my face or his own soul, and seen some grounds for mercy there. *Que sais-je?*)

I staggered downstream through the trees, breathing only through my mouth. I knelt at the river, washed my face, swallowed and spat blood. The flow had lessened now. I could not bear to touch my nose. I looked at my hands, pale in the broken moonlight. They shook not. Strange.

The man who spoke but once, the one who turned away as if not wanting to be recognized, I had seen him before. Not in Bell's company, but another's. In the city? Short hair and jawline beard, stoop-shouldered but strong. Not a servant, nor quite a master. An adviser of some sort?

I came to the place where long grass was flattened, out of sight of the path and the far bank alike. This was where young love had lain, heard my warning cry, stolen away into the night. The stone preaching cross from older times stood moonlit higher up the bank. Surely not. Not here.

I looked back up the slope. Fifteen years of growth to these bushes. A great beech trunk split just above head height. It had once seemed much higher.

I flopped down. I knew this place, this exact place where a skinny boy on a shimmering afternoon was told to show himself, and did. And she had looked her fill, then giggled and run. That she should bring Adam here.

I lay back, dumfountert, staring up at the broken moon

through leaves. It was autumn-dark, the stars were faint. I felt cold, then felt nothing.

Perhaps I slept. Certainly the moon had moved. A man stood over me.

'Harry,' he whispered, knelt and held me.

'Ow!' I said. '*Sois gentil.*'

He pulled aside my cloak, felt gently. He gazed at my face. 'Bell?'

'Surely. And two others.'

He nodded, dark and sombre.

'I am sorry,' he said. 'This was never . . .'

I shrugged as best I could. 'She escaped them?'

'She will get hame. She has many secret ways.'

'I bet she does.'

He looked at me. I looked back. 'You saved my life,' he said. 'I'll aye be owing.'

Then he sighed, stooped down and helped me to my feet. Together we went cautiously on to the old kirk at Kirkconnel. Even by moonlight it looked half ruinous, windows long smashed by Reformers' stones. He helped me up the stone steps at the side, produced a fat key, opened the door.

In a room off the vestry were some horse blankets. He lit a candle and made a den for us on the floor. He seemed on familiar ground.

I lay out, head propped up, swaddled in horse blanket, their sweet stink. My head rang like a heavy bronze bell. Nothing to do but thole it till dawn. Faint moonlight through the round window set in the gable.

He sat cross-legged at my side, head to his chest. Then he looked at me, face gaunt and vivid in candlelight. His long nose, his clever lips, his eyes unfathomable.

'I will kill Bell for this,' he said.

'And never see Helen again?'

He grunted. He knew I was right. With the Warden Earl of Angus and the Bells so tight, he would be banished at best. Hung more likely, left on the gibbet for the hoodie crows to pike out those bonnie een.

'He could have killed me, and did not.'

'So?'

'So consider your immortal soul before you speak of murder in a church.'

'Since when did you believe in my immortal soul?' he muttered, licked his fingers and pinched out the candle.

'*Helen*.' Did he sleep or wake when he said her name so saftly in the night, and his hand came out to stroke my arm?

FAMILY

My last days peter out in this backwater of Hawthornden. I keep the library, argue amiably with Drummond over *The Faerie Queene*, tease him for the rampant royalism that makes him favour the Book of Common Prayer. I serve too as a curiosity when his friends arrive. ('He rode with the reivers, you know! He was aquaint with Fair Helen of Kirkconnel Lea!')

I instruct Drummond's many children in Latin and Greek, potter in the garden, gaze vacantly over the sheer drop into the North Esk. I lie down at night, ready to depart. I wake in the night and lie by candle or lamplight – a terror of pure darkness lingers yet – thinking on her and him and those few weeks to which the rest of my life has been but a coda. Morning finds me amazed to be here still.

My soul cannot be much improved, and can only be saved by an act of mercy that I do not anticipate. All that remains is to set down events of those days as I best understand them. Most like, these papers will be burned when I am gone, then there will be nothing left of me and mine.

You will not find my stone in Kirkconnel kirkyard, though all I have loved lies there.

Janet Elliot Fleming was a handsome woman yet, and no fool. Her son's love of poetry and song, of French, Italian and the *Divine Comedy*, came from her. As a girl she had seen Paris and Rome before returning home with her father to an agreed marriage in this most debatable corner of the Borderlands. She sat in her fine body with languorous ease.

She placed me by her at dinner, and asked after my time in Wittenberg and Leyden, my brief trip to Florence as secretary to a scheming bishop. She sighed to hear me talk of the light that poured there from the sky, over bell towers and kirks that were not black and grim, the sculpture, paintings and frescos that seemed a foretaste of Heaven (and, in some cases, Hell).

'The soul might sing there, Harry,' she said quietly. I was disturbed when she looked into my eyes like that. 'Still, it is not hame.'

'More's the pity,' I replied. She gave me a doubtful keek, then speared some beef.

We talked then of the carvings of the Low Countries, besides which our best pulpits are apprentice hack-work that set on high our fanatics, and our finest paintings but cack-handed daubs.

'They say you are become a scholar of our time, Harry.'

'More mendicant than scholar,' I replied. 'I go wherever will feed me.'

She laughed, her lips full and moist. 'And did you really have to leave Leyden overnight?'

'The horse was waiting and the night was fair.'

'I trust she was worth it!'

I gave her the Italian shrug. Let her think what she may. The truth had been more simple and more curious.

She speired after the general clash from Embra – the Court, the fashions, the turmoil among the Reformers, which way the wind blew now. Also my living, my studies, my friends. I replied my living was thin, my studies desultory, my friends few.

She laughed. 'I think not,' she said. Her eyes flicked to her son, moodily slurping at the further end of the long table, ignoring the bonnie young second cousin carefully placed to his right. 'It is good to see you back among us after so long,' she said. 'Is it not, Dand?'

Her husband of three years raised his head from his meat, licked gravy from his fox-brush moustache. Red-haired and powerfully made as his brother had been fair and lean, he struck me a sensual man, with all the energy and laziness that comes with sensuality gratified.

'A friend of our son is a friend of the house,' he said gravely. In truth he barely knew me, but I appreciated the sentiment and said so.

Janet's smile was so much her son's. As was the long oval face, the heavy tallow hair.

'Not your son,' Adam said. His words were quiet but audible to everyone at the table. He went on drinking. The ripening cousin blushed and looked about to flee. Janet looked to her husband. Dand drew a hefty hand back across his mouth as though wiping away unsaid words, then called on young Watt to fetch in more bread, honey and curds.

Impossible to miss Janet Fleming's look of gratitude. Nor, as she moved our conversation to the ongoing harvest, her outrage and baffled love at her oafish son. Who, after briefly and crudely flirting with the cousin, seized his cup, swayed to his feet. I thought he was about to propose a toast, and feared what it might be.

'Excuse me from the table, *Mither*,' he said. He seized the bottle from Watt – whom I noted looked to Dand Fleming in appeal, not his mistress – bowed with exaggerated courtesy to the suffering cousin quine, then left the hall.

We heard the main door bang, his dog bark once as he crossed the yard to the peel tower.

The lamps burned dirtily, the log in the fireplace shifted down, sent up a flare. Watt cleared the table, the girl brought in apples from their orchard, oranges fresh sent down from Leith.

'So, Harry,' Dand said cheerily, 'you got yourself in a stushie already?'

He waved his red paw towards my face. Even cleaned up, I was not a bonnie boy.

'That damned rent horse,' I replied. 'She has a nasty streak. And I am no horseman, for all my Irvine blood.'

I meant nothing by it but that my mother's family had been famed for horsemanship. Dand and his wife both flinched at the name, just for a moment. Perhaps it was just on account of the long feud between Fleming and Irvine, or perhaps they had rumour of the trysting.

'I thought you had got in a brawl at the Ecclefechan Inn,' Janet said. She leaned closer, smiled like her son upon me.

'I am no fighter,' I said. 'The local callants have nothing to fear from me.'

'Nor you from them!' Dand said loudly. 'They are hairmless if you do not interfere with their affairs.'

'I will keep that in mind,' I said. I touched my nose gently. 'I think I shall have that horse returned, before my face is re-- arranged again.'

Much laughter at hapless me. I was offered the use of a bid- dable Galloway cob for as long as I stayed. No one asked how long that would be, which was as well for I could not have told them.

Soon enough Fleming got up. He was a powerful man, with the first grey in his thick red beard and tangled hair. I thought him straightforward, uncomplicated. A man who just wanted to be left alone to his country life, his new wife, dogs and horse and adequate domain. Not a man burdened by ambition or imagination.

He grabbed an apple off the table, munched into it and waited at the doorway for his wife. She took his arm, their shoulders and hips dipped towards each other as they went through the door.

*

I was brushing down my hired pony by the stables in the failing light when she found me again. Beyond her I saw the broad back of her husband pass out through the gates, following another, taller, armed figure into the gloom.

'I am glad you are come, Harry,' she said. 'I hope you may help my son. You are such old friends.'

'Do my best,' I said. Bending still made me catch my breath. Perhaps they had broken something in me.

'He is . . . troubled,' she said.

'For sure.'

I swapped hands with the curry brush. Our eyes met across the mare's back. Her hand lay hot on mine.

'Do you think . . .' She hesitated. 'He wants something he cannot have? He is in love, perhaps?'

I managed to look away, following the line of the brush, aware her eyes lay on me.

'I think he still misses his brother Jack,' I said. 'And his father, of course.'

'So do I,' she said. When I looked up, her eyes were moist but her voice was steady. She was an Elliot, great-niece to Little Bob Elliot, that thrawn and never-yielding man. 'Yet the living must live on. Dand brings protection. He is a decent and strong man, and good heidsman.' She giggled low, and that false note disturbed me. 'At least I didn't have to change my name!'

'There is that,' I said.

'I pray Adam will come to accept him, and that he drink less deep.' Her hand tightened on my wrist. 'Can you speir out what ails him? I worry that . . .' She broke off, frowning. 'His father's moods would swither like our weathervane.'

'I will learn as much as he will let me,' I said.

'And you will let me know?'

'I will let you know,' I said, with little intention of doing so.

I heard her breathe 'Thank you' as I led the old mare into the stable. When I looked round, Janet Elliot Fleming was gone.

I stalled the mare to be returned to the agent in the morn, then stood a while among the nostril-twitching dimness of horse and peat-stack, sorting through the evening. When I had got it straight in my mind, I secured the stable door and crossed the courtyard, past the family house. Watt saw me on the way, then scurried indoors.

I went to the peel tower and on the muckle outer door beat quietly our signal from former days.

CLOOT

A canny cloot, my father called me, affectionately enough. He meant I was a handy rag, a sponge, one who soaked up the words and manners of those around me. Such indeed was my nature. In Embra's closes, streets, workshops, howffs, courts, kirks and counting houses, from my earliest days I heard Inglis, various Scots, French. Gaelic was murmured among the draymen, Latin poured from pulpit and law courts, the languages of the Low Countries floated up from Port o' Leith.

A cast of mind came with each tongue. I took them all on with little effort, no merit about it, as *passe-partout*, protection, guise. And if none save Helen Irvine knew what this cloot might be when rinsed through and hung to dry – well, what of that?

When Adam Fleming and I met at the university, we found we were ages with each other, both born in the month and year Knox died. As a girl my mother had heard that implacable man preach at St Giles, and the experience had altered her faith. It also infected her young imagination in ways that oozed out among the sores as she lay dying – but I am not ready to write of that.

From our second term at the Tounis College★ we shared a damp, cavernous room in a piss-rancid tenement between St Giles and the Black Horse tavern. Our impulses likewise veered between the intoxications of prayer and carnality.

Though the friendship between a book-intoxicated city child of artisans and a lanky, fizzing, handsome laird's boy seemed improbable to our fellows, we spent much time together. He was giddy, inventive in ploy and song. At times he was full of tumult and energy as a burn in spate, then for days he would lie silent and dark as a moorland tarn.

To him I perhaps brought a certain detachment and a steadiness, plus my greater knowledge of the intricacies of the city. He was tall and lean, all fire and air. I was short, compact and nimble, my signs were of plebeian earth and ever-adaptable water.

Precious to me still is a moonlit night when restlessness sent us not to tavern or bawdy house, and certainly not to our studies. Instead, booted and cloaked, with our foppish fur-trimmed hats, we walked past the dozy watchman at the city gate as the midnight bell sounded, out into the King's Park spread like dark sea below the mountain.

★ It alone of our universities was not founded by Papal Bull or Royal Warrant, but belonged to Embra Toun. Which made it less answerable to Church or state and so – Reformation zeal notwithstanding! – made for a degree of free thought. Here I first heard of certain texts that would become my lights through a murky world.

The night was chill, with salt and gorse on a sharp wind, and the long grass was dew-sodden as we clambered through the gap between Seat and Crags. With the moon white as bone at our backs, we climbed steadily into our own shadows.

We went without spoken goal, united by a yearning for elevation. He talked that night of all he dreamed to be. He talked without reserve or self-mockery, for he trusted me and he was still young enough to trust himself, and believed the world would bend to his dreams.

We lost the path early on, and agreed just to climb ever upwards. That way, we reasoned, we could not get lost. Soon enough we were scrambling on loose scree, clutching for outcrops. In moonlight and through shadow, we pressed on up.

He would go to Paris to learn about love. He would go to Rome to study poetry. We could rent a house by the Tiber, live by translation and scrivening! We would gather news and gossip, live on a retainer from the King. He said I would make an excellent spy. He outlined his grand plan to render Dante into the Lallans.

'All of it?' I enquired as I pulled up on loose rock. 'Even the interminable religious raving and cursing?'

He thrashed up the last of the slope and joined me on a ledge. We sat looking over the city.

'*Especially* those bits,' he said firmly. 'After all, how suited my native tongue is to condemnation and invective!'

The city was torn into moonlit strips — the dour Castle, the

High Kirk where Reform preachers stoked hearts and minds, the dark maw of the Grassmarket and the tenements sliding down the long spine to the palace where Jamie Saxt (but six years our elder) slept uneasily amidst the ghosts of his many murdered regents, his fantasies of sorcerers.

Leith, the ghostly estuary, the open sea, glittered to our right. Guard fires shuddered out on the May, on Cramond and Inchkeith. On Inchcombe island the abandoned monastery was a black ship with its cargo of souls, going nowhere. In the furthest distance, a watchfire flickered on Fidra. In the nearby Auld Kirk of North Berwick the witch trials were proceeding by that most reliable proof: evidence under torture. Some threescore had already been strangled then burned.

We sat on the ledge, contemplating our native land as sweat turned to shivering.

'Or maybe,' he said at last, 'I shall go to Constantinople. I shall become an adviser to a sultan, and translate from the Persian.'

I was silent at that 'I'.

'I am that weary of our petit wars and reiving,' he said. 'Their feuds, their precious "honour", their stealing of cattle and women, and all yon keeping up the family status and lands, scheming, flattering the feckfu' gentry.'

'Let your brother Jack do that,' I said.

He looked at me sharply.

'Jack is a good man,' he said. 'Better than I. Still, he is more suited to that life.'

He would take no criticism of his eldest brother. He had another, who I understood had sickness of the lungs or head and was not expected to live long. He did not talk of him.

'A quiet life of contemplation for me,' I said. 'A garden, a sunlit room with table and chair, a good library and plentiful mid-quality rag paper. Someone to bring me food and look after my needs.'

He chuckled. 'Whatever they are.'

'Whatever they are,' I agreed.

'And as for money?'

'I shall sell my body as needs must. '

'Then you shall be poor indeed.'

'And when I grow bored of study and contemplation, I shall seek release in laughter, song and wine.'

'In that case I will join you in old age,' he said. 'We will sit in your garden and I will tell you lies of my adventures, and you will tell me whatever truths you have gathered in your douce years.' He was silent, I felt his mood shift like the night wind. 'Doubtless we will talk of the night we climbed the Seat, and talked of what we would be and do, and how it did not happen so.'

I got to my feet, feeling chill.

'We have not climbed it yet.'

Maybe I led to impress him. In the notch of the gully it was hellish dark, my hands felt for holds. I stretched, tested, pulled up. The rock was cold and smooth as a bailiff's demand. I came to a point where my only possible hold was a thick gorse root, studded with prickles. I felt around and found no other way. Silence from below. Only the wind speiring *Whaur ye headin' faur, my bonnie lad?*

I pulled off my cloak. My legs began to shake as I wrapped it round my fist, reached up as far as I could, gripped the gorse root hard and pulled. My boots slipped on the walls of the crack and I was hanging from that one arm. The root held. My other hand slapped around, hit on a projection. I clung as if it were a nail on the true Cross. Then I pulled up my body weight till, belly over ledge, I kneed and wriggled from that deathly crack.

Moonlight and silence, only the wind passing over the summit above. I looked down into the blackness and called on my friend.

'This is not a good way!'

Silence, then: 'Coming up!'

His pant and scrape, a curse, rattle of small stones. He was heavier than I. That gorse root might not hold. If he falls, it will be my fault.

His fair hair faint in the dark. Glimmer of his face looking up.

'I am stuck,' he said. His voice was calm, indifferent. 'I think I shall fall.'

'Paris,' I said. 'Constantinople!'

Silence as he scraped and scrabbled. His breath was coming fast.

'Can you reach down?'

I wrapped one arm round the rock, curled my legs behind a boulder, reached down as far as I could. He reached up. His hand wavered, found mine, clasped hard. He looked up at my face. I had no idea if I was siccar.

'Pull,' I said.

And I pulled as he pulled, quick and hard. I heaved him upward till his chest came over the top. He flopped down beside me and we lay gasping in the moonlight pool.

'You are more powerful than you look,' he said.

'Once a cooper's son, always a cooper's son. Strong right arm.'★

'Everyone needs one,' he murmured. 'Thank you, *mon cher*.'

We hurried up to the top, and sat on feet-polished rocks, cloaks wrapped about us against the bitter wind. Watchfires, darkness, moonlight on clouds like spilt milk on a parlour floor. The Firth heaved glittering between dark Fife and darker Lothians. The Pentland hills hung black curtains across the stars.

It was not Byzantium or Rome, but it was ours.

In our boarding room, his pallet was by the door, mine by the window. I looked out to see who was hollering below. In the dawnlicht I made out a man on horseback in leather jerkin and helmet. Bearded, he had a familiar country look about him. In his hand he held the reins of a second horse, a grey Galloway cob.

★ I was apprenticed to the trade till the brewer's clerk taught me to read, the first in my family. My faither skelped my arse, and then encouraged me. My scholarship to the Town's College was, quite literally, beer money from the guild.

34

He leaned from the saddle to thump on the street door. 'Young Fleeming!' he bawled. 'Wake yersel, ya dowzy loon!'

'Hold your horses,' I called down, which I thought good. I padded across the floor but hesitated by the blankets where my friend lay sleeping. A Hawick man at first light, an extra horse. I shivered, then shook Adam awake.

It was not good. His brother Jackie had been thrown from his cob at night, into a Northumbrian burn. What he was doing across the Border at night I could well guess. His followers had smuggled him back to Annandale, wet through, with a bleeding head. He was not making sense, and now he had fever.

'I'm thinking he is no lang for this warld,' the messenger said.

He stood in our rank scholarly room, a fighting man in full trig, boots and leather jack. Jed Horsburgh was rough, hardened, and though but some ten years older than us, he was a man as we were not. He had been part of the Fleming household at Nether Albie since a laddie, had instructed Adam in the short sword, lance and dagger.

He was spare of speech and thrawn, in the way of Hawick folk. It was said he had killed some in the Low Countries and more in England, had even ridden with the lawless Grahams. (These matters are exaggerated by ballad singers and gossips – and what is the point of song and story if not to exaggerate our lives to the scale we believe they should be, rather than the small affairs we fear they truly are?) Yet Jed Horsburgh had seen men die at his hand, I did not doubt it. He was also a fine cattle-thief, and fiercely loyal to the Fleming house.

Adam dressed, thrust his few necessities in his book-satchel. He took his short sword from under the bed, glanced at Jed. Jed nodded sombrely. As he watched Adam gather up hat, dagger, heavy shirt and jerkin, I thought I saw some pity.

'It is not guid,' he said quietly, then left the room.

Adam stood before me, bag slung over his shoulder. He looked as though he carried something much heavier.

'Thank you,' he said. 'It was a good time, Harry, was it not?'

His hand on my arm, then gone.

When Adam returned a fortnight later, some of his lichtsomeness had gone. The gaiety of spirit, his joking and ploys and singing, his inventiveness and fantoosherie, all that had made him a star among us, had been doused. The quickness of spirit and sympathy and fun we had loved seemed buried with his brother in Kirk Yetholm.

I tried to take him out to the taverns, but he would not have it. He studied hard to catch up with all he had missed. I would fall asleep in my corner by the light of his flickering bougie as he bent over his books, his lips moving as he read. Increasingly his end of the table bore ledgers of accounts rather than the works of Aristotle and Aquinas. He talked more of Borders affairs. There was a flurry of letters around the time Scott of

Buccleuch was abruptly replaced, as Warden and Keeper of the West March, by Lord Maxwell.*

'But surely Maxwell raised support in Galloway for the Armada?' I protested.

'He says he's no longer a Catholic.' He scratched his stubble wearily. 'The Maxwells can raise three thousand horsemen in a day. The King cannot ignore that. He could execute their heidsman, but only to be replaced by another. So he puts our noble Seventh Lord in charge of the West March. A canny man, Jamie Saxt.'

I contemplated my Thucydides. The wars of Greek city-states did not seem so distant. If they appeared more noble, perhaps it was just they had better writers.

'But your father is pleased?'

'He is in deep clover, bellowing happily. Our family have long been thirled to Maxwell, though my brother used to urge switching to the Johnstones.' On mentioning his brother, the light in him went out. We sat in silence across the table from each other.

'Song, sentiment and poetry are but a bag of wind,' he said at last. 'Only numbers of horse and kye and hard coin weigh in this world.'

---

* In those distant-seeming days before the merging of the Crowns, the West, Middle and East March in Scotland and England each had their own Warden. The most troublesome parts, such as Liddesdale, in addition had a Keeper. Some Wardens were reiver warlords, all looked to their own and family advantage, few lasted long. I couldn't keep up.

He went back to frowning over the estate ledgers. I took his point, though we both kenned fine that if one backed the wrong side, horses and kye and fortune could vanish as quickly as one's head. And for all their frailty, ballad and story outlive a man – or woman, God knows!

Weeks later found us again at opposite ends of our shared table, peering into the gloom of a creusie lamp, limited illumination indeed. Scratch of pen, rattle of rain on the window, the sigh as our peat fire burned low. His yellow hair was faintly dank, long fingers gripped deep in it. I was still stumbling through the machinations and brief triumphs of Athenian democracy. I was, in my way, at peace.

For long moments I came to myself, and saw my life as it was happening in this room. I saw it with heavy, fond heart, as though it were a time already by.

He threw his quill aside.

'Numbers!' he cried. 'Rents, contracts and accounts! They mean nothing to me.'

I shrugged. 'They govern the world, I am told.'

He clasped his hands behind his neck, glared at the ceiling as though it were its fault. 'Bloody buggering hell,' he muttered. 'Pish!'

I said nothing, though I rather agreed. Ever the swithering aircock, he clasped hands behind his neck and laughed at the regrettable world, his regrettable self.

'Can the Peloponnese wars wait for an evening?' he enquired.

38

'They can wait forever,' I said. 'That world no longer exists, save in partial histories.'

We did not head for the tavern but walked through town in steady rain. We splashed down past Grey Friars into the Cowgate, then Lawnmarket, passing through the minging parts of the city. He said next to nothing as we showed our passes at the gate, and I kept my counsel.

Without the walls, we turned across the fields by rough tracks, slipping and feeling our way in the mirk. At length we heard water muttering in the rain. We skirted the Nor' Loch and climbed the slope back onto the spine of the city, past the Watch, through the North Gate. Our boots were heavy with glaur, our cloaks sodden about our shoulders, as we clumped back to our lodgings. It had been a pointless circuit, achieving nothing. I would not have been anywhere else.

At the tenement door he stopped, put his arm out against the wall, as though propping it or himself up.

'I am the heir now,' he said. 'I am not a free man.'

'But your other brother?' I protested.

He shook his head. 'Malcolm is . . . not right.'

I did not enquire further. I could see he had lost more than an admired brother. I would inherit nothing in this world but my father's tools of trade, and for the first time appreciated my good fortune in this.

'It seems I must learn accounts and the breeding of cattle, suck up to Lord Maxwell and look to a canny marriage.' He shook his head, slapped the wall. 'Ouch!' He sucked his knuckles, keeked across at me and managed a grin, a flicker of the youth he had been. 'I think Constantinople must get by without me,' he said.

And later that night, as we lay on our pallets in the dark, I blurted, 'But your father should live many years.'

Silence, then his voice husky from the far wall. 'Still, I am heir, d'you see? I had thought to make my own way in this world, far from Annandale and our feuds and reiving . . .'

'You were born to it,' I said. 'The rest is a young man's dream.'

'It was a fine dream,' he replied. 'Much better than waking.'

Never to be born is best. In student days we used to quote that to each other, and marvel at our world-weariness.

Now I look out the window at the ordinary day, the North Esk in spate, the kestrel pinned to the sky. I eat plum tart with warm spiced wine, and think on Helen and Adam, Jed and Bell and Elenora Jarvis, young Watt, Janet Elliot, the fighters and schemers and all those who just plodded along, head down, through another day.

The nib scores the paper as a knife scores the arm, bleeding ink. The tart is excellent and the wine lingers in the throat. So much for antique wisdom.

AMOURS

If you press me to say why I loved him, I can say no more than because he was he, and I was I. And who am I to flyte against Montaigne?

I have let memory graze through lush meadows of our early friendship, to account for what was between us. Now I turn the head of this stubborn nag back to hard track and straight going, kick my heels gently against its flanks and urge us both down the story-road.

Up ahead: the Fleming compound, the peel tower, night, my old friend at bay.

'So, do you love me still?'

He sat cross-legged on a flattened straw-pallet bed, his back against the bare stone wall. On a bench a creusie lamp burned dourly, as they do at the best of times. This had once been the heidsman's bedroom, before Adam's father had the new house built, and the bed and furniture moved across the yard. Now the room was a chilly store that stank of fish-oil, pigeon-dung, and the dog that settled itself contentedly across his long legs.

Philby was a straggly lurcher, mottled grey like peeling birch bark. He shrank and dwindled in his master's absence.

'Such elegant quarters you have,' I replied. 'How long have you been sleeping here?'

He shrugged. 'Since the wedding. Since I feared for my life. A year or more.'

I helped myself to wine from the skin and eased myself down the wall opposite him. Our breath made clouds and the fireplace looked unused. Personally I thought it was a comfortless place to come for a sulk. I suggested any man spending much time alone in the peel tower would come by morbid thoughts.

'I have company,' he said. 'Snood eats here, sleeps on the roof by the balefire timbers.'

'No one has heard Snood say other than *Aye* or *Nuh* since Queen Mary fled Scotland.'

'He is no conversationalist,' Adam admitted. 'But he is armed and he is one of few I trust.'

'Would you not be safer – and warmer – sleeping in the house, with retainers hard by?'

He looked like a petulant boy with his long lip pouting. 'With bed-music from my mother's room at night? With my uncle's retainers? You have seen the boy Watt. He follows me like a fart, and is about as useful.'

I proffered wine, he shrugged it away. I huddled deeper into my cloak. The room was damp and drear to the core. The lurcher whiffled in his uneasy sleep.

'So,' he said.

'So?'

He sighed. 'I'm sorry I had not written before,' he said. 'And at the wedding . . . I have been much preoccupied with, well, you know.'

'Your amours are no business of mine.' I drank, waited, felt the slow fire spread in my belly.

'Nor yours of mine!' Philby raised his shaggy head, stared at his master, then rested his long snout on the floor again. Adam chuckled softly. 'Is it true what they say happened in Leyden?'

'Probably not.'

'The abbess?'

I raised my cup to him. 'Definitely not.'

'How did you find the Anabaptists?'

'Insane to the last man.'

'How I envy your travels and travails.'

There was nothing worthwhile to say to that, so we looked at each other in silence. I was not about to answer his first question. I had sulked long at his neglect. A scrape at the door, Philby howled and Adam's hand went to his blade. Then heavy breathing and boots slapping on up the tower to the roof as Snood went to keep his watch.

'Just the same,' he said, 'I'd rather you barred the door.'

I shook my head, but slid the stave across. Then refilled my cup from the skin, sat back cross-legged against the wall and waited. I watched his dark-shadowed, troubled face, lit by the creusie as he began to talk of his father's death on a cross-border raid, his Uncle Dand, now his stepfather, and why he believed his life threatened. It was a long, stumbling tale, and the room grew cold as we huddled into our night-cloaks. Philby snored and Snood moved overhead, and I listened and marked Adam Fleming well as he talked not of love but death.

This was the short of it. Last Martinmas, he had been set on behind the luckenbooths at Langholm mart. Jed had heard the stushie and together they drove off three men who disappeared in the crowd. Were they known to him or Jed? Not at all. That in itself was unusual.

'So *bien sûr* they must have been set on you by Dand. No other possibility?'

He glared at me across the lamplight. I spread my hands. Why would his new father want rid of him?

'Because I am still heir, poor Malcolm apart! The lands and the house are in trust to me, by agreement when I did not become heidsman.' He looked down, then added softly, 'And he knows I have suspicions about my father's death.'

Before we went chasing again after that improbable fox, I hastily said, 'And your second incident?'

Returning from Hawick's Spring Fair, early dusk coming on as he crossed the high moor home, his saddle had lurched. He looked down, felt and found the cinch had burst. Two horsemen in the distance behind waited. He had pulled the saddle off and ridden on fast by halter alone. He lost the horsemen in the heuch woods, then made it home by starlight. When he went back for the saddle next morning — it was valuable, his best — he found the leather edges of the cinch were clean-cut. Then, after eating with companions at the Fortune Rigg by Kirtlebridge, he had become suddenly ill with stomach cramps and sweating. He went bright red, then fainted. Jed had rolled him on his side, stuck fingers down his throat to make him spew. They got him home that night but he had been sick for days.

'You should complain to the kitchen,' I joked.

He had stared back at me across the yellow flicker of the lamp.

'We all ate the same. None else were sick. It was after that I wrote you.' He hesitated. 'I have not been entirely myself, and thought it best to play to it, so they think me hairmless.'

'You ken I am no fighter. Jed's your man.'

He stretched out his hands to me.

'Keep an eye on me,' he said. 'Keep me steady. Advise me on Helen. You knew me in earlier days. I love you like a brither.'

I hated it when he called to me like that, for I would aye come running, and he would never ken what I came running for, or in what baseless hope.

We stood by the great studded door and bade goodnight. Above our heads, a faint snore from the battlement where the watchfire lay ready and unlit. The night was hard, the hairst was gathered in, the season favoured by reivers for its dark nights and fattened beasts was coming on.

His arm pressed about my shoulder, then he was gone in. I heard the bar shuffle across the door. I stood a minute in the night silence, letting my eyes adjust to moonlight smeared through cloud. It was late, the Hunter was mid-leap across the western sky. My chest ached with every breath.

I crossed the courtyard to the deeper dark of the house, felt my way round the back, in the low door and along the scullery passage. Once in my room I slid the bar across.

I groped for my tinderbox, lit a candle. My chamber was small, chill, unadorned: bed, table, chair, washbasin, commode. It was the kind of room I have inhabited most of my life, something between a guest, a retainer, a friend and a witness to the lives of others.

Weary to the bone, I sat down at the table in cloak, scarf and woollen hat, and began to scratch out my report.

RISING

Ah yes, the report. First of several I wrote that season in a bleak room with door barred, and then had had discreetly delivered to their commissioner.

You think the Prince's friend a free man, the Cardinal's secretary uncompromised, the lady's maid entirely devoted? At the time I was two men: the one who had come to help my friends achieve their hearts' desires and the shadowy other I loosed only at the end of the day.

The truth of the world is low-born men may rise from the muddy bottom like trout, following the ascending nymph, and rise far enough to be glimpsed by the patient angler waiting on the high bank.

In plainer terms, we come to the notice of one to whom we are of use.

After we completed our degrees, Adam was called home to Annandale. We parted at the Gallows Gate, tears in our eyes caused perhaps by the brute wind off the sea. I watched him ride away toward the Biggar track, then turned back to the city streets where my own future lay.

I secured a lowly position to grub away in what our noble Reformation had left of the Black Friars' dungheap of a library, bringing some order to their dank scriptorium in exchange for board and lodging. An elderly ex-friar – whose name I cannot recall but whose extensive farts I can – extended my knowledge of Natural Philosophy to include new treatises from Italy and Warmia, and hinted at the whereabouts of certain pagan works in the libraries of Old Europe from which I might find comfort, pleasure and instruction. That sly and witty man, whose wandering hands were easily and gently diverted, in friendship then found me a chambers where I might train as a legal clerk.

It was at that time my father died, between one Sabbath and the next, of sweating sickness. As he lay on his pallet he commended me to my studies. 'Dae weel, laddie, dae richt weel!' The following day I closed his eyes and commended him to God and my mother. After burying him by her in Blackfriars kirkyard, I sold his tools and bought my own writing desk, fresh quills and good ink, a heap of quality rag paper.

In truth I have studied Theology without much interest in God, and Law without expecting to see justice done. At times I studied for the sake of study itself, for the brief peace that contemplation brings, in the manner by which the laverock rises above the fields to look down, singing, on its nest, its mate, all that is dear to it.

I have read too many of my host's Petrarchan effusions! Less gloriously, I studied so I could better eat. It has proved more congenial than labouring with a cooper's mallet, more long-lived than reiving.

A month after my father's death, I was toiling in my assigned cubicle. I looked longingly through the window slit out over the city walls at the King's Park and the Seat, where once a friend and I had climbed by night and opened our hearts to each other. He was long gone into the Borders, my mother and father even further gone.

Someone shouted my name. I leaned out and peered down at two women. One was my mother's elder sister, Ann, waving, her long-jawed face upturned. The other, clad in green, pushed back her hood and looked up to me, and in that look all else went dim.

Helen Irvine lagged behind her mother at the door of my cubby-hole. I had not seen her these last three summers. It was she, it was not she. She carried her new beauty of face and breast and hip in a dazed, uncertain manner, as one might carry something from a burning house, uncertain of its use.

I sweated and gabbled, she looked round gravely as Aunt Ann pushed papers to the floor and settled herself in the sole chair. I never learned how they got past the servitor. They smelled of things long lost, of women and Annandale. In Aunt Ann's voice I heard again my mother, and felt faint.

'You have found yourself anither den, I see,' she said. 'I mind you aye made them amang the in-by fields.'

Helen's eyes flickered to me, quick blue flirt of a kingfisher. She looked down innocently, but the flush was in her cheek, a pucker at the corner of her mouth. I glimpsed the child she had so lately been, impish and baffled behind her unasked-for beauty.

What had brought them here? To offer sympathy for my father's death, of course, and to be reassured I was getting by. I nodded, thinking of how I had stood alone at his grave.

The real mission, it transpired, was to visit the couturiers of the city, and have clothes made that would best present my lovely cousin. 'Even a diamond needs a fine setting to flourish,' Aunt Ann said with relish. Helen coloured and looked to the floor.

To be fair to my aunt, such ambition was reasonable and commonplace. She herself had become an Irvine, a middle-ranking Borders family. To survive, let alone prosper, in that near-lawless March, advantageous alliance was essential. Romance was something best left to poets. Helen was the only surviving child, and her unexpected beauty too good an opportunity to miss.

'None but the best for my little girl!' my aunt announced. I saw Coz Helen blink, a flicker of resistance run down her lovely cheek. I remembered how she played each game to win, how she would assent to advice, then do what she willed.

Aunt Ann announced she would leave her treasure in my care an hour or so, while she attended to some business. She looked at me closely. 'I think you are hairmless enough,' she said, then left.

We stood together in my cubby-hole, awkward at first.

'So,' Helen said at last, 'I am done with yearning to be a discalced Carmelite.'

'Glad of that,' I said. 'It sounded most comfortless.'

She giggled. 'It was. I went barefoot for months, and scabbed my knees from praying. I thought if I could not have Luc, I would marry only Christ.'

She had written months earlier to announce she was in love with one Luc Gautier, tutor to her Springkell cousins. I understood there had been kisses, pledges, touches I did not care to think on. Somehow my aunt and uncle had found them out, and young Luc disappeared – back to France, they said, though it was not impossible he lay in a nearby bog. To assuage her loss, Aunt Ann had foolishly given her a Latin abstract of Teresa of Avila's *El Castilio Interior*, and my cousin had taken to wandering barefoot by the burn in silent prayer, and making a great nuisance of herself at mealtimes, announcing, '*Either let me suffer or let me die.*'

'I heard rumour you are sought by an English Kerr. Apparently he is heir to excellent lands in Redeswire.'

She rolled her eyes. 'My mother's choice. Jamie Kerr was so dull I learned to prop my eyes open with my fingertips when he discoursed. Like this.' She leaned forward with an expression of boredom so extreme it looked near-saintly, put her hand before her face and pushed her eyelids open. 'He believed the gesture flirtatious!'

There had been little enough laughter in my study room.

'What happened to this discerning young man?'

'He had the good grace to catch fever in Corbridge and expire in Hexham. My good mother took my relief for disappointment, and said, *Never fear but we'll soon find anither*.'

'And did you?' I asked, casual-like.

'Apparently Saint Teresa has opened a monastery in Granada. When I considered the procession of suitors I must endure till I agree to one – the slack-jawed second cousins, the swaggering boys, those widowed friends of my father unable to raise their eyes from my chest – then Matins Laud at two in the morn seems a minor inconvenience.'

'So, Granada it is, then, and a nun's life?'

'Unfortunately, I have little talent for obedience.'

'Really?' I murmured, and was rewarded with her cuff towards my head.

'And –' she lowered her eyes in some version of decorum – 'probably very little for chastity.'

She reached under her cloak and handed back the copy of Ovid's *Ars Amatoria* she had insisted on for her last birthday.

'My Springkell cousins were fascinated,' she said. 'We read it aloud in our bed. Edith stuck her fingers in her ears at the naughty bits. Lizzie said God did not much mind if we gave men pleasure, but He wished we keep our worth till marriage.'

'And dour May? What did she have to say?'

'She said, *Surely God has fatter kye to drive to market than fash about what men and women do wi their bits*.'

'And you?'

'I wondered where our worth goes when we marry. You think it evaporates, like hoar in the sun?'

As we laughed together, I could smell Annandale on her, and felt us enter again an understanding of which we could never speak. We had once shared closeness and a peace that had little to do with chapels and bleeding hearts and penitent knees on cold stone floors.

She told me how, briefly apostolic, she had taken her Springkell cousins up into the hay barn to lead them in *Oratio Mentalis*, mystic prayers of the ascent of the soul, talking them through the four stages, rising to sweet, happy pain, then being entered by a fiery glow, followed by a swoon, then waking in tears. Cousin Edith had moaned in appreciation. May complained of cramp in her knees. Elizabeth said she woke in tears most mornings anyway.

'*Mystic prayer is akin to daily watering a garden,*' Helen insisted.

'*Your Teresa should live in Annandale,*' May said. '*Our garden gets watered near every day, prayer or no prayer.*'

Together they looked out to the courtyard, the sodden, lovely fields and woods.

'*Aye, we must be awfy holy in these parts,*' Elizabeth said. Four girls convulsed among the straw.

'That was the end of Saint Teresa,' Helen said. She raised her eyes to me, put out her hand, laid it on my arm in a touch more knowing than any lover's. 'Still, a certain yearning remains,' she said. 'Though it may never be satisfied in this world.'

I blinked at that.

'There is always love,' I said foolishly.

She laughed. 'Love! *Marriage is like a cage; one sees the birds outside desperate to get in, and those inside desperate to get out.* You see, I have read your Montaigne as instructed. It is very diverting, all his *Que sais-je?*, but it is of little use to me.'

We heard the stair door clunk, then my aunt's step on the stair. Helen stood back, pulled her cloak about her shoulders and spoke swiftly. 'Dear Harry, I am the sole surviving child of my parents. My father is heidsman of the Irvines, and has no brothers living. Ergo, I must marry and breed — la-la!'

Her desperate smile, her swift, patronizing kiss to my cheek, they felt like a farewell to something more than me.

I ushered them out before the servitor found them in my room. From the upper window, the senior clerk scowled and beckoned to me. Helen and I hesitated, then she held out her hand. I made to shake it, clasped her soft palm, then raised her fingers to my lips in unconvincing gallantry, embarrassing us both.

Aunt Ann's nod was more dismissal than goodbye. Ann had married up, into the lairdship, and my mother had married down, into the city. I would never know what hard words had been said between them. This visit had been dutiful, no more, perhaps checking I was not disgracing the family before they moved to yet higher ground.

I stood for a moment, watching them walk up the High Street. Two young gallants swerved by Helen, then both heads turned to look back, as though checking they had just witnessed such radiance in a scurvy street.

Choking down the sour spit of yearning, I turned back to Justice's door. Being indentured, there was no possibility of going back soon to Annandale. I resolved to find my own entertainment and some of my own kind in the city of my birth – and that is what I did, and so rose a little closer to the unresting gaze of the patient angler of useful men, waiting on the bank.

Embra, then and now, is a steep-sided, dark galley laid on a canted keel with Castle at the prow, Palace at the stern, and banks of churchmen, lawyers and merchants oaring away amidships, above slaves locked in the hold. Wherever I stravaiged on the long years of exile, I found it was ever thus, but in Embra it is perhaps most evident. Just stand on the Pentland hills and look at it, going nowhere on its dark grey-green sea, the Ship of Fools.

It is also a place of unexpected levels and curious connections. To keep some brightness in my post-student life, I had continued translating poems of Horace (the stoic melancholy appealed) and Catullus (for the naughty bits) into English and mixed Scots. A fellow clerk of higher standing offered to take me to an upper room in the Grassmarket where the poet Montgomerie held court. With certain reservations – mostly those of envious youth – I admired that man's clean-struck sonnets, and his work sang beautifully. Curiosity outweighing trepidation, I mounted those creaking stairs into a smoke-filled room of laughing, clever, witty, modern men, the *soi-disant* 'Castalian Band' who numbered the King as their head.

And it was there that, drink taken, head spinning with tobacco smoke* from a dozen pipes, I was emboldened to converse with William Fowler. (His sister would marry John Drummond, father of William, my good host. So small a country.) A dozen years my senior, he was dark, slim, sharp-eyed, witty. More to the point, he was a poet, soldier, spy, diplomat, and had become of late the private secretary to Jamie Saxt's wife. Dizzy heights indeed for a cooper's son, conversing wi' the likes of he!

I watched and listened to the gentry with great interest and some yearning. Montgomerie himself was stout, drunk, ill-tempered at some endless court case where he tried to reclaim the pension lost while he was fighting in the Low Countries. He read aloud from the first printing of some sonnets relating to his plaints with the Law, quickly confirming my belief that legal affairs and poetry are not good bedfellows.

But a young man stood up and amid hushed silence sang the poet's 'Come my childrene dere, drau neir me'. My heart was split like a chiselled stave, and long-delayed tears for my parents – or perhaps just the effect of the smoke – ran down my cheek.

Fowler's hand on my arm. 'Bonnie song, is it not?' he said quietly. 'You write yourself?'

---

* Reluctantly, I must conclude Jamie Saxt was not there in disguise. He could not abide the new tobacco fashion, and would write a grand rant, *A Counterblast to Tobacco*.

'I translate the works of my betters,' I replied, quickly wiping my face with my kerchief.

We became friends of a sort, so far as society allowed. When discussing and translating, we met as equals; it was a true brotherhood. It was through Fowler that I heard something of the gossip of the Court: who was in and who was out. And it was in part that unlikely connection that first drew my patron, my lord, my nemesis, to cast his eye my way.

The following spring I completed my apprenticeship and was given brief leave. I rode down to Annandale to return my aunt's dutiful visit (that is, see my fair cousin again) and look up my old college friend. By arrangement I was met in Broughton by six of them on small strong cobs, armed *cap-à-pe*. Adam Fleming looked older, at once more formal and more uncouth. Grown-up, I suppose. He was doing his best to be his dead elder brother.

We shook hands, constrained among those hardened fighting men. Their lances pricked the bright air, swords gleamed, crossbows dangled.

'Thank you for the escort,' I said.

He grimaced. 'It would be unwise to ride by Liddesdale alane. The place is a fuckin' shambles. The Middle March is not much better.'

I felt myself a soft-handed city loon as I rode on beside him, Jed Horsburgh at the other side. It was indeed doolie days in the Borderlands. I saw burned-out cottages, wooden shacks and empty, untended fields. In the villages, folk lurked, disappeared at our approach. I felt starved eyes staring into my back as we rode on. Suspicion and hunger hung like haar in the air, dank and chilling.

Even in an Embra obsessed with Bothwell's doings, the recent battle of Dryfe Sands had been news. Lord Maxwell had decided to deal with the Johnstones once and for all. He rode near three thousand followers to Dryfe Sands, made a complete cock of it. Exeunt, permanently, Lord Maxwell and hundreds of his men. It was said that, three months on, the streets of Dumfries were still spattered in blood.

'Disaster for us,' Adam said. 'We have been unmade for supporting Maxwell. Scott of Buccleuch is Warden now, but I doubt he has the men to keep order. As for Liddesdale . . .'

He shrugged and rode on. We passed through another ruined village, past little huts, our heads turning, turning.

'Does no one build in stone any more?' I enquired.

'What's the point?' he said. 'The Warden's men, or the Grahams, or Sandy's Bairns, or English reivers will burn you out of your cott and pull it down.'

We rode on through Tweedale, climbing towards the pass above Devil's Beef Tub. Near the headwaters we billeted in a cousin's high lonely farm. In the morn we climbed into cloud, descended by unfamiliar ways towards Moffat, then looped west to give Liddesdale a wider berth.

Nothing was said, but the heads of those around me kept turning, turning as we went through the poor lands.

'There will be small hairst this summer,' I said, looking round.

'Why sow when your fields will be burned?'

Adam's voice was neutral, his eyes straight ahead, impassive under his helmet. I thought of the yearning, inspired young man on Arthur's Seat summit, dreaming of love and Constant-inople.

'How do people live now?'

'Them as has the strength go reiving,' Jed said. 'The ithers starve or move to Embra. These are end days, friend.'

We were now deep into Annandale, my mother's people's lands where I had been happy as a child, and the men around me began to be easier. When riders approached on the road, Jed's hand went to his short sword. Two others of our party unstrapped their lance. This is no way to live, I thought.

'For now, this is the only way,' Adam said softly, as though to himself. For a moment we were close again.

The approaching band were a group of Croziers and Moffats, heading for Kelso. As far as anyone could remember, we were not at feud with them. Jed went aside with their leader, they had words. He rode back, nodded once, and we rode on.

This was Adam's life now. It was not mine. Even amid the green braes and birks and burns of Annandale, it was depressing.

'Never mind,' he said, catching my mood. 'We will attend an Armstrong wedding at Gilknockie this week's end!'

'Are you not at feud?'

He shrugged. 'We might kill each other on a dark night, or disputing over a pig, but to not attend the wedding would be a gross insult.'

'You are all mad,' I said.

He smiled. Even Jed chuckled as he rode, hand always to his sword.

'My father wants me there,' Adam said. 'He has business in Carlisle, and I must represent the family. We will teach you to drink deep afore you depart for the saft city.'

HEIDSMEN

I see them yet as I first saw them that day, the heidsmen of the Western March, jostling and carousing by the great fireplace where a small forest burned. Is it just memory with its magnifying glass that makes them so much more vivid and expansive than other men? Or perhaps in country places, where people are further spaced apart, like trees they grow wider, odder and bigger, to fill the light and space available.

Centre among them stood a great bear in a fur-trimmed cloak, wearing muddy riding boots. Round-shouldered, heavy-bearded but balding on top, scar on one cheek and two fingers missing on the vast paw that chucked wine from glass into his maw – the very model of a Borders warlord, the Laird Johnstone, victor at Dryfe Sands. Even across the hall, his voice was loud, his laughter rich and free. He seemed inflated with energy and high humour.

'Aye, he's fucking hilarious,' Adam murmured in my ear. 'In Kirk Yetholm last year he killed a Kerr who accidentally spat on his foot.'

'No hawkers, then,' I replied.

Laird James Johnstone was joking with the tall thin priest and the short red-faced minister who had conducted the marriage ceremony twice, once each, to be on the safe side. Such ceremonies had been banned on pain of death in Embra and St Andrews since the Reform, yet here it was being done quite openly. Either Jamie Saxt was still hedging his bets, or his writ did not amount to much in these parts.

Nearby, flanked by two armed men, a skinny boy waited, face of stone. Expensively dressed in black hose and stockings, his dagger too big for him, he stood out among the big, hardened heidsmen. Unamused by Johnstone's guffaws, he stared straight ahead with wide black eyes as one of his kinsmen bent to whisper in his ear.

'Yon's Maxwell's son,' Adam murmured into my ear. 'The new Eighth Lord.'

I stared again at the boy-man, standing but ten feet from the laughing laird who had killed his father at Dryfe. His eyes would bore holes in stone.

'You're joking me.'

My friend shrugged. 'It's a wedding, the Warden invited them both, they have to come or lose favour. Anyway, loads of food and drink at another's expense.'

I shook my head. 'You lot.'*

---

* That skinny boy bided his time. Some fifteen years later, in a private parley with James Johnstone, he shot him dead. Maxwell escaped abroad, was later captured and finally executed. That – along with the Union – put an end to the greatest Border blood-feud.

The muckle grey-haired man was Sir John Carmichael, famed for the Redeswire Raid twenty years earlier (neither in Redeswire, nor a raid – ballads, eh?). I stared, fascinated by his wild eyebrows, his monumental hands. He listened impassively as a thin, elegant, Frenchified man with white gloves murmured in his ear. Behind them, two swordsmen stood tense as hawks.

'Earl of Angus,' Adam murmured.

'But he is locked in Edinburgh Castle!'

'It seems not. Perhaps he has declared himself a Protestant again.'

Sometimes I scarcely believe myself that I saw such a panoply of reivers in one place, all scrubbed and dressed, swilling down wine and brandy, scoffing pies as though Famine were round the corner. (For many, it was.) Each a heidsman with his family of followers, able to put dozens, even hundreds of armed men, skilled and mounted, in the field in their cause within a day. Five of those men had been, or would be, Warden of the West March. All but one would die well before their time.

Walter Scott, Laird of Branxholme and Buccleuch, new-made Warden of the Western March and host of the evening, stood in the far corner of the Gilnockie Tower hall, with only two of his people by him while folk came to pay fealty or share in the clash.

The dirk at his hip was ornamental, not functional. He was of medium height and build, good-looking and well dressed but not offensively so. At a time when most heidsmen were expansive, swaggering, brimful of vim and smeddum, his gestures I thought restrained, modest. His hands would open towards his listener, and everyone he talked with inclined his way. When they stood together, he made young Robert Bell look an inconsequential thug.

I watched him with interest across the hall. Even in a time when song and story inflated a man's deeds like gas in the belly of a dead pig, Scott was remarkable. Stepson of Earl Bothwell, he had flourished along with him, then was exiled to France after Bothwell's fall. Yet he had returned, and instead of summary execution was given possession of estates in Hailes and Liddesdale.

A minor laird had become at a quill's stroke a man of some substance. Encouraged, he raided deep into Northumberland, bringing back cattle and horses, burning villages to ash, infuriating the English Queen, who demanded his head. Which remained stubbornly on his shoulders, following fulsome apologies from the Scottish regents.

When Queen Mary went into exile, he plotted to have her restored. Her execution, and Jamie Saxt taking control after surviving his regents,* should have been an end to Buccleuch. He was warded in Embra Castle on charges of treason, a doomed man.

The young King visited him there. I wonder yet what understandings arose over the claret, what promises they shook upon

---

*   The Earl of Moray killed by sniper; Lennox stabbed in Edinburgh; Mar poisoned; Morton executed; Esmé Stuart exiled; and the Earl of Gowrie executed. Bordellos have a slower turnover.

that had the former cattle thief, the Catholic-plotting robber baron, restored again to his lands *and knighted*. Now with Warden Maxwell dead at Dryfe, Buccleuch had succeeded to his position. I had it from Fowler that certain courtiers had opened a book on his surviving the year, and the odds offered were even.

But for the moment Sir Walter Scott of Buccleuch and Branxholme was host to the Armstrong wedding, and seemed pleasant, modest, at ease as he worked round the hall. Among these hotheaded, impulsive, unbridled warrior lairds, he seemed cool as a well-run pantry.

All day, as though seeing it afresh through my eyes, Adam had been bemoaning the current state of the March. The Borderlands had been in turmoil for near on three hundred years, but of late murder, black-rent, kidnap and rustling had become the principal economy.

'And I am expected to take side with one, be enemy to another! They talk of honour, but are reduced to stealing ploughshares and timber, and killing unarmed men. How can a man remain honest in such times?'

I already considered myself more follower of Marcus Aurelius than the Blessed Virgin, but neither had to be heir to a small estate in ravaged Annandale. It is not so hard to be stoic when one is Emperor of Rome.

'Long may your father live,' I said.

He nodded sombrely. 'I am not he.'

A darkness hovered around him. Perhaps that was why I spoke carelessly.

'Dinna fash yourself,' I said grandly. 'These Border days will soon be by. In ten or twenty years there will be no more need of Wardens or Keepers. Nor reivers, come to that.'

'An interesting prediction, friend.' The voice was warm and fluid, deep-pitched. Walter Scott's eyes were pale and shining as a coulter blade. 'Perhaps you read this in the stars?'

'A crystal ball, sir,' I replied. 'Left to me by an old spey-wife.'

He smiled, but his eyes never left me. I felt myself a mouse running before them, twisting and turning from their edge.

'I should surely like to possess one of those,' he said. 'Do you think the King has one?'

In that rowdy hall, I felt a grue pass through me like a chill wind shaking a field of grain. He had seen too well where I was going. Flanked by two followers, Walter Scott waited, head cocked to one side, smiling benevolently upon me as though I were the most interesting person in that company.

'All kings have crystal balls,' I stammered. 'At least their queens must think so.'

He laughed at that, full and easy. Clapped me on the shoulder.

'Very good,' he said. He smiled at Adam, drew him into our entertainment. 'According to the Castalian Band, our friend here turns out an elegant sonnet. It now seems he is also a seer and a wit,' he said. 'Keep him close, Master Fleming!'

'Close as my best kye when the Carletons come raiding,' Adam said.

Scott of Buccleuch looked down at his hands, spread his fingers.

'The Carletons will not reive Liddesdale again,' he said quietly. A dark bog opened at my feet. He shrugged, smiled on us both. 'I must talk wi' friends,' he said. 'It is good to see you here, Master Fleming. It is time to let old feuds sleep, and find new loyalties.' He looked at me. 'Master Langton, we must talk again, perhaps in Edinburgh.'

Then he went through the company, so neat and modest and balanced. We watched him go. *'Twenty murders and not yet thirty,'* Thomas Lord Scrope had said of him. He bore them lightly, without swagger.

And he kenned my name. I wished he did not.

I can still entertain Drummond with tales of seeing Wat O'Harden and Ritchie Graham – two of the fastest throatcutters north of the Solway – playing knucklebone on the wedding table with the loser knocking back a brandy cup each time, till they set to arm-wrestling, red-faced and straining like men at stool, then both falling to the floor to lie giggling like bairns.

With the cracked crystal ball of aftersight, I also identify those who will be hung, who would die by the sword and who by the axe or rope, those whose houses would be razed, wives ravished, the lucky ones merely exiled forever, their lands forfeit. And passing among them, murmuring and listening, his coulter-blade eyes shining, the future Lord Scott of Buccleuch.

PATRON

After the ceremony, the company flushed with wine and well-wishing, I crossed the crowded room to reacquaint myself with cousin Helen Irvine of Kirkconnel, grown an inch more tall and a world more bonnie as she took my hands in hers.

My friend was by my side. Heaven help me, I first introduced them.

Her letter was delivered to me a week or so later. Its ostensible purpose was to thank me for my present of a bound copy of the latest *Essais*. She apologized for not having more time for me, perhaps I had been offended? (I had.) It contained her own account of the wedding at Gilnockie. Though I lost it many years ago due to my precipitate departure from these shores, I mind it fine and still smile and frown at the story she told.

The Armstrong wedding at Gilnockie had been her first outing since the timely death of her last suitor. She was newly turned seventeen. She tied a black ribbon at her throat and went with her Springkell cousins, Elizabeth, Edith and May, and they giggled at the sprushed-up lairds and farmer's boys. They

68

goggled at the legendary reivers. They agreed Laird Johnstone resembled nothing so much as an inflated pig's bladder propped on stumpy legs. Wat O'Harden had a nose like a burning brand, and red-brown bracken sprouting from his ears. They sighed for the new Lord Maxwell, a long streak of a boy in black, with his dead father's heidsman dagger awkward, emerald-studded, on his hip.

The new Warden was charming. He kissed her hand without slobbering over it, and asked warmly after her father's health. He looked not at her chest but into her eyes as he said that reports of her beauty were among the few items of Border gossip not exaggerated.

'And you will marry soon, I expect?' he enquired.

She touched the black ribbon at her throat.

'There has been a . . . disappointment,' she said.

His mouth twitched before he offered his sympathy. He waved his hand towards the priest and the minister. 'So which of these would you have your marriage blessed by?'

'Only the minister can make a marriage in the eyes of the Law,' she replied with care.

That charming, alarming man cocked his head a notch to the right.

'And in the eyes of God?' he asked.

'I am a humble Borderlands girl,' she said. 'What would I know of our Maker's preferences?'

'A good answer,' he said, 'though I doubt that very much.'

He gently took and lifted her hand. His lips brushed her knuckles, with a tiny suction.

'*Haud ullis labentia ventis*,' he murmured. So he knew the family motto: 'Yield under no wind' – though it seems to her they did a deal of yielding. 'Have your father choose well,' he added, smiled, and Lord Scott of Buccleuch moved on among the company.

She looked after him, deaf to whatever her cousins were saying. Then she spied Cousin Harry standing wide-eyed, wary and alert at the foot of the stair. As she threaded through the crowd towards him, she began to take note of the man at his side.

I doubt not your friend is a bonnie one, she wrote in the margin of her letter, *bright as an Annan morn. How often do such morns last out the day?*

Though I loved the man, I had been wondering myself.

You will remember my pretty image of the low-born trout rising in pursuit of food, the clever angler waiting on the bank? Though I was but one of his many catches, of limited significance, I marvel still at the alert patience of that man, how he scrutinized the waters and when the moment was right, brought me in with one deft flick of the pen.

Adam had never thought to ask how I was able to leave my employ indefinitely to come to his aid. That is the difference between the gentry and the rest of us.

When his note came to me – a rambling, drunken scrawl,

70

concluding, *You are the only one I trust* – I did not rise up in delight, strike the board with hearty oath, run to my horse and gallop hot-trod to Annandale to the aid of my old friend. Instead I sat crumbling salt over my morning porridge, exhilarated and dismayed in equal measure. Perhaps one who has finally put behind an old affair of the heart, all yearning extinguished, then receives a note pleading for assistance, will imagine how I felt.

Besides, my student days were long over. Back home in Embra after the largely sober sojourn at Wittenberg, the eventful affair of Leyden, I had to my surprise secured a post as correspondence and personal secretary to one of our less sottish Justices. I had, it was hinted at, a *patron*. A wink, a knowing nod, but no name forthcoming. I was too pleased to enquire more deeply. In my youthful vanity I assumed some impartial higher power had noted and rewarded my abilities.

I did not dare lose such a position. The Bench was sitting, and it was most unlikely I would be given leave to go to Annandale for a period indefinite and a reason unstatable. Besides, Adam had not even notified me of his father's death – in a Saughton raid, it seemed – in time for me to attend the funeral. I made allowances, wrote to commiserate, and congratulate him on becoming heidsman. No reply. Then a couple of months later I got an invitation from his mother to attend her marriage to Dand Fleming.

I had attended, of course. Adam would need my support. I was baffled as to why Dand rather than he had become heidsman. But my old friend had been distant and preoccupied at the wedding. His eyes had been cloudy as he looked on me, his voice both formal and slurred as he welcomed me to the Fleming house, then drifted away in inky black.

I had, in truth, ridden back to the city after that wedding nursing a hangover and a sulk. Not only was my friend not open with me, my cousin Helen was away with her mother in Paris, being given a final polish, and no one had seen fit to tell me. Much else had changed since my last Borders visit, with Buccleuch now in the Tower awaiting the Queen's Pleasure following the springing of Kinmont Willie Armstrong from Carlisle Castle.* The newly knighted reiver warlord Sir James Johnstone was now Warden, and had held court at the wedding, throughout which he talked and guffawed.

All in all, I was scunnered wi' Scotia. The life of the Borders, the intrigues of the Court, were no affair of mine. I had no mother or father, no lover, no guild. The wedding had reminded me I was an insignificant man. Which suited me fine. By the time I passed through the Cowgate, I had determined I would abroad to pursue beauty in painting, music and sculpture, encounter freedom of thought and imagination. Heavens, I

---

* Buccleuch had gathered no more than eighty men to free Kinmont from that impregnable fortress. They rode by night, crossed the swollen Border burns, secretly opened a postern gate by forcing its hinges, and entered the castle. They extracted the old ruffian ('What kept ye?' as he buckled on his boots), and were pursued by the English Warden, Lord Scrope. Buccleuch led his men across the raging Eden, turned and taunted Scrope ('I'll gie you better hospitality in Scotland!') and rode off. The ballad-makers loved it. The reivers, including many on the English side, thought it hilarious.

would even be allowed to dance! And abroad I had gone, for near on two years.

Now I walked up the High Street to the Inns, my former friend's letter in my pocket, resolved. I would make my request for leave from my post. It would be turned down. I would then write back to Adam Fleming Esq., explaining why I could not oblige him.

I put in my request. The Judge's senior clerk – a man name of Gillivray, with a face grey and smooth as parchment – would have sneered had I been important enough to expend facial expression upon. His eyelid drooped a lash's breadth as he said he would convey my request to the master. He came back from the inner room.

'He will think on it. You will be contacted.'

Hard to say which of us was the more astonished. I walked to the first of my day's duties, fingers brushing my friend's plea till the fabric shredded.

The summons was thrust under my lodging's door next day at first light. I read it, cold striking up from the stone threshold through my slippers. I turned and went back up the winding stair, deep in thought and already numb to my knees.

That afternoon found me in an antechamber in Liberton Tower, a morning's walk from the city walls. All had been secret, nameless. No one would meet my eyes as I was passed from watchman to adviser, hustled up the back stair by one armed man to meet another at the top. The guard now stood silent by the stair door, armed merely with a short sword, dagger and a pistol the size of a harquebus, though by the look of him he could dispose of me with bare hands.

'A fine afternoon,' I ventured.

'Fuck off, pisspot,' he replied.

I was unable to produce a witty reply, so just stood there, examining the grain of the stone at my feet.

'Attend me!'

The voice, though muffled by the door between us, was lightly stained with the earth-brown vowels of the Borderlands. My guard nodded. I entered a panelled room, furnished only with a table, a heavy seat and a not-very-good tapestry of a hunting scene that conflated the Lothians with Ancient Greece.

The man standing at the window slit was unshowily dressed, with just a short dirk on his hip. As he advanced on me, smiling, I understood now the hugger-mugger. I had lately heard rumours that instead of having his head removed, he was about to be released from the Tower of London, after private audiences with the Auld Hag and Cecil. Apparently the springing of Kinmont Willie had been put by. Fowler had hinted at high politics. And now the former Warden of the Western March was back, in a city full of his enemies, any of whom might surround him in a close or tavern and dispatch him from the rowdy world.

He put his hand on my shoulder. I tried not to flinch. Who knows how many men that hand had put away with sword or pistol, and how many more he would with a stroke of the pen in days to come.

'I hope you have brought your crystal ball, Master Langton,' he said. 'You may need it yet.'

Rarely is it fortunate to come to the attention of the high heid ones, and in those days there were few higher and more precariously set than Scott of Branxholme and Buccleuch, my secret patron.

He commenced with enquiries as to my health and situation since my sudden return from Leyden. As I stammered that I was quite well set, he wished me well with my proposed translation of that scandalous and – smiling – probably heretical and maybe even treasonous work, *De Rerum Natura*.

As I tried to remember to breathe, he went on to commend some of my verses I had copied out for the Queen's secretary some weeks back, and quoted – accurately – a line that had pleased several: '*And all the bright stars were her dowrie.*' This was flattering and worrying in equal measure, his point being to remind me just how informed he was, and to hint he was once again privy to the King.

Then he took me by the elbow, guided me to the window slit and gently outlined how my present living and my future prospects depended entirely on his favour. As did my long life, which of course he wished for me. He had had his eye on me for some time, and now, through my Border relations and an old friendship from my college days, I could be of some small service.

He then instructed how I was to proceed in the matter of young Fleming, Rob Bell and Helen Irvine of Bonshaw. He made it seem a little thing, a favour to him, a task to which I alone was suited.

I nodded, stared at the floor. He softly put out his hand, lifted my chin so I must stare into his grey and shining eyes. He hefted a small purse. 'For the road,' he said. 'And maintenance. There need be no accounting.'

He tossed it. I caught it, chinking in my hand, and I felt myself falling from whatever high opinion I ever had of myself.

It was near dawn when I finished my report. It had required much consideration, and twice I had to start afresh. None stirred in the Fleming compound. Likely my friend lay sleeping in his damp guardroom, safe there at least, dreaming of Fair Helen and better days to come.

I used the last of the candle to burn my drafts, powdered the ashes, sealed and folded the fair copy inside my shirt, then laid me down with blanket and first light happed about my shoulders.

STILETTO

I had aimed to set down plainly only what I witnessed concerning the events at Kirkconnel, to correct the folk haivers and bring some understanding. Yet already I find footnotes, asides and addenda have begun to run wild down the margins and among the lines. I like to think of them as bright wildflowers that border and run through the acres of turnip and kale by which we feed ourselves.

But I suspect the truth is this. I set out to memorialize Adam, Helen and Bell, and those around them. Perhaps I have some faint hope that through this they will not be forgotten, nor entirely transmuted from human clay and recast into the unyielding stone of ballad. But these marginalia, these flowers of *moi*, proliferate among stern, productive history. They sway in the wind, raise their heads to the sky and cry, '*Me! Me! Remember me!*'

Were this story set down by stern Livy or high-minded Plutarch, I would scarcely appear but as a footnote. But I am not they. I call on Monsieur Montaigne for his support – his personal anecdotes are said by some to lower the tone of his *Essais* – but know I am not he. I am but a passing aside in another's story.

Yet I would you remember me, the canny cloot.

Jed Horsburgh jogged my elbow as I ate dozily in the scullery next morning. He carried two Border swords in one big fist, gauntlets in the other. He said I must come outside with him.

For dignity's sake I first finished my porridge, then followed him out.

He stopped in the yard between house, peel tower – no sign of life there – and stables. Said he would make a man of me. I said I was man enough. At least I could read and scrieve my name.

His muckle right paw whipped out. I ducked so it but cuffed the side of my head. He grunted. Then we stood in the court-yard and looked at each other.

'If not for your sake, cheeky whelp, then for his. I canna aye be at his side.'

Fair point, but still I hesitated.

'If you think you'll be spared because you go unarmed, you're a bigger gowk than I tak ye for.'

I took the blunted sword Jed handed me, donned the padded glove and made ready.

Whack with the flat of his sword, faster than the drop of a hawk. Again. And again, to shoulders, to thigh. I could not parry quick enough. The little fencing I had been taught was nothing

78

like this. When I attacked him, he turned me aside with ease, then *whack*, on my bad ribs. I could not but cry out.

I pulled back. Studied him as he stood ready to go again. He was a fighting man all his life. I could not possibly defeat him.

He swung high – I ducked. He stabbed frontal – I jumped back. He feinted to chest, then made at my legs – I skipped aside, went by him. His blade was heavy, I was small and fleet. No matter how strong and skeely he was, I should be able to move faster. I noted his left arm moved a fraction early, to give balance for his coming sword-arm blow. That movement, and a certain flicker of his eyes, were my prompts.

I began to enjoy myself. I could not fight him, but I was younger, lighter, quicker on my feet. I had fought many a rammie as a bairn in the city yards, and had learned to slip blows from fist or stick.

Autumn wind blew hair over my eyes, dust streamed out from our boots. It was a dance of sorts. When he came on, I played the female part. When he moved across, I sashayed. When he raised his arm, I slipped under, birled, made ready again.

For several minutes he could not lay a blow on me.

'Stand and fecht like a man,' he panted.

'No chance.'

He near got me then, a quick slice coming in low. I louped aside. A couple of side swipes I dodged easily, then found he'd worked me to the corner of the stable wall with no room to move back, no sideways escape. His sword stopped an inch from my ribs.

'You're a runt, Langton, but quick on your feet. We maun use that.'

We agreed that even if he had a month to train me, he could not make me a match with sword for an experienced man. He went to his house – little more than a byre ahint the stables – and came back with a long, very slim, dagger. He carefully fitted a bate to it, then handed it to me, haft first. I weighed it in my right hand. It was light, with little edge. The thin blade flickered in the sun as it followed the turn of my wrist. I had not seen the like.

'Italian,' he said. 'I have the sheath in the house.'

'Where did you get this?' I asked, transferring it automatically to my better hand.

'Italy, of course.' I stared; he shrugged. 'Long yarn,' he said. 'So you are corrie-fistit – that is good. It will surprise them.'

We went back to the centre of the courtyard and faced up. I was beginning to warm to his ugly mug.

'It will not happen like this, loon,' he said quietly. 'Assassins nor reivers favour fair fights. But this is where we maun begin.'

I see him yet, his big sonsie face mottled with weather, drink and hardship. Under eyebrows like grand tufts of barley, his narrowed eyes betrayed his next move. Him it was who showed me how to slip a sword-thrust, shimmy and let it slide by, then jump in quick with the stiletto. He showed me the gaps that armour, whether leather or metal, seldom covers – where neck meets shoulder, under the raised arm, the privates and low belly. The point would slide through leather jerkin or metalled jack. '*Ain deep strike*,' he said, '*then a second tae mak siccar.*'

I owe my life to that dour, kindly man of Hawick. Others owe their death to his instruction.

When the sun was high as it would get that day, Jed called a halt. I nodded and turned back to the house, then gasped and fell to my hunkers as his blow hit my side.

'More often it happens like that,' he said.

I nodded weakly, as though broken – then sprang inside his guard. My Italian dagger passed the base of his neck. As we clutched, our faces were inches apart. His teeth were few and blackened, his breath made dung seem sweet.

'Aye, you're a sleekit wee shite, Harry Langton,' he said. 'You may do yet. And for fuck's sake do something wi' your hair.'

In my room, I took off my shirt. Red weals where his blade had slapped, bruises like livid thunderclouds from my earlier beating. I thought of Robert Bell, of his follower who had throttled me. Thinking of the third one who had stood aside, his face averted lest I kenned him, I passed the sling over my head. The pale-tan leather sheath fitted well by my right rib.

I slid the long thin dagger in. Wincing, I pulled on shirt, then the dark-stained leather jerkin Jed had found me. It was thick, tanned hard as wood, yet moved with me easily enough. I had asked whose it had been; got a dark look for answer.

In the yard, I doused my head from the bucket, washed out sweat and dust. I pulled fingers through wet hair grown long, then tied it at the back. Young Watt watched me without expression from the back door.

I leaned over the well and looked in. There was no sign of what I carried under my shirt. When I straightened up, Watt had gone. Still, I had no doubt eyes were watching as I went to the stable for Handsome Jenny, the dandy cob mare the Flemings had loaned me. I saddled her up, took in the stirrups a notch then led her through the gates in the barnkin wall.

Outside the walls, the world was big and fair and mine. What I had seen reflected in the well was no city scholar. I swung up on the cob, turned her head for Kirtlebridge and a woman I kenned there.

THE FORTUNE RIGG

This morning as I trimmed my beard before the hazy steel mirror, I was musing on Jamie Fifth, idly wondering if my grandfather ever saw him taking the air round Holyrude, or stepped into the gutter some summer morning to let him and his courtiers pass as they hurried showily towards their graves. Was the King clean-shaven, lean or fat? Did he smile with delight at his youth and importance, or scowl anxiously, wondering whom he could trust and whom never to let stand behind him?

I must ask my mother, I thought, if her father ever spoke of seeing Jamie Fifth. It would be interesting to know. And then I thought, *My mother is near sixty years dead. Her body is bone and slime in Blackfriars kirkyard*, and my razor hand stilled before the mirror. Truly I am an orphan in this world. Every one I care for is long gone. Even the man who left me this stub for a right hand lies within his rotting shroud.

My good hand resumes its purpose. Outside my window the

freed hawk hunts high over the dene, brings home its prey to none but itself.

The wind keened through beech and birch, stripping weary leaves away. Along the Kirtle they piled at my mare's feet, black-spotted, scarlet and sere. The same wind, hastening change and death, blew through me as I rode across Kirkconnel Lea and crossed the burn. The hairst was gathered, such as it was. The beasts were being brought in from the high pastures. The reiving season would come soon enough.

I stayed well west of Blackett House and the Bell lands. Handsome Jenny and I threaded through woods by half-remembered tracks, came into the open at Laverockstane. I had to ask the way of a herdsman, who looked at me queerly, then directed me by the Roman camp to Allerbeck farm. And from there I took the track over Cauldwell Knowe, clinging to my bonnet in the gale. It was the long way round to my destination, but I was in no hurry, with much to ponder.

Above all, I thought on Adam's fixed belief that someone had been trying to have him killed. It was clear his trysting was not as secret as he'd believed, and Rob Bell had not tried to catch him out in order to shake his hand. Yet Bell struck me as impulsive and emotional, not given to indirect means and subtle planning. He was one for the shot to the head, the knife in the guts, delivered by himself.

After recent years of terrible weather and a century of autumnal reiving, such was the poverty and desperation and wildness of the Borders, bad things could happen to a well-dressed man, aimed at his purse. And were the Flemings not still at feud with more families than they could account?

Could be that Adam was merely ill-chancy. Could be that he spent too much time in the peel tower, sulking and pondering his new father, sleepless from thinking on Helen Irvine. And yet.

'*Jed stays hard by me*,' he'd complained. '*I canna take a piss but he is there holding my cock. That worries me.*'

It worried me too, for Jed was neither fanciful nor a grasper of pizzels. And the kitchens of the Fortune Rigg were clean. I knew that, for I had seen them often enough at the end of day, ever since the mistress of that inn first led me by the hand up to her private quarters.

I came down to Kirtlebridge, forded the burn, then dismounted round the back of the Fortune Rigg. The stable boy stared, then he kenned me from before, and with but a hint of smirk put her away in the furthest stall.

I crossed the yard and went in the back way, through the scullery and the taproom and the milk parlour where the girl slapped butter, her dark head averted.

I opened the second door on the left. Elenora Jarvis looked up from her accounts and smiled. She had candid, wide-open eyes, and showed her inner heart to none.

'Four days in Annandale, Harry, and not called on your old flame.' She rose and looked at me more keenly, put her hand lightly to my battered cheek. I could not but flinch at the touch. 'Dearie me, these loons at the Ecclefechan Inn are a rough crowd.'

'They were but a dozen,' I said. 'Easily seen off.'

She laughed then kissed me quick and light. 'I dinna doubt it,' she said, and squeezed my arm. She stood back and she was not smiling now. 'Unarmed still, I see. That may be for best. I think young Fleming sent for you?'

'He did that.'

'How long will you be in Annandale?'

'Till he has no need of me. I have been given leave from Embra.'

She sat herself on the edge of the table, straightened the feathers of the quill with careful fingers.

'They say he is become a sot, and isna right in the head.'

I hesitated, but there was no one else to trust.

'That is for show.'

She nodded, smoothed again the feathers from stem to tip. I have seen men so stroke the haft of a dagger, in wonder at the potency they hold.

'For why?' she enquired.

I took a long breath such as made my ribs ache again, then decided.

'He is in dangerous love, and he thinks some mean to kill him.'

'Love is always wanchancy,' she replied. 'And in the Border-lands, men live by killing.'

'Not usually their own family,' I said. 'Besides, it is Fair Helen.'

She wiped clean the sharp tip, laid down the quill. She closed the cap of the well, a small click in that silent room.

'Wait up the stair till I'm done,' she said. 'I will have the lad bring food and drink.'

Elenora Jarvis was a canny woman, and the Fortune Rigg inn was of good repute. When cott and peel alike could any day or night be reived, an inn was seldom harmed. Even Henry Tudor's army had merely commandeered it and its unfortunate serving women for a couple of nights, then moved on to sack the rest of Scotland. Jamie Fifth barracked men here while they reived the reivers' lands, yet the inn had kept its roof. Men will aye need somewhere to eat, carouse, rest and change horses.

'Gin I be careful with my friends and make foes of nane,' she would say as she barred the doors last thing, 'this house will stand long whiles.' She would bank down the fire herself, trusting none other to do it. I liked to sit at the bench and watch as she would send the stable boy off with his bread and cheese, close the shutters, cork the flagons, lick her fingers, then pinch out candle and creusie lamps. Unhurried, competent, at ease.

I try not to think how the curve of her hip, the flight of her busy brown hands as she talked, her warm easy ways, so rhymed with my mother in her younger day.

That summer when I was but a lad of seventeen, down visiting my mother's people and my new student friend, she had turned on the stair, smiled and reached back to take my shaking hand. She led me as one might a lover or a son, though in truth I was neither. She bade me sit within, then took off her cowslip-yellow bonnet, hung it with care upon the newel post and closed the outer door.

Then in her chamber, after brandy and conversation about my doings and hers, the talk of Embra and the clack of Annandale, her easy laughter and my more nervous giggles, on the wide padded sill she showed what she wanted and needed of me. And though we both guessed my nature, I was happy to be there with her and oblige.

I sat now on that same padded window seat, eating bread, cheese and cold sweet mutton. The boy had brought wine, but I drank only water, wanting to keep my head clear. The long dagger lay uncomfortably under my shift. The report for my patron was folded small within my jerkin.

I sat and stared out into the yard. How many others had pleased Mistress Jarvis on this same seat? Few, I suspected, for consorting was dangerous, the pox widespread, and she was canny. I was educated and had travelled enough to be interesting to her, but was not of importance enough to be a threat.

Elenora Jarvis had been blessed with good health and good looks. Of all the folk both high and low that I had met, she seemed the least constrained. She was answerable to none. Her mother and father had died in the plague shortly after she married, and the inn passed to her man. Best fortune of all, I sometimes thought as she loosed her hair, hung her yellow coif on the newel post, then reached for me, lay in her husband.

Married women owned nothing, were always constrained and answerable, however amenable their husbands. Affairs with a wife, even rumours of amours, were perilous. Avenging husbands, brothers, fathers, even children, poured out of every closet, duty-bound to kill the lover as he climbed out the window, then the wife could look forward to lifelong nunnery.

The only enviable woman, free to conduct her own affairs, of the heart and business, was the widow. And so, though she always avowed he was a decent man, when Alistair Jarvis, new owner and licensee of the Fortune Rigg, leaned too far from an upper window he was cleaning and fell to break his neck on the cobble below, he became the perfect husband.

'Is it not time you married again?' I asked when I thought us well enough acquaint.

'And lose this?' She had gestured round the little room, indicating the whole inn, her life.

'Do you not wish to have a life companion you can trust?' I persisted. We were easy now, the flurry done, ready to chat. Soon she would have me move and sleep downstairs, as I always did. 'To fall asleep with another, wake and find him still there?'

She propped herself on an elbow, looked at me steadily in the candlelight. She put her hand to my bare chest, her fingers drummed lightly where my heart lay quiet.

'Do not you?' she said gently.

We said no more on the matter.

Canny investment had brought her a share in a claret-import house in Leith, and with that part-ownership of a boat delighting in the name of *Sonsie Quine*. She did her own accounting, had an Embra lawyer, and made sure it was common knowledge her money was kept in the city. Though I thought her old enough to be my aunt, she was not yet thirty. She had a merry nature, could swear like a spey-wife when crossed, and flirt with the best of them.

I miss that woman still. On nights like this I fain would talk at length with Elenora Jarvis, please her in that little snug, then go downstairs with my candle to the box-bed we cried 'the dog-basket', and there sleep sound as the small rain fell outside, feeling myself at last free of yearning, understood.

I ate and drank slowly, watching cloud-shadows chase over pasture, woodland, scrub and high bare tops. After the Fleming household, with himself mooning in the peel tower, nursing his love and his suspicions alike, and Dand being jovial, and Janet Elliot suffering and smiling, and Jed beating me with the flat of his sword, this was an easy place to be.

Yet there was the matter of ill food from a clean kitchen.

I looked out upon the courtyard. Folk of the village came in, came out. A cart, near empty with brushwood, pulled by a knackered horse, led by a limping man with a nose like the landlady's florid quill, came by and tottered on up the valley. A carriage pulled by an ill-matched pair lurched down the rutted track toward Annan and the Solway shore. Two barefoot children shepherded five scraggy yowes from one poor pasture to another. The wean laughed as the boy threw a clod at her and missed, then they both forgot the yowes in a game of mud-throwing.

That was as exciting as it got in Kirtlebridge. I closed my eyes.

The clatter of hooves in the courtyard woke me. Two tall men on fine roans. The stable boy ran out, took the reins. The men were lightly armed but stood looking at the inn as though they possessed it. One said something, the taller man laughed, then turned his head away, and in that turning away I had him, in both our first and second acquaintance.

Elenora came out into the yard, in a fluster of hands and something like a curtsy as she ushered them towards the door. As they passed from my sight, the clean-shaven man laughed again, and the taller one with thin lips and elegant beard trimmed tight to his jawline put his hand easily on our hostess's rump, as a man might something he owned.

I sat back from the window, my heart banging like a cooper's mallet. That same man had averted his head from me by the Kirtle days earlier, stayed in moon-shadow as I was beaten, sanctioning it.

I knew now why he had stayed in shadow, for we had met before briefly, in Embra, on the upper stair of a tenement where I had been sent to deliver papers for my Judge. I knew not his name, but he had been calling on William Douglas, Earl of Angus, then new-made Warden of the Western March.

★

She came in with my supper as light failed, went to the tinderbox and lit the lamp.

'Important guests?' I asked.

She paused, looked down at me, her face in shadow.

'All my guests are important.'

I inspected the pie she had put before me. It smelled right enough. The cup of wine likewise. I looked up at her.

'That cocky fellow with the English beard who made familiar with you?'

'Jealous?'

'A little . . . anxious.'

She near smiled, but would not look at me straight.

'Master Dowie Fairfax serves the high heid yins.'

'Such as Earl Angus?'

She quivered, then was still. 'Very possibly.'

'You like Fairfax?'

She sat down.

'I thole him,' she said quietly. 'Why do you think my inn has lasted so long?'

After a pause long enough to silently curse my naivety, I said, 'I am sorry for that.'

'Eat your pie afore it grows cold,' she replied.

I toyed with my knife, considered the matter. I kenned I was not trustworthy – why think her to be?

I ate. She watched me, waited till I drank, then rose to her feet.

'I maun work on a while,' she said. 'We will talk later.' I nodded. The pie tasted as it should, as did the wine.

She stopped at the door.

'Make yourself comfortable. You will come to no harm here.'

Then she was gone. I ate and drank slowly, reliving that assault by the Kirtle, the look on Rob Bell's face as he had me by the throat, my sense of the influence of the man in the shadows. I thought and thought with eyes half shut as if to better see, but why Dowie Fairfax or his master the Earl of Angus would have spared me was a matter much deeper than the Solway.

Late calls and clatters in the courtyard. Low laughter, then her voice.

'Guid nicht, and come again!' She did not sound true.

Peering down from my window, I saw Fairfax lean down from his horse, and her rise up to embrace him. He looked up at my window, so sudden I may not have recoiled in time.

A clatter of hooves, a man's voice sang 'The Winding Road Does Call' quite fairly, then faded.

The cook and the serving girl bade goodnight, the stable lad left. A few last clunks as she put the doors to, slid the bars, smoored down the fires for the night. Then her steps slowly up the stair.

Elenora Jarvis stood at the door and looked at me. I looked back. She sighed, then loosed her yellow bonnet, went out to hang it on the newel post, came back in and barred the door.

She studied my face as one might an interesting but incomplete poem. Her palm brushed my face en route to the back of my neck. Her deft fingers unpicked the ribbon, then she pulled my hair free so gently that moisture pricked behind my eyes.

'So,' she said, 'you have come for more than my fine een.'

I admitted I had come – in addition to a desire to see again her bonnie face and fine eyes – in part about Adam Fleming's sickness after supping here.

'Who dare question my kitchen!'

'Not I. Yet none of his companions got sick.' I hesitated. 'Perhaps he was poisoned.'

Her hand stilled on my arm.

'Perhaps he drinks too much and nurses delusions.'

'Perhaps. Was Master Fairfax present that night?'

'No!' She paused. 'But his friend John Rusby was. He came in after the Fleming party.'

'He was the other here today?'

She nodded. I could not mind him well. Hefty shoulders, a swollen nose, clean-shaven, nothing else. I had been riveted to his companion.

'Tell me more of Fairfax.'

She lifted her head and regarded me.

'It is said when in London he reports on the Scottish Court and spies on the English one. In Embra he brings news of the aged Queen, and spies on the King's men. They say Earl Angus also pays him well.'

'Which side is he loyal to?'

She shrugged. 'He is of use to many, I think.'

'Whose side are you loyal to?'

She laughed at that. 'Mine own.'

'Nothing by-ordinar there,' I said. 'The question is what alliances we may make along the way.'

'And I thought you had come here for my fine body,' she murmured.

'And to enjoy your wit and good sense. And please you in whatever way.'

'There will be nane of that tonight.' She was right, of course. 'Let us talk of other things.'

'Such as?'

She reached for the flask, poured herself brandy and settled back into the best chair.

'A yarn of your flight from Leyden might be entertaining.' It seemed the blether of the Borders spread faster than watch-fires. 'The Dean of the College?'

'Not my type.'

'The Abbess, then?'

'Definitely not my type. Not when I have memories of you.'

'Foot-licking whelp.'

Perhaps a hint of rose came to her cheeks. I thought of her awkward last embrace with Fairfax.

'I shall give you a true accounting. It concerns a book I greatly desired access to, one that is not permitted in our enlightened country. I cultivated a douce librarian with an alarming mouth—'

'Ah, I had thought there would be love involved!'

'Not love. Lust perhaps, and some hope of gratification.'

I gave her the story, made good in the telling. The days of

astounded reading, feeling my dark world illuminated by words burning across so many centuries. The weeks of secret copying, the wandering hands kept at bay, the pallet bed in the scriptorium. The moonlit city as I hurried to my alliance with the Abbess. The warning, the hasty packing, the barred door, the window and the waiting horse below. And so homeward, with my copy in a sealed pouch next to my skin, more precious to me than gold.

Some good touches in there, I thought – the cloth-muffled hooves, the Abbess's bad breath, the pished guards at the city gate. I did not name Lucretius' heretical poem, nor say that when this affair was by and time permitted, I sought to translate *De Rerum Natura* into English or even good Scots, the first to do so. Fowler had hinted that, anonymously distributed, it might make my name among the Castalians.

Elenora enjoyed a good yarn, as I had enjoyed hers about Dowie Fairfax, spy for two Crowns, aid for the Earl of Angus at his incessant plotting. When we finally bade our goodnights and I went chastely off to the dog-basket down the stair, I doubted if she believed my tale more than I believed hers.

PEND

After all, what have we here? A creature that is the strangest thing on Earth — a long stalk of matter that has grown an outlandish flower at its crown. A lamp that lights itself, that knows its own existence, and by the same light foresees its own demise . . .

But I must delay no longer, and pen this next scene before shame stills my hand.

In the morn, as we bade goodbye outside the Fortune Rigg, Elenora hugged and pressed herself to me. Her eyes widened, and not at my manly charms.

'So you *are* armed,' she murmured. 'That may be for best.' She put her mouth close to my lug. Her warm breath in that orifice.

'Dinna let Dowie in ahint you. Trust nane.'

For a moment we regarded each other direct. I nodded, then turned to take my cob from the smirking stable lad.

'Haste ye back!' she cried as I left. I waved without turning round, for it was her commercial cry, given to all. But her whisper had been for me alone. *Trust nane*, herself included. That much I believed.

Once clear of Kirtlebridge, I set Handsome Jenny on the high way to Langholm where my report would be sent off. As I crossed the muir, then down into the dale that narrowed like a coney trap about the burn, there was an old song birling in my heid.

> *Then lowly lowly cam she in,*
> *And lowly cam she by him;*
> *The only words she ever said,*
> *'Young man I think you're dyin.'*

Your man in Langholm could not look me straight, on account of his skelly een as much as his crooked nature. In the back of his saddlery he brought me wax and candle, watched without comment as I pressed my patron's ring into the seal. His mark. His man. Deliver to Himself.

It was mart day in the toun. The streets were full of stoorie-feet pedlars, raggedy-arse drovers with their scraggy yowes, folk crying their wares. In the sole inn – a poor place after the Fortune Rigg – a solitary fiddler sat scraping wood, sheep gut and horsehair.

I stood long minutes at the open door. Mine host called for my order, but at first I could not speak, for the slow air 'The Hangman's Tryst' clutched like a garrotte about my throat.

★

There are only so many fiddle tunes one can enjoy, beasts one can watch being bid for. I took a daunder down the High Street, found the printer and speired after his latest. But the pamphlets were the usual religious ravings or else sadly pornographic. The Latin texts were familiar to me, and the poetry yet more flowerings rapidly gone to seed. Allegory and decoration, all that courtly wit I had lately so admired, seemed but daft to me now. Whatever had happened to good Robert Henrysoun, with his death-knell metre and braid Scots hammering down the coffin lid on life?

I bade the printer good day and, aiming for the river, turned down a narrow pend. A man dark and thickset as a mart bullock stepped before me. No helmet, but sword, dagger, leather armour.

'Cuntface,' he greeted me.

'Begging your pardon?'

'Whoreson gutterslug bumboy.'

He already gripped his short sword. By the failing of the light, I knew another had stepped into the passage behind me. I held up my right hand.

'Whoa! *Politesse, s'il vous plaît.*'

'Whit?'

I stepped nearer him, put my left hand up to my chest to demonstrate my sincerity.

'Friend, a little politeness glows like fruit on the underside of leaves.'

My hand slipped inside my shirt, and while the oaf still

grappled with my words, the stiletto slid through his leather, twitched off a rib and sank into his heart. A quick twirl to finish it off, then I whirled to face the man behind. He looked at me, at my crimson blade. His mouth fell open as his friend clattered to the ground. He ran.

I stepped over the body and ran the other way. Louped the wall at the end of the pend, circled back to the mart. My mare was still tied behind the farrier's. I dawdled in the shadows, wanting assurance none was watching her. A drover brought a tummle of kye through the street, lowing and shitting. As they clattered by I untied Handsome Jenny, led her round the corner, quickly mounted and bid honest Langholm farewell.

My hand pauses, the point drips. I put the pen down, wipe the tip and stare down at the North Esk. Below, my host Drummond leads some artistically inclined young member of our local gentry around his garden. By the way his hand waves, I fear he is reciting some of his poetry.

The young man stands – patient, bored, in thrall? At this distance I cannot tell. I was as him once, before that autumn I went down to Annandale, before a man, now long dust, took time to instruct me how to kill and so live a little longer.

I cross myself with my good hand. As for that desperate young man, heart hammering as he put Langholm behind, crouched low over his horse, what he was becoming? What he had perhaps always been, for when my assailant stepped before me in the pend, everything had become clear, slow, inevitable. Terror and remorse came later.

It is many years since God and I had anything to say to each other. I expect he is saving his best for last. *Timor mortis conturbat me*, indeed.

I pick up the pen again.

'There is a man deid in Langholm,' I said. 'A foreign blade passed through his heart.'

Jed did not blink.

'Any witness?'

'One. He ran awa to whoever sent him.'

'So he'll no testify. We do not want you summonsed.'

Jed Horsburgh's shack within the compound was chill but clean and orderly. It was said he had a wife in Alnwick. In summer when there was little fighting he would go to her, then be back to work in the hairst. I did not doubt he had a steady hand on the plough.

'John Rusby,' I said. 'Tall, muckle-shouldered, baggit nose?'

'Aye,' he said. 'I ken him. He's welcome as a forky golach crawlin' out of yer lug.'

He looked at me enquiringly.

'He was the one that ran off. I jalouse he poisoned Adam in the Fortune Rigg.'

Breath whistled atween his broken teeth.

'And I thought you were just awa hooring.'

I shrugged. Man of the world.

'I saw him at the inn with Dowie Fairfax. He may have had a glisk of me.'

On my ride back there had been time to work it out. Fairfax and Bell had spared my life by the Kirtle. All that had changed since then was my seeing him with Rusby, who had been present when Adam fell sick. I must have been followed from the Fortune Rigg to Langholm. I was not ready to consider what part Elenora might have played in this.

Jed scowled at the pristine earth floor. 'Fairfax is a dangerous man.'

'They say he is at one with our Warden.'

Jed picked at his teeth with the point of his dirk. He found a shard of old meat, held it up atween thumb and finger then flicked it out the window.

'I say he is at one wi' many.'

We sat in silence. I heard Philby yelp, the peel-tower door thud to. Adam went by the stables and out the compound gate, hound at his heels. He was sprushed to the gills and doing his best to look casual.

Jed was already on his feet, short sword in his hanger.

'Froggy's gaun a-courtin',' he said. His hand heavy on my shoulder kept me down. 'Weel done in Langholm,' he said. 'Seems you're a natural.' And he was gone after his man.

At the gate, I watched Jed slip into the woods below. Though strong and weighty, he appeared to float over the ground. It seemed we took turn to be Adam's guards. '*Quis custodiet custodes?*' I murmured.

I turned away from the bright day, quick enough to glimpse Watt at an upper window, looking down at the woods where Adam and Jed had gone. He saw me and for the first time his thin face masked not contempt but fear. Then he withdrew.

I went to the kitchens, needing something on my stomach. It could never be well done to kill a man. I had seen his face as I stepped over him. I wished I had not.

Yet I was hungry and would eat. In Langholm a man had left the world of appetite and, judging by his expression, he left it most reluctantly.

BONSHAW

Across the North Esk gill at Hawthornden there festers not quite pond nor marsh. Year after year of leaf-fall rots there among reeds. I sat on the bank on this chill afternoon of Martinmas and watched the last leaves tear off and fall. In a few weeks they will be black, then sink. This both depresses and soothes me.

A minor Latin poet linked falling leaves to both the dead and our memory of them. My friend and patron Drummond has lately translated sonnets from the Italian on the same theme. Though he is not a terribly good poet, I am gentle with his later verse, because for all its courtly conceits his loss is real. The woman he was to marry died but weeks before the wedding. Though he married later, and has the many rowdy children who enliven the castle with their shrieks, in his cups late at night, her name still arises. Mary Cunningham of Barns. *Sweet Marie*.

The sounds bubble from his lips like a drowning man giving up his last air.

At night the will-o'-the-wisp flickers across this bog. The peasants say they are spirits of the dead, but I think not. Yet the dead return to us, no doubt, by night or by day, rising from the rotted mulch of the years. Up from black oblivion they rise, catch fire and play across the surface of our minds, insubstantial, unignorable.

Adam, Helen, Jed, William Fowler, my fine landlady removing her brave yellow coif to signal time for pleasure, my mother singing old songs of Annandale and my good father grunting as he drove his cooper's hammer down – they all passed long syne into the black bog. They are its unexpected graces, its jack-o'-lanterns, elusive flares that are left to us, to baffle and delight with their false fires.

That season after Martinmas rang high and bright as a clean-struck bell. The days grew hard, the stars more sharp-edged each night I left the peel tower after conferring with Adam. Each morning the sky stretched paler above the hills. Winds stripped the trees of their glowing dead and piled them in ditches to rot.

Across the in-by fields, fat kye were clumped like juicy fruit awaiting picking, and it was time to make a long-anticipated visit.

Dew was still heavy on the riggs when Handsome Jenny and I followed the Kirtle downstream then crossed the glittering Lea. I nodded to shepherd, farmer, labouring wife, a bairnie staggering at the door, unsure whether to wave or run from the stranger.

It was aye that way in the Borderlands. Folk would look at me, hesitate, look again, uneasy. At a glance they saw this was not a soldier, not preacher nor merchant nor pedlar (where are his goods?), not handyman or tailor, nor farmer, smith, journeyman or tinker (no tools of his trade). Not a hangman nor a doctor nor stockman (again, no tools). Not quite a musician, ballad-makar, or juggler (they travel in groups, for their own protection, and have better patter). He has no companion or servant, yet he is not a servant.

Of what family or guild is he? How are we to treat such a one?

Border folk do not welcome strangers – with good reason, Lord knows. Their eyes did not linger on me long, and few ever shook my hand, in case I carried some contagion they could not name. They saw one who is not defined by family, trade, guild or station, who is thus a not-quite man, and gave me the by.

Fair enough, really, to pass by such a man. For who knows how the world appears from behind his not-quite eyes?

I passed the ruinous kirk where Irvines and Maxwells still lay in the lower crypt while their allies, dependants, retainers and workers worshipped elsewhere. I wondered if the horse blankets were spread yet in the chamber off the vestry, and when young love had last lain there.

I swivelled in the saddle. None rode behind though curious glances followed me. Jed had gone with Adam and Dand to do the rounds of the tenants. I was on my own, as I had long been. The Italian dagger under my jerkin, wit and low cunning were my only friends.

As the high cleuch crowned by Blackett House came into view, I turned my cob's head and made a long loop, through the woods of Burnfoot. I had no desire to meet with Rob Bell again. So I rode by the ruins of Langshaw's once douce wee farm, charred rafters pointing at the sky like broken ribs. I was entering a land part real, part myth, the world of my childhood summers. Smoke unfurled blue-grey from the woods upstream as I rejoined blithe Kirtle water and followed it on down.

I took the way without hesitation, knowing it somewhat better than the back of my hand (which I doubt if I would recognize, set alongside others). The water was easy at the ford, then I urged Handsome Jenny up the steep bank, through a stand of young Scots pine, to look on Bonshaw Hall remade.

I slowed, admiring the broad brassed door, the knotted corbels, the ground-floor slits that since my last visit had bloomed into arched and graceful windows. It seemed the Continental ornamentations and *gentilesse* of Linlithgow and Falkland were spreading. Money was being spent here, and I wondered from whence it came, in what expectations.

Nevertheless, the peel tower still lurked massively behind the Hall, tall and brutal as a broken-off cliff, its lower windows mere slits, the great door studded with blackened nails. If the outer walls could not be held, this remained the Irvines' last redoubt.

A man lounged on the guardhouse ledge, set high on the stone barnkin wall (a step up from the Flemings' wooden palisade). Booted feet up on a stool, sword propped beside him on the wall, a crossbow dandled across his knees. He stared at me as I called up to announce myself.

'I ken wha y'are,' he said, then went back to cracking fleas in his hair. 'They're no at hame.'

'I come by invitation,' I said.

He swung his feet off the stool and glared down at me.

'You could come by fuckin' chariot,' he said. 'Himself and his guidwife are no at hame.'

The out-by door set in the main gate snicked open, and there stood one assailed, perhaps imperilled, by her own beauty.

Helen hastened over, took my arm as I dismounted, then led me quickly away from the walls. I looked back at the guard, saw him spit down into the dirt below, then swing his feet back up on the stool and close his eyes. Long may I be protected by my unimportance!

The path Helen took me on ended at a little ledge, so steep on all sides they had built a wooden rail. We stood high above the deep cut where the river hastened, spray rising to moisten our faces.

I knew, as few others did, that the thick ivy on our left could be parted, and a short tunnel went through the cliff, and the path then jouked and snaked on down through landslip and blackthorn, laurel and briar. The hidden descent to the Kirtle water, and the way upstream to Kirkconnel was old, surely very old, from before the de Brus family arrived with their swords, bows and charters.

As a bold, bored, solitary child she had found it, and one afternoon, after making me swear many oaths, she had taken my hand and shown me the way through. Now I looked at her spray-glistered averted head, her hidden eyes as she looked down into the foam. That path's existence was the only secret of hers I knew for sure.

I took her arm. 'That is the trysting way?' I said.

She turned, looked past me at the ivy. 'One of them,' she said. She smiled at last, her eyes seemed to swell and fill my world. I felt complete, as though reunited with the piece of myself she carried within her.

'Adam kens it?'

She dropped her gaze, blushed, mock-demure.

'He has come that way.'

'And Rob Bell, what of him?'

She looked me in the eye. 'You have come here to know my mind?'

'Or your heart.'

'Oh, that,' she said. 'Did Adam send you?'

'I am not his spy or messenger, only his friend in this.'

She stared me out, then nodded. 'Bell has no need of hidden ways,' she said. 'He is approved of my mother and father, and may enter by the front.'

Then I began to giggle at her words, and she in turn, and we laughed, blushing at our low minds. Then she pushed damp hair from her eyes and spoke more seriously.

'I ken what others think of Robert Bell,' she said. 'I do not find him so. Let him be as he is in the company of men, but among women, he is strong but douce, nigh-on jocose.'

'I find that hard to imagine.'

'Then try harder, dear coz. Folk are more wax than stone.' She paused to grip my arm. 'You are not the only shape-changer in the valley.'

I inclined my head, accepting the thrust.

She recounted their first privy meeting at Bonshaw (her mother pacing silently outside the door). Bell did not stammer or bluster or blush. He had looked at her from slipper to coif, then shook his head. '*You are the bonniest quine I have ever set my een on. Ask what you will of me.*'

'Winning words,' I conceded. 'And what did you ask of him?'

She smiled down at her feet in private memory.

'I asked that he might stop the rain outside.'

I winced, thinking Bell would kill a man for such impudence. Apparently he had stroked his beard, looked at her again and said gravely, '*That I cannot do. But I can offer you shelter from it.*'

I groaned theatrically, while inwardly admitting the reply had merit.

On parting, his hand had fallen lightly on her wrist. Without taking his eyes off her, he kissed his own palm where their flesh had met. Then he pulled on his gloves, strode to his followers, mounted and was gone through the gate without backward glance. Her wrist had reddened and burned where he had touched, as though she had been flicked by nettle.

'Hot stuff indeed,' I said. 'What say your Springkell cousins?'

She told me Elizabeth declared Rob Bell looked like the Devil and was the most desirable man in Annandale. Edith, the pale, earnest, sleekit one, had replied, '*A devil just the same. Who is to say he would not use you hard as he uses other men?*'

Cousin May had looked up from sewing flounces for her wedding day – did I know she had been agreed to Andrew Charleton, a merchant trader out of Carlisle? There would be no reivers in the family she would have.

'*Rob Bell is like to quickly give you children,*' May said, '*then leave you a young widow.*'

Helen laughed, kicked her boot against the rail, scraping away the mud.

'I replied, *No man could do better by a woman.*'

'Yet it is not Rob Bell with whom you tryst.'

She looked down into the Kirtle as it rushed swollen and mud-brown by Bonshaw.

'No,' she said quietly. 'It is not. Were I a salmon, I would rush upstream to Nether Albie and one who lives there. He runs through my thoughts like rain.'

More might have been said between us, but the girl Alysoun hurried up the path, all a-fluster. It was not right we met alone.

'Don't be daft,' Helen said. 'Harry is my cousin, and no suitor.'

Alysoun hesitated, but stood her ground with sulky mouth.

'Yon was my instruction,' she insisted. 'Nae privy meeting. It's mair than my job's worth.'

Helen took on her high-toned look that minded me she was gentry. I took her by the elbow.

'A job's a job,' I said.

Three of us walked away from the ledge and secret path. I wonder yet had we but five minutes more alone, four fates might have been otherwise.

Helen Irvine and I walked round Bonshaw's walled garden. Alysoun walked behind us, sulky eyes downcast, ears attentive. I was asked to admire the espaliered apple and pear trees, the peaches that grew under glass frames against the southern wall. By them some late roses still clung on.

Out of habit, I hunkered down to sniff a yellow, a pink, a deep damask. Each scent coursed through my body like an apothecary's draught. I did not know what it was I longed for, only that it was at hand.

I opened my eyes, her face was there across the yellow rose, looking straight at me. As she crouched in that garden, she made sunlight dim. The faint lines across her forehead, the little asides that flickered round her mouth, could not obscure it. She was golden and perfect as a mask. But her eyes with their pale flecks were still the ones I had known when we were young. They looked out at me, mutely appealing, as a prisoner clings to the bars as the visitor goes by.

'Unchanged, I see,' she said, so saft. 'You still dawdle to sniff the beauty of the world.'

I looked square at her.

'I am much changed,' I said. 'And the world has grown ugly.'

Her hand squeezed my wrist. Her grip was strong and urgent. 'Think that, and they have won.'

For how many years her words, whispered vehemently as she gripped my wrist in that sunlit garden, have guided me. They twitch yet at my dark brain, as a horse's bridle jerks the head back when it turns the wrong way.

Without doubt the Borderlands are more at peace since the Union of Crowns. That, I now see, is what my secret patron worked towards always. Jamie Saxt had to become King of England. Buccleuch foresaw what I had seen in my so-called crystal ball. That, and opportunity for his own advantage. His family are now among the greatest in the land, and what remains of the Maxwells, Bells, Irvines, Kerrs, Armstrongs and Flemings, even the Hieland Lords, all must do obeisance to the Lords of Buccleuch.

Yet the gentler arts and human reason are still in eclipse, even at Hawthornden. There is no dancing in the inn courtyards now, religious fanatics denounce and rule, witches still confess under torture, King and Parliament are at each other's throats, and our songs are all grim or piously false as 'Fair Helen of Kirkconnel Lea'.

Do not have me start. The world is what it is, the times are what they are.

Bring my head round, dear long-dead cousin. Let me look through the window at the garden at Hawthornden, and through the years to Bonshaw that day, and say most quietly to myself this heresy: *Néanmoins, c'est si belle.* Not in the manner of good Drummond's verses praising timeless gardens, sun without rain and love without loss, but seeing all in all, and insisting: *Nevertheless it is beautiful.*

Otherwise they have won indeed.

We walked once again around the garden. The walls protected us from the wind and stored the remaining warmth of the sun. Helen talked lightly of this fruit, that unlikely vegetable, the bottling and jelly-making, the elderberry wine whose sweet-sour rankness billowed through the scullery. Alysoun, bored, fell a little way back.

I did not change my tone of voice as I asked, 'And which would you rather have?'

She pointed at the stand of currants, keeled over at the end of their season, some last fruit still clinging dark as blood.

'I would like to eat that fruit,' she said. 'But others insist there are finer.'

'And your preference, dear coz?'

She leaned to pluck three berries.

'My will is not my own,' she said. She offered me one, dropped two into her mouth and smiled.

I stopped by the gooseberry bushes, long denuded of their fruit, a tangle of thorn. 'Perhaps you are considering something sharper, more strong-flavoured?'

'My family's taste has long inclined towards gooseberry. It is both richer and stronger than the redcurrant. What do you think?'

Alysoun dawdled, attention caught by the garden boy bent over the kale.

'I think him a swaggering bully. Men fear Bell, none love him.'

I kept my voice casual. The corner of her mouth tugged at some secret amusement.

'He does not bully me,' she said. 'Indeed he follows me like a well-built puppy dog.'

We had toured the garden twice and were back where we had started.

'But which will you choose, coz — the strong or the sweet?'

She looked away then, far above and beyond the walls around us.

'My will is not my own,' she repeated softly.

Her mother was bustling down the walk towards us.

'Your will is Toledo steel,' I said quickly. 'I have never known you not get what you want — by whatever subterfuge is required.'

She turned away with a small smile, but perhaps the seed I had proffered found fertile ground.

Aunt Ann was upon us. By her ferocious smile I understood she did not much like me, never had. Perhaps it was my sly cheek, or that my mother had married down but had a living son. Perhaps it was the company I kept.

'Dear Harry!' she cried. 'So long a stranger!' She seized me with one arm, took Helen with the other, and marched us to the newly promoted Hall where the seeds of the Renaissance flowered but were not, I fear, well understood.

We ate in the new dining hall. What had been bare and dark was now fetlock-deep in rug. Stone walls were swathed in tapestries of Italian hunting scenes, tactfully bordered by emblems of the Scottish crown. The chairs we sat in were heavy-carved with fruit, flowers, unplayable lutes strummed by blowsy cherubs, surmounted by the Irvine arms, the sharp and ever-green holly.

'So you have seen our new *décor*, and the remaking of the frontage,' Aunt Ann enquired. 'What do you think?'

I raised my head from pheasant pie.

'As one would expect,' I pronounced. 'It is in as good taste as money can buy.'

Ann beamed. Helen looked down at her plate, a faint pucker at the corner of her mouth.

Over a damson cheesecake – my tooth is sweet, I gorged myself – my aunt apologized for her husband's absence. He was meeting with the Bells of Blackett House.

'Business or pleasure?' I enquired.

'The twain aye meet at Blackett,' she whispered conspiratorially. 'We have some ongoing affairs with them. I expect an announcement will be made soon enough.'

My spoon did not falter.

'Mother, that is not at all assured,' Helen said. Her face was flushed, but she did not look at me.

'Detail, fine details,' Ann said. Her fat hand waved, as though calling on the tapestries to witness the fineness.

I finished my second helping of cheesecake, but it did not taste so sweet as before.

We sipped *tisane* in the withdrawing room (the hastily remodelled front scullery). The seats were padded with quilt, backed with dark velvet. The Borders' arse must be growing soft indeed.

I sat eyeing the brutal Gothic script above the lintel. HAUD ULLIS LABENTIA VENTIS. Or in the vulgar, *Yielding under no winds*. Perhaps so, perhaps not. I sensed a great gale was blowing through Annandale, and the Irvines like the rest of us would have to bend with it, or break.

A clatter outside, banging of doors. Enter Uncle Will, still booted and raised from the ride and the wonders of Blackett House. He shrugged off his wife's scolding at the mud he'd brought in, tossed his hat on the window seat. His fuzz of black hair sprung out, minding me of a rook's nest high in the tree.

'Still not full grown, young Harry,' he said, not unkindly in his thin, nasal voice. 'You spend too much time in libraries.'

He was in high good humour, mucky and flushed.

'Did it go well?' Aunt Ann asked.

'We advance, we advance!'

'Doubtless some costly details remain,' I said innocently.

He gaped at me, his great mouth like a lapwing, outstretched.

'Why say you?'

'Because I spend too much time in lawyers' chambers, where all details are expensive.'

He hesitated, then laughed. Clapped me on the shoulder and nearly knocked me off my chair. There was something of the fool about Uncle Will Irvine, a kind of stumbling, precarious dignity I had liked as a child. Now I could see his long, deadly arms. Even Jed said he was *verra handy in a fecht*.

Through all this Helen said nothing. She stared at the embroidered rug – a portrait of Jamie Fifth looking blurred and baffled – as though something of great import lay there.

They made sure I would have no further time alone with Helen. By the time I understood this, darkness was silting up below the surrounding hills. By the stables I hesitated, looking down that gloomy avenue of trees. That did not look a healthy place to be.

I went indoors and asked if I could stay the night. Aunt Ann smirked.

'You spend too long with the Flemings,' she said. 'They are unmade men.'

Will Irvine nodded, reached his long arm out and the boy poured sherry wine into his cup.

'Perhaps not for much longer,' he pronounced. 'I hear Dand Fleming – a sound man – has petitioned our Warden, who has given him hope the family will be restored. Subject to good behaviour, of course – and Warden Earl Angus remaining in his post.'

He glanced at me. I donned my diplomat's face, though much was being reshaped behind it.

'You think he may not?'

He shrugged. 'Competition is tough at the top, in these parts.'

'I think you'll find it's tough at the bottom, in all parts.'

He keeked sharp at me, then laughed.

'Aye, the difference is the heid yins get a roll on the drum afore the heid comes off!'

It still dumfountert me that the Earl of Angus had been made Warden at all, when but three years earlier he and Bothwell led an attack on Embra. Not only was he pardoned of treason – on declaring himself a Presbyterian, he had promptly replaced Sir James Johnstone as Warden. I couldn't keep up.

'I too wish Adam Fleming to know his best interests,' I said. 'I work only to those ends.'

My aunt loosed a suspicious scowl at me, though I had said at least some of the truth.

'They say he is become a sot, and not right in the head,' she said.

'He is . . . erratic and excitable,' I allowed. Only I caught the little dip of Helen's head that hid her smile. 'His father's death still ails him.'

'We are still at feud,' Ann insisted. 'You should not be biding wi' the Flemings.'

'Wheesht, Annie,' Will said. 'The blood-feud sleeps now. Jock Fleming and I rode together, with the Bells, when we ganged to free our kinsman from Saughton Tower.'

I tried to keep my voice casual.

'Was Dand Fleming on that gang?'

Will looked at me. His eyes were already dowzy from sherry. With that great mouth, wild hair and twisted neb, he really was not a well-made man. Many speculated as to the source of Helen's beauty, for it was scarcely in her mother either.

'Dand was by me when Auld Jock was lost to us on the way hame. Riders came out of the dark in ambush, ran him through wi' the lance and were gone in the woods. Cowards all!'

When reivers pulled off an ambush, they called themselves cunning strategists. When they were ambushed, they were outraged by such low behaviour.

'Did you know them?' I asked.

He shrugged. 'Na. English Grahams, some say.'

His indifference – Jock Fleming was part of the gang, but not family, and such things happen – seemed unfeigned. A guilty man would protest more. I changed the subject, but there was much, much to think about. An ambush, in the dark, targeting one man only. It was very strange.

We supped lightly on cold game (to my regret the damson cheesecake did not reappear). The precious candles, tinted red in the Oxford manner, swayed and guttered in the draught. It grew chill in the withdrawing room as Helen was prevailed on to sing. She passed me an old chanter, and asked me to accompany her on something from old days.

I fingered the unfamiliar, familiar stops. Some bleats at the reed got it supple and summoned the few retainers from other parts of the Hall. They hunkered down in the shadows as she began to sing, soft and low, 'The Unquiet Grave'.

> *The wind does blaw today, my love,*
> *A few sma drops of rain.*
> *I never had but ain true love,*
> *In cold clay she is laid.*
>
> *I'll dae as much for my true love*
> *As any young man may;*
> *I'll sit aside her grave and mourn*
> *For twelvemonth and a day.*

My breath blew across the reed, and the wee instrument moaned like wind through a dry dyke. As we played, I thought of Jock Fleming ambushed in the darkness, and of the face of a man gasping his last in a Langholm pend.

> *The twelvemonth and a day being rough,*
> *The dead began to speak.*
> *'O wha sits weeping on my grave*
> *And will not let me sleep?*
>
> *You crave ane kiss of my clay-cold lips,*
> *But my breath smells earthy strong,*
> *If you've ane kiss of my clay-cold lips*
> *Your time will no be long.*

The stalk is wither'd dry, my love,
So will oor hearts decay,
So mak yourself content, my love,
Till death calls you away.'

She finished. Silence. The retainers stared straight ahead, and in the candlelit silence their faces were wild, haunted, grim, as though the final end of Man was but enduring.

Helen looked down at her hands, head bowed as if in prayer.

I was shown to a small room at the end of a backstairs corridor. I was handed lamp, blankets, chanty pot. Aunt Ann was not hard to read.

The window was one of the originals, a narrow slit without glass, but there was no bar for the door. The Irvines were family by marriage, surely I would be safe enough for tonight. I bedded down still in britches and jerkin zipped tight, dagger to hand.

I happed coarse blankets about my neck and waited for sleep's ambush. Come the morn I would ride straight back. I had to talk to Adam, and I had a report to pen. Both required careful thought to handle aright.

I lay looking at the ceiling. That song, and Helen's clear, unshaken voice singing it, sounded yet in my head. I blew out the candle. Lord knows our graces are few in Scotland, but they dirl like an auger, richt tae the bane.

*

The scrape of wood on stone woke me. A light bloomed behind my slowly opening door. As I fumbled for my weapon, Helen entered, bearing a small creusie lamp afore her. She wore but her shift and her feet were bare.

I was about to speak, annoyed by my own fear and more than a little uneasy. She reached forward and put a finger to my lips. She put the lamp on the stand, looked down on me gravely then slipped in.

Her linen shift was chill and damp under my hand, her feet ice.

Our embrace was not carnal and never had been. We lay mixter-maxter in each other's arms and legs, as we had done as bairns, and she kenned she was safe wi' me. I looked direct into her eyes. The lamplight snagged the glassy flecks within them, and as I stared they seemed to enlarge, then begin to drift, as in some dark uncanny current. She put her hand over my mouth then cooried her head into my neck.

I could not comprehend what I'd just seen. It felt like something had been shown me, but I did not know what that might be. The lamp flame bent once, twice, past her shining head.

I have never slept so purely as that night, as though held in arms incorruptible.

HOT-TROD

I woke to a wondrously red dawn, then shouting voices, acrid smoke. I reached for Helen; she was not there. I peered through the window slit. Out in the darkness, the battlement of the peel tower glowed where the balefire burned high.

I adjusted my weapon under the jerkin, and hurried out to the courtyard where already men and horses gathered.

Such calling and clashing and wheeching, such stushie of horse and man and burning pitch-torch. So much horse shit! Servants, retainers, excited boys and hardened men I had never seen before, and many more still pouring in through the open gates. And at the top of the steps, tallest among the crowd of gentry gathered there, flame-lights flickering from his iron helmet, red cloak billowing loose over his armoured jack as he shouted instructions, stood Robert Bell, fresh-ridden from Blackett.

(He was of the cockerel sort, one who believes his cry alone makes the sun rise each morn. So mighty a crest, so puffed a chest, so small a brain!)

Be fair, he was damn impressive. While Will Irvine seemed befuddled, with his great nest of hair tipped sideways, still in his night garments with a cloak over his shoulders, Rob Bell took charge. He was taller than most, stood high with steel bonnet a toy in his strong hand, his black hair hung long in thick curls. The pistols at his hip glinted as he gave clear orders as a heidsman must.

I kept my distance, listened to the clash of news and rumour. The raid had fallen by night on Warden Angus's own lands, reiving cattle and sheep and young Galloway ponies from farms and hamlets surrounding the great house. A shepherd had freed himself and hurried to raise the alarm. Balefires signalled from tower to tower, warning and summoning local families.

The Bells, long close allies to the Warden, were out in numbers. So Robert had ridden his hard-faced followers through the valleys to Bonshaw to call in the Irvines, and stake his claim as Helen's protector. He strutted on the steps, giving orders, welcoming allies as dawn came.

Bully reborn as leader: I have seen it before. The man suddenly made sense. Though he had spared my life and smashed my nose instead, he was the one I looked to now.

I turned away and hurried down into the kitchens. The lamps were lit, the women of the house busying themselves, barefoot yet, in night attire as their hands flickered among cheeses, oatcakes, dried meat and fruit. They worked fast, near-silent, to great purpose.

Will Irvine pushed by me, his hair even madder than usual, like a furze-hedge in a gale.

'Woman!' he bellowed. 'Where are my damn crossbow bolts?'

Aunt Ann glanced round, her face set and shining.

'Press cupboard at the stairhied, you old fool,' she said, then went back to wrapping up rations.

Helen stooped by the range, pulling oatcakes off the griddle. Will paused by her, gazed down, then put his hand on her shoulder.

'Mind your mither whiles I'm awa,' I heard him say.

She turned, thrust his wrapped rations into his hands.

'Go canny, Faither.'

He stowed the package and stared at her.

'I'll bring ye back a fairing frae England.'

'Just bring yersel back.'

He put his hand tenderly to her cheek and was gone. I stood by Helen and began gathering up my piece for the trod. She glanced at me, all intimacy of the night gone. She was pale but her eyes were hot and wide. It seemed the revenge lust was upon us all.

She cut me a hunk of ewe's milk cheese, so hard you could break a tooth on it. Oatcakes, fruit, dark dried meat, all folded together in a flick of her hands.

'Go canny, Harry,' she said. 'Stay close to Adam and Jed.'

'They'll ride with us?'

'Earl Angus as Warden has called the Flemings to the hot-trod. It may be the remaking of them, if it goes well.'

I followed her up into the courtyard. Half-dawn, firelight, a great stushie of men, horses and dogs. There was purpose but no panic as they made ready for the off, and I understood this was what they were born to.

Will was still pulling on his britches, his leggings. Ann passed him the metalled jack.

'Nane left ahint?' I heard her say, her voice low but taut as bowstring.

He looked up at that. 'Nane to spare, Annie. I must gang wi' the lave.' His voice was hoarse. 'Take yersel to the tower, bolt and bar and dinna leave.'

He put his hand on her shoulder, gazed into her face. Something passed atween them, some wild look, something privy. Something Helen and I would later understand.

Ann nodded, turned away. Helen pushed in as Will buckled his great boots. She passed him another package – a wrapped Bible, liquor, I know not. He stowed it within his jack, clapped on his steel bonnet. Now dressed and fully armed, he did not look in the least ridiculous. Long-limbed, unflinching, implacable, he looked the heidsman.

Helen turned and touched my cheek with her chill hand.

'If you aren'a keeping what is yours, you are losing it,' she said. Her words struck home like a crossbow bolt. She slipped away through the crowd, towards Rob Bell on his high horse. I watched her reach up, grasp his thigh and hold out his wrap of ration, then a wee silver flask. He gazed down at her, slipped them into his saddle bag, and never took his adoring eyes off her as she went inside.

Then Robert Bell, as good as the acknowledged future husband of Cousin Helen, gestured towards the Border with his latch crossbow, and with a wordless shout led us out, his red cloak afloat behind him. As daylight came on and the watchfire burned low, he led some threescore men on horse, heading for our muster at the stone of Tinnis Hill, and I rode among them.

The way was uneven, the ground set with night-frost. The hills around us glittered white with false-snaw. Few birds sang in that dawn, the air scoured my lungs, the dogs ran silently ahead of our company.

I had never ridden among so many. Days in lecture hall, library and chambers were now faded as ancient manuscript. I knew only the bounce of the saddle, creak of leather, the chill in my hands as I swapped damp reins from left to right.

And the faces of my companions, most unknown to me, their features were vivid and dear. Some were silent, a few grim. A few I sensed rode reluctantly, having no choice for they had been called in by family heidsmen, in turn summoned by Earl Angus. But most were in high spirits, flushed, grins curling and breaking out along their heavy lips, like white on a wave approaching a savage coast.

I gathered the news as we rode. On discovery of the raid, the sleuth-hounds had ran out into the darkness with a small number of horse. However hard the ground, it is impossible to move beasts without leaving a trail and a scent. Even among the innumerable glens, valleys and hidden ways, they would be found.

In the meantime the muster had gone out locally, to the smaller, immediate families — time was all. If we could raise a gang and knew where to go within the day, we could follow hot-trod and none could stop us, even at the Border. At least, that was the theory.

'Will we carry the burning turf?' I enquired. And was laughed at. It seemed that existed only in the ballads. As did, I suspected, honour, reason and mercy.

I kept my mouth shut after that, feeling pitiably inexperienced and underequipped. I had no lance, no short sword. Many carried the latch, preferring the silent crossbow to pistol shot, but I had never even held one. My bonnet was leather, not steel. My jerkin, though tough, did not have metal sewn in to turn a sword, unlike the jacks the men around me wore.

I was a joke. A *canard*. A soft-handed scrivener. The man to my right slapped me on the shoulder and proffered a flask.

'Drink deep and be bauld, wee fella!'

Raw spirit coursed over my thrapple. I coughed, shook my head to clear the tears, drank again. And again. Felt the heat rise in my gut. Felt myself a bonnie fighter.

I handed back the flask. We looked briefly into each other's eyes. His name was Branxie. He looked a bruiser, but his eyes were large and brown and tender as those of his horse.

'It's not my quarrel,' he said. 'I'm only here for the bevvy,' and we laughed and rode on for Tinnis.

I never knew if he lived out the day.

We gathered under that hill's bald pate, hard by the standing stone from earlier times. The bulk were the Warden's own men waiting there, the Douglases and their allies the Bells. The rest were smaller, local families, those who could get there in a hurry. I had thought we would be more. I had gathered the Earl of Angus was not highly regarded in the Western March, much of his interests being elsewhere, but he was Warden, and both loyalty to the office and self-interest meant it was worth keeping in with him. That and a certain indignation at this impudent reiving of *our lands* – the exact same thieving as they themselves were proud to carry out.

Good to see Dand's meaty face glowing under his steel bonnet. Jed grinned at me and held up a short sword and a proper jack. Young Watt clung to his small grey cob, staring around defiantly, and I knew he was feart. As would be any man in his right mind, without a drink in him. The Flemings had brought but some twenty followers, including a dozen hardened men from the Kirkpatrick branch, for the family were unmade men fallen on hard times.

Adam sat tall and silent on his grey cob, Philby in attendance, at a small distance from his stepfather. From spurred jackboot to steel bonnet he was kitted for battle. His face was calm but his sallow colour raised. One gauntlet lightly clasped the reins, his right hand hung down loose, long gloved fingers curling and flexing.

Robert Bell and Will Irvine rode up to them. Leaned over, in turn clasped Dand's hand. They looked to Adam. His spur twitched, his horse trotted forward. His right hand came up from his side, shook first with Irvine, then with Bell.

The four of them rode over to William Douglas, Earl of Angus, who sat upright and aloof on his high horse, quivering with outrage. I had not seen him since the Armstrong wedding. On account of his title, I had expected a heathery Hielander, but he was much more Earl than Angus. He was lean and springy, elegant and tough, like a willow that catches the saw's teeth. He wore crimson gloves, still had his beard trimmed in the French manner (which was perhaps tactless, given his recent conversion), and a jewelled dagger hung at either hip.

'Why two daggers?' I whispered to Jed.

'Guid wi' baith hands,' he said. He nearly smiled. 'That's how come he changes sides sae easily.'

I did not hear what was said among the heid ones. Such was my part throughout, to be watching, implicated, but never in the inner council.

But I saw what I saw. I saw Bell looking magnificent, Will Irvine subdued, still hung over. Dand was bright-eyed to be among such company. Earl Angus was pale and vehement, furious at the humiliation, the King's appointee made ridiculous. And Adam sat motionless on his grey cob, attending, his right arm hung down loose at his side, gloved hand restlessly flicking as though shaking off contagion.

*

Jed handed me sword and jack and gauntlets, watched silently as I donned and buckled. Around us men were checking their gear, pouching food, wiping drink from their lips. I have attended women about to give birth and seen the same fear and yearning to be done in their eyes. Those who survive birth or battle feel themselves reborn to the world, for a while.

'You maun make do wi' a leather cap, shrimp,' Jed said.

'I shall rely on what is inside it to protect me,' I declared grandly.

He grinned. 'Keep a calm sough, and the brains inside where they belong, and you'll gang fine. The sword is but to make you look the part.'

A clatter and splash of horse crossing the burn. Four men rode up the slope towards us. Three of them in full armour, lanced and jacked, not farmers but hardened fighting men. The biggest I had last met in Liberton Tower when he told me to fuck off. Another had fine long fair hair that fell to his shoulders. The one they flanked was modestly smiling, eyes a grey blade as he swept by me.

Walter Scott of Branxholme and Buccleuch rode easily through our company. He gestured Earl Angus to come aside. The two men dismounted and stood some distance off in urgent parley, not for the likes of us.

I leaned on the great stone, felt it faintly shudder under my palm as I watched. Which I must have imagined. What I did see was one had come to deliver a message or advice or a warning, and the other, supposedly the superior, inclined his head to receive it.

*

The sleuth-hounds and their men returned, worn, wild-eyed and slavering as they went first to Earl Angus and the heidsmen, then went among us. They had picked up several tracks of kye and sheep and horse winding down through the dales and burn-fissures, coming together to sweep through Liddesdale, as though toward Bewcastle Waste and the Border.

Unknown was the number of armed men who had carried out the raid, or their identity. The English Kerrs, some said. Others insisted it would be the Armstrongs. Probably not the Carletons, for little remained of their strength after Scott had done with them, and their land was all to the East. It could be but a few dozen bandits and unmade men, or ten score hardened reivers raiding at Lord Scrope's blessing, by way of recompense for the springing of Kinmont Willie.

No matter. The offence was clear, and beasts and honour must be retrieved. Though the Warden, his kye and his honour, meant nothing to me, I caught that company's righteous rage and excitement as though it were the Plague itself. The Maxwells were absent, unsurprising after Earl Angus had driven them out of Annandale. It was rumoured Sir James Johnstone hoped to raise his people and meet us on the way. In any case, we would ride hot-trod to take back what was ours.

I let go the great stone. It must have been blood beating in my palm that made it seem to tremble.

Jed stayed at my side as we jostled toward Adam.

'Mark the maister,' he muttered. 'I to his right, you at the rear.'

I looked at him. It would be hours till we met the enemy, if ever.

'I do not like this,' he said. 'Mind whit happened to old Jock.'

So he too had misgivings about Adam's father's death. Young Watt glared at us anxiously. If I had carried liquor, I would have passed him it.

'How fares your coz?' Adam asked as we came upon him.

The student and the lover and the wayward, brooding drunk, all were gone. In full tack, he was a Borders fighting man, strong and assured.

'Bonnie,' I said.

His eyes lit. A smile broke across his face.

'Of course!'

'And near-betrothed,' I added, and regretted it on the instant.

He went moon-pale. He stared up ahead at Robert Bell, jostling alongside Earl Angus. Bell's scarlet tabard parted in the breeze, revealed the armour and the muscle beneath.

'Like hell she'll be,' he said. 'We'll talk later.'

And so the whole company – now fourscore horse, at a guess – began slowly, then swept on down the brae towards the burn and the Esk valley.

'This goes too quick and unthought,' Jed said low.

Adam shrugged. As we forded the stream, I look off to my left and saw Buccleuch and two followers heading back toward Branxholme. The scowling, long-haired third follower now rode with us.

'Yon's Davy "The Lady" Graham,' Jed whispered. I tried not to stare. 'You'll ken him?'

'Why would I?'

Jed had a wee grin to himself.

'Better not tae. The man has an awfy quick temper, whatever his tastes.'*

I avoided his eye, but marked Graham closely as we hurried towards the Border.

---

* 'Mistress' Kerr, 'Bareback' Bob, Davy Graham – their preferences were widely known. None dared mock them. In their society, fighting ability outweighed every other consideration. The less violent had to be circumspect, for it remained a capital offence.

JARRALL BURN

Folk might liken us to a small army – we were both less and more than that. None were paid, except by booty. Each had a heidsman, but no order or rank beyond that. The men I rode with all had trades – farmers, herders, smiths, farriers, innkeepers. They rode their own horse – the small Galloway cob, like themselves, did not look noble, but shared their great resilience and skill. They kept their weapons and gear in house or loft or tower. They could be armed and horsed within an hour.

So, not an army like the Roman, nor Longshanks' or Jamie Saxt's. Such Border raids were quite small, dozens, couple of hundred at most. They avoided formal battles they could not win. But they raided by ways they kenned well in a land full of secrets. They could converge, attack, disperse. Our hot-trod was typical in being short-lived, but a day or two.

The men around me were not drilled automata, led by centurions, paid at the month's end. They were skilled, hardened, self-reliant, feeding themselves along the way, fighting for family, livelihood and reputation. Twenty such riders could raze a village, forty take a tower. In his heyday, Maxwell claimed to raise two thousand, though he exaggerated. Little wonder Jamie Saxt had to treat the Border lairds with caution.

No, I tell Willie Drummond when he asks for my tales of that hot trod, we were not an army. We were more dangerous and endangered than that. In such alliances, forces could change side mid-battle, for though all talked of honour, family advantage meant more.

When I read Thucydides again, many years later in exile, I recognized Athenians and Spartans for what they were – men who had livelihoods outside of fighting, yet each skilled and hardened and relishing combat where it was to their advantage. Such men are more dangerous than armies, and far less predictable.

My nib dries as I stare out the window at our phantom hot-trod pouring through the valleys, some forty years syne. Let me admit it was exciting. Never have I felt so raised and ready to live or die.

We climbed to the pass at Whitrope, then followed the burn down through rough pasture, willow and rowan. The white frost had lifted by the time we passed the castle at Pittenton, where more Douglas men joined us.

'Still not enough,' Jed muttered.

But among so many men, my nag indefatigable and sure-footed, my borrowed jack fair set to turn aside a blade, I felt myself invulnerable. Just cause was on our side.

Still, the drink was wearing off and I was arse-nippit by the time we came down through trees to the Kershope burn and gathered there. The dogs panted, their warm moist breath rising in clouds from the little bellows of their chests. Our leaders talked. Once across, we were in England. Law allowed our hot-trod pursuit, but since when did Law count for much in the Debatable Lands?

In the soft banks we could see the clart and stir from many hooves. A muddy trail wound up the far bank, over the brae and away into scrub and trees. Angus talked to Bell, Will Irvine and Dand hung close by. Adam glanced round at me, grinned sardonically.

Earl Angus raised his sword and rode hard into the Kershope, Rob Bell tight in behind. And we all followed, our nags sure-footed among the tumbling waters.

Once across, I have to say England looked very much like Scotland.

We passed Bewcastle Fort at a distance, scanning anxiously, but none rode out to challenge us. It seemed our way had been made clear. At the far end of the dene, three burns descended, one made a bonnie watergaw, the colours hanging in moistened air. The sleuth-hounds hesitated, ran this way and that.

It seemed the raiding party had split up three ways. The prints were least by the western burn. Another quick parley. This time the lesser heidsmen were called in. Jed sat in the saddle, munching silently, his face impassive as he kept scanning the hills and woods around us.

Some of the impetus had gone from our hot-trod. What were the Warden's kye to us, or us to them? Only loyalty kept us there, awaiting our heidsman's word. Some shifted in the saddle, muttered among themselves. The raiders and their booty would soon disappear into the Solway Moss and the innumerable valleys that lay beyond. Yet the trackers insisted the animal prints were fresh-pressed. If we hurried on, we might catch up with them.

Dand and Adam came back to us. Our mixed party of Bells, Irvines and Flemings would continue pursuit along the burn that coursed deep into England. The bulk of the Warden's men would take the middle way. The third trail we would have to leave, for our numbers were not enough.

'Not enough as it is,' Jed said quietly.

Robert Bell and a dozen or so of his closest men rode over to us. He clasped Dand Fleming by the shoulder as a man might clasp a flagon of wine he intended to drain to the last. He stared at Adam, ignoring me. My friend looked impassively back. Jed stirred at my side.

'We ride with you till this is settled,' Adam said.

'Glad o' that,' Bell said, then turned his horse and led on down towards the paler sky that stretched above the Moss.

Snuck in behind Adam, I looked back to see the Warden's party dwindle and disappear away to our left. We were barely sixty now, and the short day was well advanced. Buccleuch's man, Davy 'The Lady', rode easy nearby, reins in one hand, the other lightly on his sword hilt.

Still we pressed on. Marvelling at the endurance of Handsome Jenny, I leaned forward in the high saddle and brushed my hand over her ears. She shivered impatiently. Horse and dogs and men, all had such stamina.

We turned the shoulder of a steep and narrow cleuch. At the bottom of the wooded valley spread a wide, glinting burn, and on the far side of it were gathered many fat kye, sheep herded by dogs, and fine horses led by halters. The last of a group of armed men were still splashing through the river. They were scarcely half our number, looking back at us as they tried to herd their booty away into the willow scrub and woods beyond.

The Bells unhitched their lances and crossbows, we unsheathed our swords, and all rode hard for the river. Robert Bell plunged first into the water and held his cob's head steady, pistol held high in one hand, sword in the other, crossbow bouncing on its hanger. Unencumbered by caution or doubt, he seemed unstoppable. The others followed in narrow file, for the crossing place was not wide. The men on the far side fled for the trees, leaving the sheep behind.

The first of our party heaved up onto the far bank. The next group were mid-stream. The remainder, we Flemings and Irvines, were still on the near side, waiting for the ford to clear.

'Well, fuck me sideways,' Jed muttered. Then he bellowed, 'Ambush!'

Horsemen burst from the trees up to our left. On the far side of the river, the men who had seemed to be fleeing rode back down the hill, joined now by many others riding out of the scrub. Our men who had been crossing now hesitated midstream. I heard pistol reports, and the first man slipped from his horse and was carried away face down in the water.

We'd been proper shafted.

I turned Handsome Jenny to flee the horsemen sweeping down on us, but Jed grabbed my bridle and pulled her head round. He pointed to a thicket on higher ground, off to our left, then put his head down and went hell for leather. Adam was beside him, myself just behind, Philby at our heels, Dand and his retainers lagging as we galloped across the line of the attack for the succour of the trees.

The charge swept down on us, yelling obscenities, swords and lances flashing. I made it into the copse and the charge swerved away like a torrent turned by a boulder. Looking back, in the stillness of the moment I saw the boy Watt raise his sword as the leading lance tore into him. He was hoist into the air, sword flying from his hand, then trampled over.

I hear that thin scream yet, and the silence at its end.

That ambush bore away a dozen of our men. Dand had vanished. The remainder of us huddled in the trees. Adam looked to Jed, who shook his head. We were but five, and one was Buccleuch's man Davy the Lady, who set me quite on edge.

Across the river, a swirl and scatter of horse and men. I could see Rob Bell unhorse one rider and hack down another as he called his men back. The mid-stream company hesitated, then turned back our way. Perhaps our deepest instinct is to die nearer home.

Bell rallied his force at the far bank, then set them back across the river. Jed grunted, leaned forward on his saddle like a man attending the argument of a play. Downslope, the ambush party were finishing off the last of our men. They would come for us next.

I looked to Adam.

'Exam time, *mon ami*,' he said. I reached inside my jack and plucked out the stiletto. Well used, I could take one or two with me when they came. Philby looked up at his master, whined anxiously. Adam quelled him with a downward gesture. The bedraggled lurcher stood and waited for whatever happened next.

Jed was still studying the river. Robert Bell was mid-stream now, his horse moving slow through the water. Two men were right behind, gaining on him, one with lance, the other with sword levelled.

I saw it most clearly. At the last moment Bell leaned across and let the bright lance go by. Then he twisted in the saddle, brought up his pistol and shot the man full in the face. The second rider hesitated. Bell's sword descended and cut him clean between helmet and jack. Then he urged his horse and his remaining men on towards our bank.

'Yon big cunt is a bonnie fighter,' Jed said. 'But they are too many.'

Indeed they were. A dozen were riding warily up the slope

to our small stand of trees. The rest of their force, several score, turned to face the Bells gathered at the riverbank.

Adam looked at me and grinned like a man who has placed a bet and just understood the foolishness of his wager. 'I long wondered what you carried by your heart,' he said.

I turned the stiletto blade, so thin, so sharp. 'So now you know.'

All had gone calm and slow-clear, as in the Langholm pend. The hot pish cooled in my britches, willow leaves drifted down against my face. Davy Graham lifted his sword and for a moment stared calmly into my eyes, then winked. He then turned to face the approaching riders. For myself, I saw the yellow coif of Elenora Jarvis crown the newel post before she closed the door and turned to me for pleasure, and my father's calm face as his hammer descended on the barrel hoop.

The horsemen began to encircle the trees. Philby's hair stood up like grey grass, his growl unrelenting.

'Kerrs,' Jed said, and flexed back his great shoulders.

It was then that the Johnstone men came down the eastern brae like wild boar, if boar had sword and lance for tusks, and could roar oaths. And the Kerrs were gone, galloping down-stream. They did not get far before they were unhorsed and cut down. As we emerged from the trees, their force by the river were already urging their streaming horses up the far bank and away.

James Johnstone reined up by Robert Bell. Dand Fleming dragged himself out from under his dying horse and limped over to join them and the other heidsmen. I had to admire his determination to stay close to where advantage might lie.

My calm left me. My stiletto shook as I put it away, and I had a crunching headache. I was also beginning to smell. I was thankful when our heidsmen decided we would collect what beasts remained and head home to cross the Border before night fell.

The ballad of our heroic foray – folly, I should write – has, mercifully, already died out. 'The Ballad of Jarrall Burn, or Earl Angus's Revenge' did not speak of the disposal of the dead. I am no singer, so I will.

We had need of haste. Deep in the English Western March, we were far from our lands and allies. The raiding force had scattered but could regroup. Already mist and dimness silted up the fields and hedgerows.

So we did not bury our dead, nor even drag the last few from the river. While some rounded up what cattle and horse the raiders had left, we stripped the corpses of what was of use. I strapped a bundle of jacks and a clutch of swords to the pommel, pouched one liquor flask and drained another.

The dead were too weighty to add to our already weary nags. A couple of minor heidsmen flopped like long sacks of flour across the horses we had recaptured. Blood dulled the hilt of Davy Graham's sword as he hunkered to wash clean his long fine hands in the burn. I turned away to see Dand Fleming without expression strip jack and boots from young Watt, then lift him in his arms, place the ruined boy across behind his saddle, make him secure.

I had to honour him for that. The others we left behind where they had fallen. The Kerrs still lay in a strew by the river. In time flocksmen would come, sort out their own and bury the rest or leave them to fatten corbie and fox.

Riding close together, glancing round, our dogs herding beasts along, weary to death we scuttled back towards Bewcastle Waste. The valley below smelled of dankness, blood and shit. In the ballad they call it the Jarrall, but we just called it *yon place*.

None looked back as we crested the brae. I could not find it again. I have never entirely left it.

Young Watt's mud- and blood-smeared head bounced on the flank of Dand Fleming's nag. My eyes fixed on that horrid bounce and flop till he began to stiffen and darkness took us all.

HAMEWARD

On the sole shelf in my garret cubby-hole, peat-brown Monsieur Montaigne leans up against faded blue calfskin of Titus Lucretius Carus. What stops them falling over is a pile consisting of my big black King's Bible (lest some suspect me of Papist tendencies), Tacitus, *The Republic* (overly provocative in these times?), a few quarto plays by Ben Jonson, signed during his second visit here, and a bound handwritten prompt of *Love's Labours Won*, memento of a night long syne.

The point being? That I have abandoned much in the course of my life. That my host's library downstairs is more than sufficient to my needs. That in truth I am no scholar.

Of all the books I have known, it is the upright two that most speak to and for me. I take down my precious Florio translation of Lucretius. (A lifetime ago I showed Fowler my first attempt at *De Rerum Natura*. He handed it back with a sorrowful shake of his head. On the way home I dropped it in a watchman's brazier.) I open a page at random, scan . . . *'If men saw that a term was set to their troubles, they would find strength in some way to withstand the hocus-pocus and intimidations of the prophets.'*

I return the volume to its brother, inspired and chastened by my presumption. I lack one man's wit and the other's metaphysics.

Nothing to be done about that! I return to my scratchings on middle-grade rag paper. When I am dead – my bones whisper this will be my last winter, though they have lied these past ten – a servant clearing out this room will find all I have written in the box under the bed. Illiterate, he will consign them to the flames along with my few and heavily patched (and faintly malodorous) clothes.

And yet I will not stop my story, but hasten it on.

Earl Angus and his party were already waiting for us at Tinnis Hill. It seemed they had secured a number of yowes and some lame kye, left behind by the fleeing reivers, who had disappeared into the hills with their booty.

Earl Angus, for all his hauteur, looked weary, and seemed to have lost one of his pretty daggers. As we approached, with the triumphant Johnstone at our head, I thought the former Warden gazed on the present one as a dog eyes a well-presented bone.

I had seen the gathering of a gang, now I witnessed its sundering. Many went their own way at Tinnis. It was dawn of the day by the old standing stone, cold and red-pink as lifeblood carried downriver. With just a quick shake of the hand and slap on the shoulder from their heidsman, each rider and their dogs hurried homewards, duty done.

The rest of us pressed on, driving what beasts we had recovered. Angus's head was down as he rode beside Robert Bell, who seemed in high spirits. James Johnstone and his men kept some way off, and he appeared very pleased with life. Behind them Will Irvine and Dand Fleming were in converse, Adam a few paces behind.

I came up alongside Jed. He looked at me and shook his tousled head.

'Never ride awa from an ambush,' he said. 'They'll cut you down from ahint.'

'Robert Bell managed it,' I said. I could not forget the man's agility as he'd slewed round on the saddle mid-river, shot one, cut down the next.

'You are not Robert Bell.'

'Nor wish to be.'

He chuckled, took a swig and passed me the flask.

'So what d'you think of your first hot-trod?'

I poured some liquor down my throat. 'At the time, I feared it would be my last,' I spluttered. 'Now I pray it will be.'

I passed the flask back. It was the very worst brandy I ever tasted. Jed took it, laughed and rode on. I looked at him with some curiosity.

'How do you live like this and smile?'

He turned in the saddle and looked me in the eye. 'Because, laddie, I ken I am going to die.'

He rode on, singing under his breath. It has taken me forty years, much thought and reading, to grasp in entirety what he offered me that day.

What was left of our company gathered at the home farm by the Hermitage. It was the first time I'd seen the Warden's stronghold. It was near big as Embra Castle, and as cheerless.

'Heating yon must cost Angus,' Jed murmured.

'I doubt he'll have it for much longer,' Adam said, and we sat, saddle-weary, watching Earl Angus formally shake hands with a triumphant Sir James Johnstone.

The sheep, kye and a handful of young cobs were sorted and counted. Earl Angus stood high on his stirrups and shouted out his thanks. Words like *loyalty* and *honour* and *rightfully ours* were shredded on the wind. Johnstone stood nearby, grinning.

'Six Wardens in as many years,' Jed muttered. 'I've kenned better-ordered whorehouses.'

Earl Angus raised his hand to his following, then turned away and went into the Hermitage, motioning the other senior men to follow. After a short hesitation, Adam slid from his saddle, passed the reins to Jed and followed them inside.

With relief I slid off Handsome Jenny. I walked up and down, kicking cramp from my legs. I never wanted to sit astride a horse again. My wee legs would be bowed forever.

'Boss wants to see you.' It was the slab of cliff that passed for Buccleuch's guard. Just looking up at him gave me vertigo.

'I'll send him my report.'

'In person. Crichton Castle.'

'Bless me,' I said. 'A conducted tour.'

'Prick,' he said. Spat on the ground.

'You should meet my friend Snood,' I said. 'You two would have a fine blether.'

'Never fuckin' heard of him,' he said. 'Be there, soon.'

He lumbered away.

'Pal of yours?' Jed asked at my elbow.

'Admirer,' I said. 'Can't seem to shake him off.'

Then we sat and waited, as such as us do the world over, for our heidsmen to reappear to say we can go hame.

MOTHER

I wrote nothing yesterday. I sat at the table, a mass of aching dough. The feathery quill lay ready but I hadn't the heart to make it fly. It is that time of year when some whiff in the air, some change in the light, minds me of her.

At last I gave up, and creaked down the winding backstairs, shuffled across the courtyard and into the Drummond chapel. Chill in there. I chose a candle, dropped coin into the poor box then struck the flint, set the bougie at the feet of Mother Mary, and with difficulty bent these penitent knees.

The sweating sickness, the falling sickness, apoplexy, wet lung and Lowland fever – I have seen these raptors swoop down, take grip on the body, adjust, then carry another from this world. They leave behind the living, shaken, bereft, relieved that it was not us, not yet.

Most men, women and children die of causes that remain mysteries to us. But the sword into the belly, dagger in the heart or knife across the throat, the hangman's noose that choked off

Black Jock Armstrong and many another reiver as that long song ended – they are understood by all. They are truly natural causes.

We give our illness common names, the doctors cry them in Latin as if that meant something better understood. We blame them on rats and fishwives' curses, witchcraft and outsiders and contagion from the stars that fall. In my days I have sat alongside doctors, herbalists, necromancers, dispensers of oils, spells, leeches and charms, users of the philtre and the surgeon's saw, and I have seen and heard enough to know that they know nothing and understand less. The only one I value is the apothecary who dilutes pain, and the wine-maker who can for a few hours let us forget it.

None of them could save my mother.

She died so many years ago, in Embra when Jamie Saxt was yet a boy, at just this time of year when nights are long and mirk. She died in our tenement room within sound of the Lawnmarket, with stall boys pitching, carts crunching by outside, masons' hammers thumping, all the quarrel and energy of the town, far from the sweet, bloody dales and darts of Annandale.

I would guess I was in my sixth year, too small to seek work yet old enough to be useful about the house, to do the messages, wash out cloots, sing street songs and country ballads at her requesting as the swelling sickness took hold. Her sole surviving child – I never knew the ones that came before – I was old enough to have my hand gripped, to be present at her dying, as her company and witness.

(What else have I ever been, but company and witness to the

living as they hurry to their end, most in great reluctance, some baffled or enraged, a few eager to be done?)

My father went to work still, as he had to. Aunt Ann came, reluctantly, I felt. I slept now in a neuk in the common stair, where men taken with drink would stumble on me and curse, and women touch me silently, soft hands passing over my hair.

She died of causes evident and unknowable as the lump that had appeared beneath her breastbone. Once, when it hurt greatly, she bade me put my hand there to still pain while I sang 'Thomas Rhymer'. I feel that growth yet, hard in my palm as a cannonball.

Soundless for days she lay, but towards the end a ceaseless moan rose from the very core of her, as though her bones were humming the song of pain. The terrors planted by the Reformist sermons of her childhood sprouted in her mind, then ran wild. She feared Damnation for her sins – I caught something of a bairn unborn, another conceived too young, perhaps by another than my father. She came to believe her present agony would last through all Eternity.

Then the merciful fainting and the apothecary's draughts. In the end, no sound but her long terrified gasps, her frail chest rising, the obscene swelling where her ribs divided as though her body were trying to give birth again. I sat beside her, hating those men that had implanted such terrors. I have never forgiven them, nor see reason to.

Each morn my father left for the cooperage, tools in the leather bag over his shoulder. By his quick glance at me, then

153

toward the closed door of her room, his head down like a man ashamed as he left and closed the street door so douce-like, by his impotent shame, I kenned he loved her. Sensed too his relief that he must work each day, his gratitude and sorrow that I must stay and attend her.

She died around Candlemas on a quiet afternoon, her sister Ann and I present. Her breaths spaced wider. Her chest rose and fell minutely. Her jaw dropped. I heard that last breath go. Then there was but a shell and an open mouth, and within it darkness without end.

TRIP-STEP

My soul is an old horse-trough that lies forgot in a field, its rotting boards mottled with fungus and moss. What fluid remains lies stagnant under yellow leaves from the trees above, bugs squirm in its shallows. Once in a while a living creature comes to sip what it needs, then moves on hastily.

Soon this trough will cease to hold water, then someone will burn it, or let it lie in long grass under the trees until it becomes indistinguishable.

I do not find this a melancholy thought, not compared to my mother's fearful dying or Helen's end, or young Watt's scream as the lance of death tore through him.

Give me the old horse-trough any day.

I woke whimpering among blankets. I was in my room at Nether Albie where I had fallen like a dead man on returning from the hot-trod. I lay looking at the ceiling. Nothing up there but mottled stains. *I am definitely going to die.*

Unlike Jed, I could see no comfort in that. No mother, no father, no lover, no guide. Only me.

I lay there till I got bored with being dismayed at myself. Then noticed I was hungry. So I took myself off to the kitchens where Mrs Smeaton found me some cake, cold beef and cheese. No one else was around, so I was able to sit at the servants' table, eat and give myself a talking-to. When I had become something approximating to a man again, I began to think about what needed done.

The light was fading as I hirpled across the empty courtyard, hips and knees aching from the hard riding hours. The peel-tower door was barred, so I thumped and waited till it opened.

'He's up amang the doos,' Snood said.

I went on up, hearing him bar the door behind me. The stair curled up past Adam's makeshift quarters where the door lay open, up another flight, and then the acrid stink. This room was completely lined with pigeons, each slotted in its box, chubbling and crooning, *a scandal o' doos* my mother would have said.

Adam stood facing one wall, cradling a pure white pigeon, slim and sleek. He looked up, smiled distantly, slotted the bird into its cubby-hole.

'How do I find you, Harry?'

'Been worse, but not often.'

He looked at me closely.

'You should spend time in here. It's peaceful.'

'Peaceful?' The doo-cot room was so loud with pigeon, we could scarcely hear each other.

'Well, a lot more sense than I hear out in the world.'

He passed his hand over the head of the slim white bird, then led off down the stair.

'Can't beat pigeon pie,' I said on the way down. 'This loft is a living meat safe.'

He nodded. The Border keeps and farms relied on the doo-cot to get through winter.

'Also for our gunpowder.' He turned into his room, waved me in and saw my puzzled face. 'You didn't know? It's part of old Snood's work to gather the shite for making saltpetre. He and Jed mix our powder in the wee shed out-by.'

'You can't buy it?'

'Rationed by the Crown. And unmade folk like us get none. Angus and Buccleuch seem to get as much as they need, but the rest of us make our own.'

'That's the Borderlands for you,' I said. 'Even the birds of peace were used for killing. Three hundred years of this has turned men to brutes.'

He turned at that, glowered at me. 'Jed? Wat O'Harden? Will Irvine? Folk in these parts may be rough indeed, but would you say they were anything less than human?'

He stared till I had to lower my eyes.

'No indeed,' I muttered, and my shame stays with me still. 'I am no better.'

Adam slumped onto his pallet, leaned back against the wall.

He looked pale and wabbit. 'So tell me of this *soi-disant* engagement.'

I told him. He turned his face to the wall, sat there picking at the stone with his fingernails, inward and dark as a donjon. Then he turned back to me, lamplight sparking uncanny in his eye, and his voice and smile as he recited made me more uneasy than any scowl.

'Do me a favour,' he said. 'Fetch wine and yon witch book from the house, and we'll put it all by for a night.'

We sat up late, getting drunk and cackling satanically at Jamie Saxt's *Daemonologie*, hot off the press in the Cowgate, astounded, incredulous that in our modern age such haivers would spew from the pen of an educated man.

Adam read aloud, stumbling round the chamber like our King himself, orating most solemnly. '*The fearefull aboundinge at this time in this countrie, of these detestable slaves of the Devill, the Witches or enchanters –*' he rolled his eyes, adjusted his imaginary codpiece, continued – '*hath moved me (beloved reader) to dispatch in post, this following treatise of mine, not in any way (as I protest) to serve for a shew of my learning and ingine . . .*' At this point, he could read no more, for he could not breathe for laughing, laughter like vomit from the pit. He passed it over to me, motioned I should continue.

I took the damn book, made a kingly stance, fondled the head of an imaginary favourite or two, and read: '*. . . but onely (mooved of conscience) to preasse thereby, so farre as I can, to resolve the doubting harts of many; both that such assaultes of Sathan are most certainly* *practized, and that the instrumentes thereof, merits most severely to be punished.'*

'Yon's what comes from spending too much time in Denmark!' Adam groaned. 'We might as well take up augury.'

Our laughter was tinged with horror, for there was indeed evil afoot again in North Berwick even as we spoke, and it emanated not from so-called witches but their tormentors.

On taking my leave in the small hours, I said I had to go back to Embra for a day or two. I had some smooth lie at hand, about how I had been summoned back to my work – as indeed I had, but not by my Justice. He just grunted, embraced me heavily, his unshaven cheek rasping on mine.

'Mind the trip-step,' he managed, kissed me full on the lips then slumped onto his pallet.

Clutching *Daemonologie*, I stumbled down the turning staircase. Out in the courtyard, a freezing night, the stars bright, wind-polished. The Seven Maidens hung tangled in the trees outside the compound. No young Watt loitered in the stables to report on me. His last cry had gone out among the imagined constellations, never to be re-called.

I threw the accursed book in a corner and fell a long, long way.

CRICHTON CASTLE

Have little, travel light, bear no weapon, trust none – that is one way to travel through this world. Another is to be girt with arms, travel with enough coin to pay for followers, and trust none.

Neither is any guarantee of safe passage.

I left Handsome Jenny at Crichton's stable block – so sturdy and ornamented as to be more laird's hall than quarters for horse and servants – then walked round the back of the castle under the shadow of the great wall. Since our return from the in-- glorious hot-trod, the wintry rains had come, and the Tyne burn had burst its banks in the valley below. Fifteen miles from Embra, horses and fat kye, market-ready, stood sodden but unguarded in well-made fields.

Here in Lothian the King's writ ran, more or less. The castle Earl Bothwell had so enlarged was vast, untroubled and, it seemed, impregnable, were it not that modern artillery and antique treachery will breach the most stubborn walls.

I scraped mud off my boots and chapped on the postern door. 'Wha the fuck are you?'

The guard was not a looker. One side of his face had red infection and both ears were cankered. When I gave my name, then that of my summoner, he recoiled as though I were contagious and scuttled off, his scabbard scraping the wall.

I had not thought I looked so frightful. Four days after our bedraggled return from the hot-trod, I was sprushed up, dressed in clean doublet and best britches, and positively fragrant with a new skin salve from Janet Elliot, applied by her own hand. (I will not deny her touch set me a-quiver and uneasy. She handled her son so, and his reaction was much like mine, but went deeper.)

I stood in the grim little guard room and wondered at this secret summons. The postern door was still open behind me. I could see myself run to the stables, turn my horse to ride far from this peaceful and so dangerous place.

I stared longingly at the low hills to the West. At least those Border men could rely on their courage, horsemanship and strong right arm. Despite the horrors of *yon place*, life in Annandale and the Debatable Lands seemed direct and simple in comparison to what I was entering. My concealed stiletto was of no use here. The wrong word, a poor formulation, a deception discovered, would have me killed and dropped in a ditch without even knowing why.

The guard came back with an ill-tempered friend. One slammed and barred the postern door, the other nodded me to follow. We passed into the arcade, a place of elegant arches, all decorous order as in a Florentine monastery where scholars might pass hours of solitary thought or earnest high-minded debate. At least that was the fantasy it had imported wholesale. It hadn't been true even in Florence.

We ducked into an unexpected narrow arch, then up some back stairs. A brief glimpse down into the courtyard with shrubs and benches and – Lord help us! – a fountain in the manner of Ammannati, as executed by a pupil with terminal ague and a blunt chisel. Then the gracious windows abruptly reverted to slits, and all was dim as we climbed.

A door that led only to another door, a twist to the right, then more narrow steps felt for in the dimness. The guard ahead stopped so suddenly I tripped into him.

The door opened on a small room with full windows, rugs on the wooden floor. I blinked in the sudden light. Frescos on three walls – hunting scenes, a battle, a Last Supper. The usual themes, and not badly done.

The man in the doorway was all too familiar. I had last seen him in the grove of trees in *yon place*, glowering across at Jed, who had stared steadily back. I felt some odd affection for him, just because he had been there with me and survived.

'Arms out, arsehole,' Davy Graham said.

I held out my arms. One opened my jerkin and felt inside my shirt.

'Careful,' I said. 'I'm tickly.'

In truth I near soiled myself. Graham plucked out my stiletto.

He looked at it, looked at me. He touched his thumb gently to the point, watched as the deep red stuff bubbled up.

'Bonnie,' he said.

'It will be returned when you leave,' said a rich, well-modulated voice behind me. 'Come this way.'

I hung on to that '*when you leave*' and like a wee lamb followed Walter Scott of Branxholme and Buccleuch through a heavy brocade curtain, into the intimate splendour of the oriel window set high in the west wall.

We stood by the window. I heard the door of the outer room thud, then the world was silent but for the whisper of drizzle on the panes.

'You may put your hat on,' he said. 'Chilly day.'

I fumbled my best bonnet back onto my damp head. My patron was dressed unshowily in dark green and black. From under a broad-brimmed velveteen chapeau his steel-grey eyes pricked into my soul.

His silence was more frightening than any threat I have known.

'Good salve, by the way,' he said at last. 'You must have been quite a bonnie laddie.'

'The King once ruffled my hair in Holyrude Park,' I stammered. 'When he passed with Esmé Stuart.'

'He did that to everyone.' Pause. 'Still does, come to that.'

'Oh.' In truth, Esmé Stuart's elegance and beauty had struck into my young soul, and a little barb of it sticks there still. That midnight-blue chapeau! Those wide, wandering dark eyes!

Scott sat on the only stool and stared at me. After a pause, I hunkered down at the other side of the window. With my back against the stone wall, in that narrow private space there was nowhere to look except where I least wished: at him.

'Shall I start with the raid?' I offered.

'Ah yes,' he murmured. 'The astute Earl of Angus and his bold pursuit.'

'We rode hot-trod,' I protested. 'To take back what was ours.'

He smiled down into his hand. I realized then he was in high spirits, hugging a secret satisfaction.

'Indeed you did. And got back – what? – a quarter? And caused quite a stushie. It is neither dignified nor well-advised, the King's Warden charging off across the Border, and making such a guddle of it.'

'We drank a toast at the Hermitage to celebrate our return, but his heart was not in it.'

'Dear, dear,' Scott said. 'The new heidsman in the Western Borders, so lately a convert to the Reform, has made himself look both rash and ridiculous. His Majesty is not best pleased. I fear William Douglas is not the best-flighted arrow in the King's quiver. Did I mention I have just been appointed Keeper of Liddesdale?'

'A pleasing honour,' I managed. For years the two offices of Warden and Keeper had been combined. Jamie Saxt wasn't daft. The wind was blowing from a new airt.

The pins and needles were starting, but I stayed crouched as I was, letting my patron enjoy himself. I saw our hot-trod in a new light, and wondered what message or advice Scott of Buccleuch had offered to Angus before we rode. I also wondered how long the latter would remain Privy Councillor and Warden.

Walter Scott put aside his private pleasure. His eyes levelled at me.

'Tell me everything,' he said.

And I did, very nearly.

I talked through the hot-trod, from my moment of waking at the watchfire's false sunrise. I made no mention of my night visitor. Once in a while he would ask for more detail of who met, in what order, who talked, who rode together and who kept apart. When I spoke of how we were ambushed at the ford when our force was divided, he shook his head at such stupidity.

'Kerrs,' he said. 'My grandfaither ganged wi' them deep into Northumberland some sixty year hyne. Three thousand men!' His eyes brightened at the prospect, his very voice changed. 'Yon was a big raid. The old King was well pleased, though he had to let out he wasna.'

Then the mask fell back in place, leaving only his eyes skewering me as I talked. It was his silence that made me talk, confess more than I ever would have under cross-examination. I would say my piece, look for his response, but he gave none, just kept looking. To fill in that silence I gave him more, and more.

I told him of our flight into the trees. Of how Robert Bell rallied his men, led them back across the river. In a flush of something like hero-worship I recounted how he killed his two closest pursuers – the body-swerve, the pistol, then the sword.

He listened, very keenly, without comment. I could not read his face.

'And Andrew Fleming?'

I told him how Dand seemed to have been cut down by the Kerrs as we galloped for cover. We learned afterwards that Dand's jack had turned a sword-slash, and his horse went down, with its rider sprawled half-hidden under its head and neck. He escaped with bruises, nothing more.

'A most fortunate man,' Buccleuch commented. 'Let us hope he is enjoying marriage to his late brother's redoubtable wife.' His smile was thin as the newest moon. 'Continue.'

To my account of the conference before we set off from Bonshaw, and the mustering at Tinnis Hill, he offered neither comment nor question. But the one on our return – when the heidsmen went off apart into a chamber off the Great Hall at the Hermitage – that made him very still. Exactly who was there? In what order did they come out? Who stayed behind for further converse?

I sensed this was the nub, and spoke with care. I wanted to give him whatever he wanted, and be in his favour. And then be far from here.

'And young Fleming? He was among the heidsmen then? Sober, in his right mind?'

He seemed to look into my very soul, had I one.

'Yes,' I said.

He stared at me. I dropped my gaze. His hand lifted my chin to make me look him in the eyes.

'He would not talk much about what they discussed,' I confessed.

'Not for the likes of you?'

'No.' His hand was gentle on my chin, close to the windpipe. 'But I understood . . .'

'What did you understand, my canny lad?'

'That they intend a further raid, with more time and thought and men. While the Kerrs and English Elliots are still weak.'

'Where and when?'

'I do not know,' I stammered. 'I think it yet to be decided.'

He released my chin, gave my cheek a gentle pat, sat back.

'You will send message when it is.'

It was a statement of fact and a contract, witnessed and sealed. He stood up, stretched his legs. 'Wine!' he said cheerfully. 'Wait here.'

He left me in the oriel window, looking out at the flooded fields, the grey rain and the beasts at peace in their dull acceptance.

My heart still beat too fast, yet I was wabbit as after battle. I thought: *So long as he has use for me, I will live, unless another get me first.*

*

167

My patron came back with two goblets, presented me one as though we were equals.

'Drink!' he commanded.

I hesitated, then did so. After all, he still had use for me.

'That is very fine,' I said. The warmth went down, turned about and rose up through my chest. I drank more, looked out at the rain, surprised not to see the sun full out on Tuscan hillsides. '*Molto bene*,' I said, almost to myself. '*É superbe*.'

He clapped me on the shoulder.

'Well done,' he said. 'Montalcino.' He sipped, rolled his eyes, swallowed. Smiled. 'A small but fertile branch of our family has vineyards there. If all goes ill here, perhaps I shall retire to warmer climes.'

'My lord is surely too young to retire,' I obliged.

'Flattery is pleasant but never clouds my judgement. Remember that, boy.'

He turned away from the window and sat on the stool. Apparently our interview was not yet done. I wearily slid down the wall and waited.

'So,' he said. 'Young Bell had a good raid. As did Johnstone. And the feud is concluded between Irvine and Fleming?'

I nodded. Will Irvine had looked ten years younger when he had emerged from the conference. Dand was expansive, arms waving enthusiastically. Even Adam admitted some good had come of our hot-trod.

'But the boy Lord Maxwell still commands the Flemings' loyalty, despite not being present at your grand adventure?'

'I believe Adam Fleming is not especially inclined to Lord Maxwell,' I said with care.

'And why would that be?'

'Because his stepfather is.'

He almost smiled. 'Perhaps. And his mother? She is an Elliot to the core. Little Jock Elliot . . .'

'My friend's relationship with her is . . . strained,' I said. 'And I have cautioned him against relying overmuch on Maxwell, or our Warden, and to look to ally himself . . . elsewhere.'

This was not strictly true, but could become so. I began to glimpse possibilities. A smile like wintry sleet from my patron.

'Very good of you, I'm sure.' He looked down at the back of his hand. Nose, lips, cheeks, chin were all in balance. A harmonious visage, a trim physique. Men trusted him. He looked up. 'He is still inclined towards the bonnie chick, though Bell considers himself good as betrothed?'

I nodded casually.

'Some say a man who uses a pistol is a coward,' he observed. 'Nonsense! To every situation its apt weapon. Bell is a fine leader and fighter because he is too stupid to know fear. His brain is the size of his cock, which is very small.'

'It is?'

He shrugged. 'How would I know? But spread the word and it will go about the world and men will snigger. How fares young Fleming's body-man?'

'Jed Horsburgh? Well, I think.'

'A bonnie fechter, I am told.'

The former Keeper of the Western March sat in silence, hands at rest as he gazed out through the window. His face was impassive, yet I could almost hear the sleuth-hounds of his thought scouting the world beyond the glass. When he spoke at last his voice was low, as if to himself.

'How does one ever bring lasting peace to the Borderlands?'

'Abolish the Border,' I said promptly.

'You are not as daft as you look. Nor as clever-breeks as you think.' He rubbed his right palm lightly down his sleeve, reshaping the nap. 'Encourage young Fleming in his wooing. Suggest to him it is not o'er-late, if he be bold.'

I nodded, but wondered as I had from the start why he should take keen interest in the affairs of a minor family like the Flemings. The Irvines were a step up, and the Bells two steps more. I could not see where that stair led.

He smacked his palms on his knees and stood up. A small cracking sound and he winced, more in exasperation than pain.

'Aye,' he said. 'Time to let others go reiving for me. Perhaps I shall retire and live among vines and sunshine.'

'The country would be poorer for it,' I said loyally.

'No doubt,' he said. 'But when I need my arse licked, many can do it better than you.'

I looked down, but failed to hide my smile. He drew back the curtain and led the way out of the oriel. I thought our interview concluded.

'You too have seen the marvels of Italy and the Low Countries,' my patron said over his shoulder. 'Hard to come back here, eh? We do not do graces well.'

'Indeed, my lord. Yet it is my country.'

We crossed the chamber, went past impassive guards at the door.

'Quite so,' he said. 'I aim to make it a better one.'

I followed Buccleuch down the spiral, thinking the betterment he aimed for was his own. And that of his family, I now add, for even the most brutish of those I knew then, the Border men and women, lived and died by their wider family. It was not King, nor Saviour, nor country defined them. Family honour, duties and family standing, those were the lights they guided their short lives by.

On account of my mother's coolness with her sister, my attachment to the Irvines was sentimental, not visceral. My father, being a city man, was loyal first to his wife and son, and then to his guild. I have no guild, nor wider family other than those who live in the books on my shelf and in my mind. I am not connected to any cause greater than myself, and in this I know myself lesser than those I write of.

'Nice place, eh?' Buccleuch was once again in lightsome spirits.

'The arcade at least is very fine,' I said cautiously.

We turned from that elegant walk, through a decorated arch and into the great courtyard. I had long been curious about the wonder that was there.

The face of the south-east court was studded with diamond-shaped carved stone. I had seen the like under dazzling sun in Firenze, but had never imagined it in sleet-grey rain.

'Bothwell was illiterate,' my patron murmured. 'He went to Florence and saw something he wanted. What do you think of his lozenge wall?'

The Renaissance graces of this wall, and the arches, fountain and garden, sat oddly with the ancient tower that was the castle's stony heart.

'Astonishing, if somewhat overstrenuous,' I said at last.

He seized my elbow, painfully, on the joint.

'There you have the man!' he said. 'There you have him. He overplayed his hand and lost all but his head. Still, in France he will remain, and he kindly left us this fine, if somewhat con-flicted, castle.' He turned away from the wall. 'I do not think we will hear more of the Bothwells.'

Having consigned the Hepburn family to history, we walked in the shelter of the arcade. He hummed some tune I could not place.

'Let that be a lesson to us both,' he said. 'Rise by all means, but keep in mind the ceiling.' He chuckled, shook his head. 'His uncle killed the Queen's husband – understandable, really – harried, then married her, then fled the field at Carberry, to be confined in a donjon. Ten years chained to a pillar in utter dark. Died insane, as one would.'

I chilled at the thought.* 'Earl Bothwell's death has long been rumoured,' I said.

---

* The image haunts me still. It is in part why, however poor I become, I must have a taper or candle or lantern on winter nights when I sleep alone. As I have done most all my life.

'Why, he earned his end!' Scott exclaimed. 'When our impetuous Earl fled for Norway, he was apprehended by Erik Rosencrantz – cousin of the first wife Bothwell had fleeced and abandoned! He was given to the King of Denmark, and at the request of – well, never mind who – incarcerated in Dragsholm for the rest of his days.' He shook his head. 'They say he wore a deep circle in the floor around his pillar.'

'That is . . . terrifying,' I said.

'There you go, laddie. Ambition! Ceiling!'

In this at least my patron did not dissemble. I see now he aimed very high, but long ago had identified his ceiling, and that was the King. Unlike Bothwell, he was content to fatten and grow like a wasps' nest under some high corner. And unlike the Bothwells or Maxwell or the other warlords of the Borderlands, he saw clearly how that ceiling could be – must be – raised yet higher, and himself with it.

And so it came to pass. That man is gone (peacefully, in his bed, so much for cosmic Justice), but his family prosper and prosper, growing ever greater under that Union ceiling.

We sat in the shelter of the arcade as the rain drew a curtain across the afternoon. As he murmured the last of his instructions, there came a clatter of footsteps, an opening door. The guard and a man in a wide-brimmed hat stood for a moment in the stone-clenched dimness, then, seeing us, swerved abruptly into another corridor.

Though his face was calm when I dared look at him, I sensed Buccleuch was vexed. My glimpse of that visitor was the only moment of our meeting my patron had not controlled. I raised my eyebrows as if in mild puzzlement, and took the purse handed me with a steady hand.

That hat, that long pale face, the manner of turning away – it had been no other than Dowie Fairfax, whom I had thought Earl Angus's man.

Buccleuch stood, so I did too, fumbling for my hat. He put his hand on my shoulder and looked into my eyes. I tried to neither avoid his gaze nor meet it, to give him no glimpse of the turmoil within. It was, I think, my moment of greatest peril.

'O'er-late to ride, laddie,' he said at last. 'Bide the night in the fine stables Bothwell left for us. I think you'll find good company there. Enjoy them according to your tastes, but don't keep them up too late, for I have use of them tomorrow!'

With that he gestured to an attendant to lead me out, and himself set off briskly in the direction the new arrival had taken.

The stables and servants' quarters of Crichton Castle were indeed magnificent, a grand house in themselves. A fire burned in the main room. I glimpsed small rooms off, with pallet beds and wash-stands. The floor was of fine wood, not earth. It did not smell of piss. The long table was set.

All this was good, but better was the company gathered round the fire. They were players – a rare sight this far North, being long proscribed by our high-minded Reform. They said Scott had hired them to play tomorrow at a feast in the Castle – tragedy in the forenoon, comedy in the evening.

174

One passed me a cup of spiced wine and I drank, letting all else go. A boy strummed his lute, his face all bright mischief. Another wittered like a laverock on the recorder. A couple of youths scuffled in the corner. The senior men pulled up their stools by the fire, and paced their drinking and their wit.

The balding one with wide, round brown eyes asked my trade and business here. Encouraged by wine, I gave them a fine and fanciful version – a nervous scholar come to help his erratic friend, and finds himself riding hot-trod with reivers, beaten at trysts, witnessing the amours of others and constantly disappointed in his own. I threw in some blood and a villainous stepfather, hoping to impress, but my audience were more inclined to comedy so I turned my tale to that.

I sat among them at table, all cares forgot. Neither bound peasants, nor fighters, nor gentry, not churchmen nor anxious merchants, we knew better than our masters that this world was a charade, imagined into existence and as quickly gone. And when we had employment, food, drink and attractive company, we made the most while they endured.

In plain terms, we had a party and got pissed. The music and catches grew obscene, then nostalgic, then melancholic. At some point the younger servants from the castle joined us, lasses among them. A fine youth stood in the ingleneuk to sing 'The Wyfe of Usher's Well', and the hall was silent as the firelight flames ate our faces.

The senior player stood pinned against the wall, cavernous eyes unblinking.

More drink, more songs. The night began to disintegrate, the senior men said they were for bed on account of rewrites in the morn. We younger ones carried on till we too were ready for our beds, where some took pleasure in the usual way, with added wit and laughter, not without affection.

I did not so much fall as soar into sleep that night, thoughtless, free, among my own.

GALES

I woke with aching head, drained in my netherparts. Crawling from a tangle of limbs, I collected boots and hat and stumbled forth to find my Handsome Jenny.

By dint of hard riding, I got back to Nether Albie in a gale at dusk the following day. Nonc questioned my story that I had been summonsed to Galashiels by the Judge to fill in for the absence of his clerk. Adam had already retired to the peel tower. Saddle-sore and with much to think about, I warmed some wine, picked up a stack of biscuits, said my goodnights and went down the dark passageway I now knew by heart.

I lay awake in my wee chamber and the wind loud in the trees sounded as if we were at sea, too close to a dangerous shore. The stockade fence howled and groaned. How went it with Adam in his guardroom den? He would be lying under furs on his pallet, long limbs bunched, clutching dreams of Helen, nursing fantasies of his stepfather plotting to kill him (which I still doubted) or taking pleasure with his new wife in the marital bed (which I did believe, Janet Elliot being almost alarmingly alive in that respect, her fingers lingering on Dand's hirsute arm as they sat at table).

Above the stramash outside in the woods, I heard, or thought I heard, a door close, a *slop* of slippered feet in the passageway. The wind doubled; my door shook. By the light of my creusie I saw the latch lift and jiggle. I cried out in fear, or hope. God knows.

The gale dropped to a sullen roar, door and latch were still. Did I hear or imagine footsteps going softly away, a draught as the door at the end of the passageway was opened then closed?

'Push, you wee bugger!'

At first light I put my manly shoulder to the skewed gatepost. Jed and I got it near-upright while old Snood jammed a timber into the gap, then kicked earth in about it. The gale hit again, the stockade fence slewed as the post gave way completely.

'Haud to it, boys!'

Dand Fleming tacked bare-headed across the yard, red and grey hair flying. He grinned his gap-teeth. He must have had a good night.

Strong, too. With his weight and push we got the posts and the gate upright. But none of us could step away. The gate doors shook against our straining shoulders. Even a second timber shivved into the post-hole wouldn't keep it up. The four of us looked at each other, stuck.

Adam went by in a whirl, shirt hoist high in the gale. I noted his pale belly, his ribs, the rope across his shoulders. He too seemed in high humour. He shouted words snatched away, unbolted the gate, staggered, then went through.

Janet Elliot and the cook, Mrs Smeaton – a strong woman with a low centre of gravity – bundled out of the storeroom with stakes. The pot-boy, Alec of the skelly eye, followed on with a great hammer that seemed the only thing keeping him to the ground as the wind roared.

The solution was simple, though it took some doing. Ropes looped round the post near the top (pot-boy on Adam's shoulders, thrilled at his elevation, fearful of the fall as my friend staggered). Pale-stakes hammered in obliquely, ropes tied, then tightened by staves pushed through the rope-loop, then twisted into tension.

The strain came off our shoulders. The palisade bulged but held. More hammer blows and grunts from over the fence, then the work party came back in. Together we shouldered the gate closed and double-bolted.

We stood gasping and grinning in the lee of the fence, rather chuffed with ourselves. Adam's arm on wee Alec's shoulder, Mrs Smeaton beaming, hair awry. Jed and Dand laughing quietly, Snood coiling spare rope, smiling at the ground. So this is family, I thought. Warm eyes everywhere. Us agin the storm. One of those moments of harmony and affection, as though an underlying good order of things had been revealed.

'Jed, you should be with people that can afford better walls,' Janet said.

'Whit would be the fun in that?'

Amid our laughter, Dand put his great paw round his wife's waist. Her hips inclined to his. Then she turned to look to Adam, her hand went up to tenderly brush mud from his cheek.

He leaned into her touch, then quivered away. I felt the attraction and the repulsion as if it were my own.

'I must inspect the woods,' he muttered. 'See what we have lost.'

He hurried back towards the peel tower. I glanced to Jed, who shrugged as if it were all beyond him. We straggled inside to eat; the shining moment faded.

Janet and Dand went to their quarters, making hungry eyes at each other. In the kitchen, Mrs Smeaton boiled eggs and we sat at the long table and broke open warm bread and drank small beer. Pot-boy Alec – an orphaned distant relative, I discovered – glanced at Marie the serving girl, who blushed, eyes shining with admiration. Mrs Smeaton piled my plate with cold chicken and pickles. 'For a growing laddie,' she said.

'I'm growing wider here, but no taller,' I replied, but did not spare the chicken, bread and eggs.

I watched Jed, one great paw wrapped round his tankard, the other lying loose and easy on the table as if it had never killed a man. Snood had returned to impenetrable silence, staring vacantly at the table like a bull at pasture. Alec and Marie found reasons to work near each other, giggling and glancing among the pots and dishes.

I wondered what was passing now between Janet Elliot and

her husband. I expected they would emerge hours later, soft-dazed, replete.

It would be better, I decided, to tackle them both separately, when it came to attempting to nudge them away from the Maxwells toward a new alignment, one more suitable both to my patron's wishes and my own judgement.

Outside the wind still roared insanely, like Earl Bothwell chained in darkness beneath Dragsholm. I poured another small beer from the brown jug, helped myself to preserve tart that had just appeared on the table, as though that could make me a bigger man. I was in no hurry to leave that warm kitchen. For a wee while life had been simple.

I got to my feet. Back to business.

I found Adam in the peel tower, up among the doos, stroking a fine white one in its cage. For a man about to go into the woods to inspect fallen timber, he looked sprush – second-best britches, a hoop-fastened doublet, kerchief knotted casually about the throat.

'So,' I said cheerily, 'still thinking of eloping?'

He smiled beatifically as he withdrew his hand from the bird, carefully closed the door. 'You know her family have been in Annandale since long afore the Bruces?'

'Will mentions it most mornings, then Aunt Ann takes up the theme.'

'And that they hid him a whole winter through?'

When Helen and I were weans, many a time we went

downstream, loosed the rope of ivy and, hearts pounding, lowered ourselves down the cliff to the hidden door.

'Surely Bruce's cave would be safer for trysting than Kirk-connel kirk.'

A stifled giggle. I looked at him.

'It is handy enough in a shower,' he confessed. 'But not the most comfortable, and a bit far off.'

'Is there any place in the valley where you two haven't—'

He held up his hand.

'Yon's my intended bride. Best not think on it too close.'

I looked away. It had been near-sacred in that cave, dim light through the concealed entrance, the burn rushing below, as Helen and I sat on bundled windlestraw and shared our inner-most hearts.

'The vestry key,' I asked. 'How came you by that?'

Adam rolled back on his pallet and lay idly picking plaster from the crumbling wall, a daft fond smile on his face. He told me that some months ago Helen had left from visiting her cousins at Springkell and, troubled in her heart, walked through drizzle to the Kirkconnel kirk. She had sat in her family's mil-dewed box-pew in the ruinous nave, among the rot and puddles, with the stink of doos for incense.

'Generations of her people are in the crypt there,' Adam said. 'Mine too, though maybe not as long.'

I leaned up against the wall, thinking about Lucretius, how even families do not last. Mine certainly hadn't.

He shrugged. 'Then the door creaked. She nearly jumped

from her skin. It was Father Alexander – you'll mind him from the Armstrong wedding?'

I nodded. A thin-faced, haunted man. 'And your mother's.'

He grimaced.

'Aye, that too. Anyway, the old priest settles beside her, and they sit there saying nothing, wi' the rain drifting down through the roof. Then he tells her he has been ordained for thirty-nine years, and only for the first two had he kirk and congregation.'

'He could have joined the Reform, like many others.'

'That's what Helen said – to him who had sprinkled water at her baptism! Apparently he spat on the floor, then talked about living pillar to post, humping the sacraments from door to door like a hawker. Eating in the pantry, pastry and cooking oil on his fingers as he absolved the dying, then sneaking out the back as the minister came in the front . . .'

We sat in the chill dimness among the pigeons, thinking about pretence, secrecy, a lifetime's dedication to a lost cause.

'Not a happy ecclesiastic, then.'

Adam grinned. 'He admitted it had kept him from flummery and vanity.'

'Sounds like a Protestant!'

Our laughter echoed round the stone walls.

'Then he said he believed she was in love. She admitted it.' Adam smiled. 'She said it was a painful and wonderful thing, but meeting was difficult, especially now the rains had come. Then the priest was silent. Apparently he muttered, *I remember it so.*'

'So priests have burned for love as well as their Church.'

'Then he puts his hand on hers, not at all lasciviously, and presses something long and cold into her palm. And they look at each other. And he says, *If you can make your trysting over to God, so much the better.* Then he departs, and my beloved is left sitting with the key to the upper hall.' Adam chuckled. 'And you wonder why I stay with the Old Faith!'

'I expect he did it to get back at the minister,' I said.

'You remain a godless heathen?'

It was not something we had talked about for years. In those times – as in these – it was unfriendly to enquire about such matters, and unwise to believe any answer. I stood at the window, looked out at the rain streaking down towards the sod, the stub of a rainbow above the Roman camp, and the faint outline of hills massed across the shining Solway.

'An incredulous one,' I said. 'I think plans for her engagement advance.'

A flurry behind me, then his hands dug into my shoulder.

'Once we are secretly married, they will all have to accept it!' His eyes sparked like chapped flints. 'We may return. Or make our life in the Continent.'

I suggested he read too many romantic ballads. Cut himself off from his own family, and from hers – madness! Besides, she would never agree to it. Or perhaps he considered binding her to his horse and galloping into the sunset? And Robert Bell: would he evaporate like morning dew?

'Fuck off back to Embra,' was his helpful response.

'I'll do just that, for all the good I do here!' I cried, headed for the door.

'Harry?'

He looked across the stinking doo-cot at me.

'Thank you for coming when I wrote you.' His voice was soft in the throat. 'I can see I have taken you away from your post for too long.'

He stood with the doos at his back, tall and lean, still young. Through the window slits, daylight ate his lovely cheekbones.

'I'll bide a whilie yet,' I conceded.

He bit his lip, nodded. 'Thank you. But I have asked too much of you in this. I must decide myself what to do for the best.'

'That's what I'm afraid of,' I replied, and dodged a fistful of doo-dung thrown at me. But at least he laughed.

I was not laughing on my way down the stair. I admired my friend's spirit, but not his judgement.

WOODS

I have spent half the morn – a wind-polished dot of a day among Eternity – staring at the back of my good hand. Not that good, as it happens. It has done things I wince to remember even as I set them down here.

(It has also done things that must be accounted good – in its caresses, in having been offered in aid and friendship, and clasping another's in the same spirit.)

Materially, as morally, it is not in the best of condition, as one might expect after near seventy winters. The knuckles have swollen, the sinews stiffened till it is more bird-claw than hand. Each morning I rub it with ointment and ease the fingers straight against my chest before gripping them around this quill. The skin is spotted like autumn leaves, ridged and pale and so thin I see the blue rivers of blood that run beneath.

A few nicks and gouges mark the back. I turn it over. This pale scar across my palm was not, I regret to say, incised in a fight to save a lady's honour or even my own skin. I ripped it on a nail on the back of a stable door, on a wild morning much like this one, as a peel-tower door opened and I hastened forward from my lurking-place, looking for words that might forestall my friend and prolong his life, and hers.

As I ran cursing across the compound to get something for my bleeding hand, I could see Adam's head and shoulders disappear down the brae towards the Kirtle woods. Perhaps he had not heard my call above the wind. Perhaps he had. He had not taken Philby, he had pulled a half-cloak about that fancy doublet, wore his best boots. Something was definitely up. No sign of Jed shadowing him, so it was down to me.

I sluiced my hand in the scullery, then wrapped a rag tight around it while Mrs Smeaton tutted and tried to feed me biscuits. The bandage had bloomed red again by the time I had pulled my leather jerkin over a couple of shirts, snuggled my weapon in under my ribs, grabbed a bonnet and passed through the gate, licking away the last sweet crumbs.

No sight of Adam, but muddy prints were clear on the path into the mangled woods. I followed on, ducking under uprooted trees, clambering over torn-off boughs. The great gale had stripped the hardwood trees, left them exposed as my conscience.

Where the path divided in the wood – down towards Kirkconnel one way, the upper track to Bonshaw Tower on the other – I hunkered down to closer look. The mud was churned with boot heels, and a slide-mark on the bank. It took no sleuth-hound to see he was heading for the river.

Fitting my feet to his prints, allowing for his longer legs, I also jaloused he was in no hurry. At certain places he seemed to have stopped, the prints facing in various directions. Perhaps he had indeed come to inspect the damage to the woods.

Still, it was unlike him not to bring Philby. And he had left the tower so quick and quiet, even Jed had missed him. If I had not been in the stables attending to Handsome Jenny – she had been hard worked – I too would have missed him.

The track dipped towards the Kirtle. I hurried on through the wood, as fast and silent as possible amid the damage.

The crack came from behind, very close. I turned, hand reaching under my shirt. He was standing not five feet away, one hand on his sword, the other on the branch he had just broken. Smiling and serious both.

'Still a city boy,' he said. 'I could have broken your head as you passed.'

'That is what I need to talk to you about.'

He laughed quietly, came to me. His hand on my arm.

'About cracking your head?'

'About things I have learned in the city.'

He studied me. Hazel-grey eyes looked into my innermost self.

'I had wondered when you'd tell me,' he said.

I smiled, though my heart was rattling like a snare-drum. We crouched in ahint a fresh-uprooted beech, our backs protected, the burn close by and a clear view back up the path. He glanced at my bandaged hand.

'Did you and Jed get carried away at your lessons?'

'Nail in the stables,' I said.

'My mother will take care of it,' he said. 'She is a grand healer.'

His voice was briefly tender. When I first visited the Fleming household as a student, I had noted how she hung upon him, how close they were with shared jokes and smiles and touches. My own mother had loved me in a brisk, busy, cheerful way.

Then his mouth twitched and he went back to restlessly scanning the woods around us.

'So,' he said. 'What have you to say to me? Speak saft,' he cautioned.

Was he really in danger on his own estate? Had it come to this, or was it only of his mind? And yet, away from the confines of the tower and the family, perhaps he would listen to reason.

I gave him reason.

I told him that he and his family would do better to ally with Buccleuch, not Maxwell. Certainly not Earl Angus, nor Johnstone.

He removed his arm from my knee, glanced behind us. As he spoke, he kept scanning the trees.

'Lord Maxwell is aristocracy, the Buccleuchs are just new gentry. The boy is growing fast and will soon take charge.'

'I have heard Buccleuch is the coming man. He has the King's ear. They are in accord.'

'He has been banished twice, imprisoned by both Crowns.'

'And he always comes back stronger.' Adam was silent. 'Use your eyes,' I said. 'Who has the sharpest understanding among all these?'

'My grandfather and my father were aye Maxwell men,' he said stubbornly.

'And where did it get them? Your family are still unmade.'

'We are no longer at feud with the Irvines,' he muttered. 'That must change everything. Did I say our families are feasting together next week?'

'Nobody told me.' He was right: it did change things. 'Still, Buccleuch is the coming man. Johnstone is but a bandit knighted. Scott will do down Maxwell.'

'Lord Maxwell has many more men, as do the Johnstones.'

'And lost half of them at Dryfe Sands. Man, follow the brains! Last week's hot-trod – was that not ill-considered? Lord Angus will revert to popery sooner or later. Only Buccleuch is in accord with Jamie Saxt and the way things must go. These others are just grabbing what they can in the last days.'

He glanced at me, his eyes very sharp. I had not meant to grow so heated.

'Since when did you move in such circles, Harry?' I said nothing. 'Who have you being talking to?'

I shrugged. 'I hear gossip from the Castalian Band. My Justice is close to the Court. I write and deliver his notes. I hear the clash and use my eyes.'

'I bet you do.'

I said nothing. Any further argument and he would dig in and never be shifted. He reached out his dagger, sclaffed the point in the dirt as he considered.

'I have no strong lealty to Maxwell,' he admitted. 'You met Buccleuch, didn't you?'

'At that Armstong wedding.'

He nodded. 'Took a shine to you, I'd say.' He turned his grey-green eyes on me. We looked at each other. Then he sighed and leaned back, wiping dirt along the blade till it shone brighter.

'Were I to incline towards Scott of Branxholme, you would let him know it?'

I tried to appear suitably amused at the idea, and succeeded because I was entertained by his preference for referring to Scott with a caustic *Branxholme*. Delicious hint of snobbery from one small Borders gentry towards another that had once been even smaller!

'I could by way of gossip, in a letter to Fowler say, or when next in Embra, mention your inclination to one of the senior clerks who is Buccleuch's nephew.'

'*Mon Dieu*, wee Harry Langton the conspirator!'

'And your friend,' I reminded him.

'Yes,' he said, and glanced at me almost shyly. 'I have treated you poorly, and you have repaid my whining and haivering with loyal commonsense. I do not deserve you, Harry.' His arm around my shoulder, grinning again. 'When you have schemed me a dukedom, I shall have you made a lord!'

'I am a humble man and will settle for a knighthood.'

'Sir Harry of Humble! Very good.'

He leaned back against the fallen trunk, all doubt and suspicion gone. My friend was clever and quick, but he had no guile. A mere mouse running before the coulter blade, I had nothing on my side but guile. At such moments I sickened myself. Yet I still hoped both to satisfy Buccleuch and keep safe the only friends of my heart.

He chuckled quietly, his mood changing again. 'I wish you luck in getting this past my mother.'

'Surely it is the heidsman needs convinced.'

'She leads Dand as one leads a bull by the ring.' His laugh was scarcely such. 'Only it is not attached to his nose.'

'Yeuch,' I said.

'Yeuch indeed, *mon ami*.' He got to his feet, still scanning. 'I will give some thought to what you say. But I am not heidsman, nor will be for many a year – if Dand or whoever it is doesn't do for me first – so it is hard to see my allegiance matters much.'

'I am only thinking of your family's advantage,' I said. He was flexing his knees, sniffing the air like an eager dog. I was losing him. 'But—'

'I will walk the woods as far as Kirkconnel,' he announced. He glanced up at the faint sun, then smiled on me. 'You should go back to the house and get my mother to attend to that wound.'

'I will come with you a bit way.'

He shrugged. 'If you must.'

We wandered through the woodland, following the Kirtle burn. The wind was still high and we kept a wary eye on the branches overhead. The woods bore pale scars of split boughs, we smelled the sap that had been hidden way inside. Where soil was shallow, a great elm had ripped from the earth and in its fall brought down three smaller pines, and crushed a little rowan to pulp.

We gazed at it together in silence.

'A lesson there,' I said.

'Indeed — we will stay warm this winter and the next.'

'I thought next winter you expect to be walking by the Arno, living on nothing and happily disgraced with your young bride.'

'Sounds good enough to me.'

I sighed. 'You intend to take her by force?'

'Awa tae fuck.'

'So she has consented to this elopement?'

We were facing each other. He pulled off his bonnet, shook loose his hair.

'You've not been in love, Harry, have you?'

'Has she consented?' His silence pushed me on. 'To anything at all?'

'You don't understand,' he said. 'We know we need to resolve this, but when we are together we keep getting . . . distracted. And then she must leave.'

'So she says there is no truth she will soon be engaged to that bam-pot, Bell?'

He had the grace to look shifty.

'I don't know,' he said. 'There are so few messages between us. You are the only messenger we can trust.'

Nothing I could say to that.

'Do you mind my asking, but have you and she already . . . ?'

He looked away then back at me.

'Yes,' he said, then grinned. 'Yes, I do mind you asking.'

'Sorry.'

'Sometimes when I see her again, at first she looks ordinary to me – a bonnie lassie, no more. The way she probably appears to you.' Fortunately, he wasn't looking at me but into his own heart. 'And then we talk and touch and listen, and something happens.' Now he looked me full on, his eyes shining. 'You ken when a cloud shifts and the sun falls on a stained-glass window in the kirk? Helen lights up from within, from her soul, I swear, and she lights me too. Then nothing else is real to me but her.'

I stood feeling the wind wrastle wi' the trees around us. 'Fair enough,' I said. 'Should you both untangle from each other long enough to decide to run away, I will do whatever I can to help.'

Adam smiled, reached out to clasp my upper arm.

'Thank you,' he said. 'I never doubted it.'

After all, what else would I do but help them reach their hearts' desire? Which happened to accord with Buccleuch's wishes. That was what puzzled me, for I did not see my patron as one of our romantics. I could not grasp what he was about in encouraging this suit. Perhaps it amused him to do down Robert Bell because he was a headstrong, dangerous man, bound to Angus. Yet I doubted it, because whatever Buccleuch was, he was not petty.

Adam glanced up at the thin sun again, adjusted his bonnet in the lopsided manner approved among the more modern-minded.

'Must get on,' he said. 'I will inspect the storm damage to the brig and beyond. You must go back and get that wound rightly attended.'

I agreed to go back to the house. Just before he set off downstream, I took him by the sleeve.

'Matter of interest, Adam,' I said. 'How do you two arrange your trysts when you have no go-between?'

That too-long-lost smile rippled across his long lips.

'When you are in love, you will understand.'

Then he was off through the trees, eager as a sleuth-hound on the scent. I set off slowly back up the slope, threading a way through the destruction, looking round to see his progress. I saw his head come round once, checking on me.

I paused in a dip out of his sight. Listened to the wind roar in the trees. Listened to myself. Gently felt my throbbing injured hand. The bleeding seemed to have stopped but that nail had been old and rusty, and the stables were scarcely clean.

I turned to contour the slope after him, following the Kirtle but staying well above it.

LOVERS

'*Vides ut alta stet nive candidum Soracte . . .*' As it was with Horatius Flaccus, so with us in Hawthornden. Through night and day the sky has shredded and fallen, smooring bush and beast alike. '*See how the snow lies deep on glittering Soracte . . .*'

A living man once wove a pattern of words so intricate and tough it has blown across sixteen hundred years to settle around the shoulders of an old man that same white glister. Alone at my table by the window I raise this glass of cooling wine and toast that man. Timeless are lovers' secret trysts, whether in Rome's midnight piazzas or the banks of Kirkconnel Lea, those youthful assignations, a ring pulled from an unresisting finger.

I came cannily through the woods to the bankside, hunkered down low and stared along the burn. He was not waiting under the brig. The day was still wild, one where rain and sun chase each other across fields and hills. Not a day to lie in mud and long grass. I stared along the Kirtle woods towards Kirkconnel hamlet and had the briefest glisk of a back: fair hair.

The abandoned kirk, then. The chamber off the vestry, among the horse blankets where we had lain after Robert Bell had mashed my face but spared my life.

I crossed the brig and hurried along where the high branches of great beech trees stirred and groaned against each other, and the pools of the burn scurried with blown light. I passed a shepherd laddie driving a score or so yowes from the Lea, but no other.

I came to the kirkyard, the old stones furred with moss and lichen. The wooden crosses of the poor stood canted and rotting. My mither and faither had no better in Blackfriars. If I got back to the city alive, I vowed to put Buccleuch's money to good use and commission a stone memorial, the first of my people's.

I stayed tight by the burn and went lowly through the brush, the silent dead to my right. There was no one outside the Maxwell crypt, none on the nine steps up to the upper door. I wondered again how these trysts were arranged. If Bell could know of it once, he could do so again.

Fifty yards off, I cooried down by the bank, ahint another fallen pine. I lay belly-down, and listened and looked for Bell and Fairfax coming through the woods. A shower came, and then low yellow sun. Were the lovers in the kirk at all? They could be using a retainer's cottage, a hay-byre or a stable.

Then I remembered how grey dawn had come into the room where we had lain, through a plain round window, on the gable wall. There had been a wood pile below.

My hand slipped under jerkin and shirt, adjusted my weapon for the draw, then crouched and jouked along the Kirtle bank, past the kirk to the gable wall where I was hidden from the cottages. The round window was way too high up. Behind me, across the burn, massed laurel bushes were thrashed by the half-gale. Good place to lie in ambush, I thought, the burn being fordable there.

But no ambush came. Nor sound from the kirk. I had to know. I dragged a log from the pile, propped it upright against the gable wall, put one foot to the top end, gripped the stone and stood up tall to keek through the window.

I lay aside the quill, stare out the window into my heart. Who knows why I went so canny along the bank of Kirtle, took the old trail without sound, ducked under low branches gently parted and released? I could never have protected Adam and Helen had ambush come, warned them at best.

I like to think I was doing my duty by them, regardless of the risk, for Bell would not have spared my life a second time. Yet that does not feel quite it. A game, perhaps? To show them the risks they took, when even a city boy could surprise them? To pay my friend back for catching me off-guard in the woods?

Questions I suspended at the time, as though I had averted my gaze from my own life even as I soft-footed through the mangled woods. Answers I cannot now give, even as I watch myself, still young and agile, stepping up onto a propped log and stretching up to peek unblinking eyes on the scene within.

The lovers lay on horse blankets, softened by discarded clothes.

It must be said his cock was magnificent, long and true. The thick head dark where it slipped between small, clever hands. I must have imagined the hiss of his breath, her soft giggle. Pale breasts swung gently like clappers of silent bells as Helen bent forward her lovely head. The bolt of his pleasure shot through me as I tumbled from the log.

I lay on my back, winded, staring through broken leaves at the sky, seeing them, seeing them. Her soft roundedness so far removed from the girl-child I had once kenned. His perfect root. Her fingers and his astounded face.

Back through the trees and away from all that would never be mine, I fled from that holy, terrible place.

'*Fair Helen, chaste Helen*' the ballad-mongers cry her. Tastes and times have changed to favour the respectable and douce, and rendered those days of quick-blooded men and women into something noble, picturesque and sexless. They do her a disservice. She was much more than fair and chaste. And he, he was blessed among men.

Wrapped in my blankets at the table by the window, I stare out where mist settles a shroud on the trees and river below Hawthornden. I might close my eyes, but it would bring no relief from seeing her, seeing him still.

I have not let myself think on it for many years, for it brought only dismay and shame. Now I begin to chuckle, white breath chuffing into the cold air, witnessing myself stretched up on tiptoe, then falling from the log to lie on my back on the wood pile like an astonished beetle. I had never before seen how ridiculous and hilarious my fall was.

Then I think on him and her at their pleasure, and for the first time smile because they had known the sweetness of that hour, when human joy and tenderness shone in a dim storeroom as it never had in the kirk itself.

After long enough in the cask, raw spirit turns into something more rich and kind to the palate. The years are not altogether cruel to whatever lies within this skull.

PRIVY

After snow, the melt. It rains a great deal, the fields grow wide with water. Restless, heart swollen and aching like a bladder, I had to rise from this table, pull on my old boots, and clamber down by the river. I stood watching the grey floodwaters swirl bruck and muck away.

Straw had thatched itself onto low-hanging branches. I stood in a dwam, contemplating my heart's high-water mark.

Something grey and black bobbed in the straw. I found a stick and poked. A drowned cat, with one torn ear and open pink mouth blackening already where the little tongue flapped in the current as though still licking. Then moisture flowed from my eyes for the first time in many years. Water seeping down my neck and rising through my split boots, I stood like an old fool weeping under the trees.

The short day's light began to fade, and the rain exhausted itself. On black twigs, water hung in swollen, quivering drops but did not fall. I stomped soggily home and, quite wabbit, climbed the backstair to my attic room.

The damp has gone to my chest and lodged there. Drummond has insisted the girl light and tend a fire in my room. I sit at the table, happed about in blankets, coughing and sweating. I dip my pen and carry on scratching, with more urgency, aware there might not be much time.

'Come to my privy room, the light is better there.'

Janet Elliot Fleming gave orders for hot water then turned and led up the stair, swishing her long skirts.

I followed her through the bedroom, averting my eyes from the marital bed and my mind from the storeroom of Kirkconnel kirk. We went into her retiring room. It was indeed lighter, with windows on two sides, looking down over the courtyard, the door into the peel tower, the stables, the main gate where we had struggled to re-erect the palisade this morning.

She said she liked to come here to read, but I thought what an excellent place it was to watch from. She patted the padded window seat and bade me sit by her.

'You are the most interesting of my son's friends,' she said. I blushed, shrugged. 'You arrive here as a meek scholar, legal secretary, a city youth, and within two weeks you are riding hot-trod across the Border, in boots and jack, and acquitting yourself well enough.'

'When in the Western March . . . ' I said.

She glanced across at me, then downwards. 'And I hear you have a concealed weapon.' When she smiled, her lower lip curved away and showed fine teeth. Her skin glowed, not in the creaseless, perfect way of youth – of Helen, say – but in full ripeness. Her hazel-grey eyes – Adam's eyes – were wide with knowledge.

'I do not normally carry it indoors,' I stammered.

'I should hope not.' She glanced down at my lap again. 'I hope it is not too uncomfortable.'

There was no mistaking her meaning and I blushed like a boy. I tried to think of anything but Helen's serene descending head and Adam's face in ecstasy.

Janet patted my hand. 'Your secret is safe with me,' she said. 'I trust my laddie is still off gallivanting in the woods?'

'He is making an inventory of the storm damage,' I said, trying to adjust to this new thrust.

'Is he really?' she said. 'You grew bored with each other's company?'

'He said I should get you to look at my hand.'

She nodded and gently took my left arm. My hand was throbbing, not the sharp scratch of pain but a deeper beat. She slowly unwound the bloody bandage and turned my palm to the light. She stroked a finger up past the wrist, looking closely.

'He was right.'

Marie chapped the door, then came in carrying a steaming bowl, white cloths over her shoulder. She could not keep her eyes from straying towards me where I sat. She set down the bowl, took a quick, backward, doubtful keek, and left us to it.

Janet Elliot set out phials and salves on the sill. From her sewing box she took two needles and a candle.

'They say you stole a heretical book from Leyden,' she said casually, unspooling a fresh bandage. 'Yet another accomplishment!'

'I made and took with me a copy,' I replied. 'Not the same thing.'

She raised her eyebrows, lit the candle.

'Some say it is pagan and obscene. It sounds most intriguing.'

'Obscene? Ridiculous!' My anger undid caution. 'The poet merely observes that all living things are animated by desire to procreate, that all existence is energy.'

'All?' she enquired softly. 'As though we were animal too?'

'Yes!' I had brought these ideas back with me from Leyden like a spark saved from a fire. They had glowed in my mind secretly ever since. 'All that exists is tiny particles of matter in motion and combination, ceaseless and without end. Nothing endures, everything is in flux, forever.'

She looked at me gravely, yet her eyes were lit with interest.

'I do not think our churchmen would be pleased. Your poet seems to omit God and the immortal soul from his account.'

'Yes!' I could not stop myself. 'Only particles in motion, endless, dazzling energy – it is a glorious vision of things.'

She dipped a cloth in the steaming water. 'This may hurt a little.' It stung like buggery. I may have yelped as she began to swab and clean my wound. 'What else does your pagan poet say?'

'He says that without superstitious fears of Damnation, the afterlife, permanence or Providence, we are free to follow Epicurus.' I winced as she dabbed on some clear liquid from her phial. 'We pursue pleasure – happiness, if you will – and avoid pain.'

'Not very successfully in your case,' she murmured, picking up tweezers.

'At times Stoicism is called for,' I said through gritted teeth as she explored along my cut. 'What cannot be avoided must be borne. It will not last, for nothing does. Not fame, nor wealth, nor family endure.' My breath was uneven, my gut tight at the pain, but thinking and speaking helped distract me. 'My mother's last days were lived in terror of Damnation.' I closed my eyes, breathed deep. '*De Rerum Natura* says she did not have to add that to her torments, and I would believe it.'

Janet's other hand tightened on my arm as I was ambushed by tears.

'Indeed, dying will be hard enough,' she said gently.

She turned my palm to the light, leaned forward to look more closely. In that absorbed, healing stoop I saw Helen's head descending like a blessing.

'He is in love, isn't he? With Helen Irvine.'

Undone by pain and grief and these ideas and her presence, I could dissemble no more.

'Yes.'

She dabbed carefully with a clean corner of the bloody cloth, then reached for her other bottle.

'He could do worse,' she said, 'now the feud is at an end. But she is promised to Robert Bell.' Her full mouth twisted in distaste. 'Nasty boy, though handsome. Not one to cross. Is that why you and Jed cling to my boy like ticks to his dog?'

I opted for silence. The white salve stung at first, then sweetened and cooled my whole hand.

'So it is she my son goes to meet?'

'I couldn't say. He won't let me go with him.'

She looked at me hard, but there was just enough truth in my voice to pass scrutiny. She stoppered the salve, small lines puckering across her high forehead.

'I hope he is very careful,' she said. 'I have nothing against the Irvines, but my husband has long favoured the Bells as a better match. But what do I, as a woman, understand of these things?'

I choked quietly. Amusement flickered at the edges of her mouth as she bent over my hand once more.

Then she reached for her needle again and turned it in the candle flame. My heart lurched, for I had thought she was done.

'My husband gives fealty to Lord Maxwell, and will continue to.' She squinted at the needle tip. 'Despite your best efforts.'

She flicked the fine point into the pulp of my wound. The shock jabbed in my gut. No point denying my conversation with Dand the day before. I had felt he wavered when I argued for Buccleuch. He knew he had little experience of court politics, the Western March being his whole life, and he had seemed to think I was worth listening to.

Janet squeezed my bad hand and my eyes watered again as she glared at me.

'I remain an Elliot,' she said, 'and I will never, ever, ally with the murderous, treacherous Scotts. We have been at feud for five generations, they cut down my father by the walls of Carlisle, and I will see Buccleuch in Hell before this house changes allegiance. Do you understand me?'

I hesitated. She jabbed with the needle, but this time I was ready for it and kept my watering eyes on hers.

'You are the head of this family?' I managed.

'I am the heart,' she said. 'And I have my husband's.'

She laid the needle aside, dabbed some clear, stinging liquid into my cut. No more was said as she calmly laid lint, wrapped bandage and made good. It was very queer sitting in her private chamber as she treated me. I thought back on the oriel window at Crichton, and my patron's very different blend of charm and subtle, chilling threat. I wished people would stop taking me aside.

'I am sorry to hear how your mother died,' she said. She laid her hand on my leg. 'Truly. Living and dying are hard enough without invented terrors.'

She smiled so sympathetically, I unburdened myself.

'I have not talked of these matters with many.'

'I am flattered,' she replied. 'I will think on your poet's vision when I look at the starry Heavens. I will imagine there is no one up there watching me. It is very . . . stirring.'

'But best not shared with minister or priest.'

'Indeed not.' Her hand stirred and smoothed my britches across my thigh. I was still young then, and despite my nature it had the usual effect. 'Let me make my wishes plain, dear Harry,' she said, and grabbed my cock through the cloth.

I gaped at her, but my privates had their own notion. Her hand rotated, descended, cuddled my goolies through cloth.

'Felt worse,' she said. 'If you ever try to influence my husband or son away from Maxwell to Buccleuch – if I hear so much as a whisper – I will tell Dand how you tried to ravish me in this chamber. He is a dear man, but maist jealous. He would likely kill you on the spot. At the very least, you would never see this house or my son again.' She stared me in the eye. 'I ken for whom this cock rises, and I would make it plain. You haud wi' me?'

I went down the stairs on legs of straw. Marie gave me a sharp look as I passed her in the passage. I made it to my room, closed the door and flopped on my pallet. I propped my bandaged hand up against the wall, as instructed.

'Keep it clean, Harry,' had been her parting shot. 'Clean, you understand?'

I understood. The entire hot-trod had been as nothing compared to an hour with Janet Elliot Fleming. Had Adam her will, craft and sheer smeddum, he would have been Prince of the Borders.

I lay exhausted, scunnered and throbbing, till light failed and Adam's voice rang in the courtyard. I did not go to join them at supper. When the boy Alec chapped on my door I called that I was indisposed. I got up to strike my tinderbox and light the lamp, then lay beneath the blankets trying to keep my various pains at bay so I might think clearly, for I sensed the crux was coming soon.

My dreams, when they came, brought pleasure and pain, fused in copulation.

The chapel bell rings out. I had forgot this is the Sabbath. The service and sermon – promises of Hellfire and copious Blood of the Lamb – will be made bearable by the excellent dinner that follows it, with more company, conversation, beef and wine than usual. Excellent!

Fear not, there will not be many more of these musings, for I must set the story down in whatever time remains. Not that it matters to the dead it celebrates and mourns. Not that any of this matters.

Nevertheless, I feel both hungry and lightened as I pad the page and take my leave for now. Though wheezing and failing, this animal is ready for more. I sense a nameless witness remains within, unscunnered and true.

TIMOR MORTIS

Many nights and days have passed since I broke off this story to go down for Sunday Service (we must learn not call it *Mass*!), followed by dinner. I never ate it.

Perhaps it was the unheated chapel, or the interminable world-hating sermon, but I felt my chest fill up with congestion. It came on apace and coughing would not clear it. The coughing became a fit where I could not breathe and passed out for the first of many times. As they carried me from the kirk I was drowning in my own fluids.

Now I know they do not call it the breath of life for nothing. For days and nights I slumped propped upright on pillows, fire blazing in the grate, the kindly quack dozing in the corner while I fought to stay alive.

On one of those nights of panic and delirium, I saw and understood the look in the eyes of the man I had killed in the Langholm pend. It was terror at the knowledge of his end. My own mother's terror had been of the Hellfires that awaited after death.

I did not want to die in fear like them. I gestured and croaked for the blue book of *De Rerum Natura*. I fingered and stroked it as some would the Bible, while Drummond looked on disapproving. Yet he did me the great kindness of reading aloud those passages – so lucid, rational, ungainsayable – that assert as grossest superstition fear of the afterlife.

As a true Christian, he read most reluctantly, but it was the kindest service he has ever done me. (*Memo*: before this day is out, clasp his hand, look into his eyes and thank him from the heart. He has been unfailingly good to me, and does not deserve my ironies.)

Listening to Lucretius' great poem, I believed in the great blank of death, and in the world continuing without me, scarcely changed. Suns would still rise, birds sing, men and women would desire, fight and die, children throw clods of earth at each other and laugh. This room where I was dying would soon be lived in by another, then another.

Yes, I believed that, even as the fluid in my lungs rose to my throat. The terror of the afterlife was not for me.

I gestured to Drummond to cease reading. He put the book away with some relief. He put his hand on the black book. I shook my head, and that small movement brought on the dreaded cough that led to choking and drowning and I could not breathe and the room lost all colour then fell into dark.

Some time later – dawn was coming, I remember the relief of light seeping back, for who wants to die in darkness? – I was back again. For a while there was peace and silence, as after a battle.

But this had been merely the opening skirmish. Soon my breath began to fail me again. I sipped water, tried to breathe and not to cough, for then my throat closed off. Next time I would die. I knew this for certainty. I would suffocate, or my heart would stop.

Timor mortis conturbat me, indeed.

In that hour, Lucretius was of no further use to me. His calm reasoning, his classical poise, his lovely Latin verse, they could obliterate fears of Damnation and Eternity but not this animal terror of dying itself. Perhaps Montaigne, I thought, and tried to gesture to the quack – Drummond had gone, likely to sleep, poor fellow – and that brought on the cough, then the drowning, then the impending end.

And back again, for brief exhausted peace and gratitude to be here still and the world seeming lovely merely in its existence, and then all too soon the troubles and terror and fighting for existence once again. (Perhaps not so very different from the history of the world itself.)

Panic grasped me by the thrapple, I grasped him back. I knew I must die and it terrified me, yet I would not die in terror. I would not, yet I would . . .

And did not, clearly. The Christ Mass has long come and gone, and here I am again at the table, scratching away at my life as one scratches at the healing wound beneath a bandage.

Before I resume this story – and now I know my time is

short, there must be fewer digressions, diversions and addenda – I want to record just this.

Though the rediscovered voices of Antiquity have offered a vision of a greater, kinder, more humane and playful life (scarcely in Scotland, *ma foi*, not till the hoodie craws of the Reformed Faith back away from the carcass of this my only true home!), we are not they. Their balance, calm, serene poise and dignity, such as allowed Epicurus and the Stoics to outface death itself, these we can never match. That world is as a burned-out watch-fire.

Which is why, were I allowed only one book, I would choose the modest, brown John Florio translation of Montaigne. He is of our time. With his irony, modesty and wit, his owning up to human feebleness, his celebration of uncertainty and swithering, his exploration of his self as the only honest starting point, he is one of us in the modern world of the seventeenth century *Anno Domini*.

'*The most certain sign of wisdom is cheerfulness*.' I would not gainsay that.

I turn the pages. '*The soul, like the foot, is part of the body*.' Nothing is more incendiary and hilarious – and little good it did me in my sickness. I open on another *Essai*.

'*The public weal requires that men should betray, and lie, and massacre*.'

Now that is more apposite to this story I resume after being so rudely interrupted.

★

When Dand Fleming announced that the formal feast to mark end-feud between Fleming and Irvine would be hosted by the Earl of Angus and Rob Bell in Blackett House, my heart mistook me. Adam and Robert Bell and Helen all in one room, with drink taken. It was surely the very opposite of what my patron desired. It could not come to good.

'Long overdue,' Adam said. 'Now we can have our full rights restored.'

He drank, looking calmly about the table. I was dumfountert at his self-control, and then tried to read him. Without the family feud, one barrier would be removed between himself and Helen. The feast offered a chance to meet with her. Was that enough to account for his cheer, or had he laid plans of his own?

'Warden Angus assures me we will not be unmade men much longer,' Dand said. 'Apparently it awaits only the High Chancellor's seal.'

Long may he wait, I thought, if Buccleuch is bending over the High Chancellor's table.

Janet Elliot stared at me across the dining table, a hint of smirk about her full mouth.

'Is your hand mending, Harry?' she enquired.

'Very well, thanks to your administrations,' I replied.

'You must come with us.'

I inclined my head. 'Never miss a feast.'

'It will be a chance to see your lovely cousin.'

Adam's knee stopped jumping.

'That is always welcome,' I replied.

Adam glanced at his mother. She looked back steadily, and in that moment he knew that she knew.

'It is long past time that lass was marrit,' Dand remarked, crunching down on an apple core, then delicately picking pips from his lips. He lined them up on his plate, black and glistening, and studied them for a sign.

He put his hand, cuffed with red hair about the wrist, down on Janet's. Her fingers curled within his. She looked at me as they got to their feet.

'Yon marriage will be another grand Borders feast, Harry – you must visit us when you come down from Edinburgh for it.'

I nodded. They left the room, already cleaving to each other. It was not quite what Epicurus had in mind. I both envied and rather despised them.

Adam chuckled quietly. I looked at him.

'She has a point,' he said. 'It is time you went back to your work.'

'And your safety?' I said. 'Remember, the reason you asked me to come?'

He dipped bread in the honey pot, tipped his head back to let it drip into his mouth.

'Perhaps I was not entirely myself,' he said. 'Your presence here must have done me good! With Jed nearby, I shall survive a while yet.' He glanced across at me, in high good humour still. 'Anyway, I may not be much longer in these parts.' His voice was casual.

'Really?'

He looked back at me calmly, then dipped his finger in the honey and licked along it. 'You never know.'

'I certainly do not,' I said, and left him to his schemes and dreams.

In my room, before dawn, in writing crabbed by my injured hand, I set out my brief report. I wrote of the coming end-feud feast. I suggested that Adam Fleming was open to a shift in fealty, but that his parents were less so, despite my best efforts. After some hesitation I added that I had encouraged him in his amour, and I anticipated developments soon, though I could not be sure I would be informed of them in advance.

I looked at the missive for a long time, sensing it could set in motion things I could not foresee. My little room where I sat was cold as clay, but the door was barred and it had become familiar, almost safe. All I had done, I argued, was tell the truth in my friends' cause, which for some unfathomed reason accorded with Buccleuch's interests.

I struck flame and lit the candle. Then carefully folded my doubts away, melted wax and set my patron's ring to the seal. I picked up dagger and sheath, tucked them away under my shift alongside my report, shrugged on the padded jerkin, reached for my bunnet and went out into the plain light of day.

I sit by the window under the roof of Hawthornden, dazzled. Never has the day seemed so sharp, each twig and river-sparkle

216

so defined, each chest-breath so momentously long. I am still warm, still here.

Whatever I scrieve now merely gestures at this. The village idiot's finger points at the city, the hill, to the distant sea, the sun in the sky and the husk of the daytime moon as he cries, 'See! See!'

Then again, he is an idiot and knows not what he points at, only that he is pointing and crying.

Approaching Kirtlebridge's single poor street, I went on by the Fortune Rigg to tether Handsome Jenny by the saddlery. I ducked into the leathery dimness where Crosier the maister and two apprentices were hard at it. I gave my name and the senior man put down his tack.

'Come in by,' he said.

In a wee back room – stove, accounts on the table, good coat hung on a nail – Drew Crosier studied me calmly. He was tall, thin-faced, eyes brown as his apron, his arms and hands tanned by his trade.

'So?'

I reached into the jerkin and handed him my sealed report.

'This to be delivered to Himself only. Soonest.'

He nodded, then put it under the lamp on the table, along with a couple of others.

'Shall be done,' he said. 'Any reply and I'll send the laddie tae the hoose wi' a message your gear is ready for collection.'

I thanked Crosier and went back onto the street. After the

'regrettable incident' (that is, attempted murder of *moi*) in Langholm, my patron had made this new arrangement – closer by, and safer.

I unhitched Jenny, wondering just how many agents Buccleuch employed in the Western March. I rode slowly back towards the inn, smelled good food, and on impulse called on one I hoped still my friend and ally.

The stable boy smirked, dodged my cuff, then tenderly led Jenny off to water. The yard was quiet as I slipped in the back door. In the pantry the maid in a headscarf and coif was doling curds into a row of bowls, head down in thought, or vacant: who knows?

As I neared the end of the passage, the door opened. Only once was I to catch that woman unawares, and that time had not yet come.

'Well, bonnie boy,' she said. 'Come for a ride?'

How well she read me. Elenora Jarvis stood with one hand on the door, and her eyes were bright as the day beneath her sunshine-yellow coif.

'I could be.'

Her hand – work-swollen and reddened – came up to stroke my face. As we stood smiling, her palm lingered on the back of my neck.

'No high-born horsemen come by today?' I asked.

Creases appeared and disappeared at the corners of her mouth.

'Apart from yourself?'

'You tease me.'

'As you tease me. Jealous of such men?'

I shrugged. 'More concern for my own safety.'

She took my bandaged hand, lifted it most gently.

'Got into another stushie, Harry?'

'I had argument with a nail. No, really.'

She lifted my hand to her neck. 'You daftie,' she said. 'Come and entertain me.' Her foot closed the door behind us. With my free hand I slipped the bar to.

The appetite is quicker, and the senses sharper, in the forenoon.

We sat across the table from each other in a corner of the dining hall. The curds, sprinkled with sugar, were pantry-cool and delicious. And so to business.

'Have you told Dowie Fairfax about the end-feud feast?'

'I have not seen him this last while. The big blaw-oot at Blackett House is part of the common clack.' She slurped happily, seeming unconcerned.

'And John Rusby?'

Her spoon faltered, dripping white.

'He came by yestreen. It seems I am to supply the wine. You will all be pished as collies.'

'Rusby is not someone I would care to deal with.'

'Nor I.' She leaned closer to me. 'You want to mind that man, Harry.'

'Did he mention my name?'

She hesitated, then nodded. 'And that of Jed Horsburgh. Said he looked forward to becoming better aquaint. He was a bit fou at the time.'

I put my hand on hers, so warm and mortal.

'I hope he didna stay the night.'

'No for want of asking.' She frowned down at the table. 'Him I can deal wi',' she said, and slipped her hand from under mine. She got up.

'Thank you,' I said. 'And not just for *yon*.'

'Likewise,' she replied. 'Now I have an inn to run.'

She showed me out the back way. The breeze fanned loose her hair against the lowering sun. I had forgotten how much we liked each other, I thought, but did not say.

'Ca' canny, Harry,' she murmured, then held out her hand and we shook as though swearing on a contract. 'Haste ye back!' she said loudly, then turned and went within.

The stable lad left the shadows.

'You need a hand mountin yer mare, sir?'

He dodged my cuff and took my coin. I liked the boy fine, did not trust him longer than a docked dug's tail. Keeping a sharp eye about, I began to ride back to the Fleming compound, my body pleasantly at ease, mind birling wi' doubt.

SICCAR

I had to step away from the table, stretch my legs. Elenora Jarvis, my untrusty feire, my friend. So many years unseen, most likely dead.

How can we be excused scenes such as that flurried pleasure in her office? Need we be excused?

Ways are much changed since those days, and Drummond would scarce credit the goings-on of which I write. Women have become douce-like, modest, eyes downcast as though feart to trip on their own feet, and men are penitential. The flesh is sinful and chastity rated far higher than charity. It is a wonder bairns still get born at all.

But in the Borders in those days, far from the reach of the pulpits of Embra and St Andrews, their lives aroused by danger, uncertainty and brevity, the women and men I kenned then were . . . otherwise.

I did not get far from the Fortune Rigg when they came out of trees to surprise me. I reined in, stared at Helen and her girl

Alysoun. My cousin looked weakened and pale as a reed peeled back to the pith.

She slid from her cob, passed the reins to Alysoun, who stared sullenly back at her. Helen reached within her cloak, I heard a chink, then she passed coin.

'Dinna leave my sight,' Alysoun said. 'It's mair than—'

We walked off some paces. I secured Handsome Jenny and waited.

Helen made a couple of false starts, tears working at the corners of her reddened eyes. 'My mither took me aside this morn. She asked . . .' Helen looked down, blood in her cheeks at last. 'She asked if I was still . . . entire.'

I had tried not to wonder myself. Still, I was affrontit for her.

'And you answered?'

'That I had never felt anything other than entire, until that moment.'

A reply at once cutting and evasive.

'*I ken how these things are,*' her mother had continued. '*I myself—*'

'*Mither, please!*'

Her mother flushed, but persisted. '*This must be known before a marriage can be committed to. If you are no longer entire, daughter, there are ways . . .*'

'*That will not be necessary,*' Helen said, and turned away, ready to leave and spare them the pain of looking more at each other.

But the interview had not been over. Her mother said there had been word of trysts with Adam Fleming. This must stop.

She was to meet with none but Bell. No more sneaking off to tryst in bush or byre. She was not to receive visitors alone, nor leave Bonshaw unaccompanied, even to see her Springkell cousins.

'*It is your father's will.*'

Helen's voice faltered. Her hand clenched on my arm as though she would fall if she let go.

'And I gave her back, *Oh aye — whoever he is!*' She stared at me, wild-eyed. 'I mean, anyone can see . . . I have long wondered—'

The blow had been hard and swift. Helen had crouched on the floor, drawing hand across mouth, looked down wonderingly at blood.

'*Your faither is a better man than you can ever imagine,*' her mother said.

Helen rubbed her lips, got to her feet.

'*I have imagined only because you have never told me,*' she said quietly.

The moment was long, then her mother stretched out a shaking hand. Helen sat beside her, licking away blood, felt her mother's shoulder tremble against hers. She had seen the drawer containing christening gowns of the brother and two sisters who came before her, who lived but days or weeks.

'*You mind how Bonshaw was overrun by the Hameless Grahams whilst your father was awa?*'

Of course she remembered — not the fact, but the story, mentioned, glimpsed, quickly bundled away. Her father in his cups had joked it cost him five years' rents to get his own wife back.

'*They held me for three weeks afore he could raise the money.*' Her mother's voice whispered like moths clasped in the palm. '*Much may happen in three weeks.*'

Out in the yard, nothing moved, but the very light of day changed.

'*Who is he?*'

'*Deid afore you were born. Your faither made siccar of that.*'

The retiring room grew dim as they sat. '*You are our best hope,*' her mother said at last. She stood up, rearranged her coif, checked herself in the mirror. '*Please do not speak of this to . . . your father. He has taken and loved you as his own.*'

As Helen watched her mother leave the room, all she could taste was blood, her own blood, but it was not the blood she had thought it to be. It seemed everything she had been and felt up to this point was but childish.

The sun had grown bleary as I held Helen cooried to my chest. Standing by the horses, Alysoun glared anxiously, though surely she could see this was no lovers' embrace.

Helen pushed herself away from me. Her chin came up.

'I must get back to Bonshaw,' she said. 'Rob Bell is calling by, and I am to be there. Please do not tell Adam.'

'That you're seeing Bell, or that—?'

'No! Do not tell him *that*.'

'What will you do?'

'I have no idea,' she said. 'I no longer know who my family is.'

She kissed my cheek, hurried back to Alysoun. Once back on the saddle, she looked thoughtful rather than broken and lost. She blew a vague kiss, then they were gone.

I stood awhile by Handsome Jenny, watching them pass into the trees. To not know one's family was surely a terrible thing. Whatever her mischief and high spirits, being an Irvine had mattered a deal to my cousin.

I saw again that brief, puzzling exchange between my uncle and aunt, the haunted look that passed just before he rode off on the hot-trod. '*Nane left behind?*' '*Bolt and bar yersel in the tower and dinna leave.*' Aunt Ann had been right on one count – Will Irvine was a better and more considerable man than most. I wondered how long it would take Helen to come to the same conclusion, and what difference that might make.

BLACKETT HOUSE

Even in the Borderlands at their most unruly, most days were just birds whittering in trees and hedge, fields wet with rain, sky shifting above the long riggs, a dour day brightening. The horsemen riding up the heuch for the most part passed with a nod, the axe rose and fell to make a winter's burning. The crossbow thrummed, the squeal was but a hare dying for the pot.

Yet the balefire wood remained stacked under cover on the battlement. Lance, jack, sword and crossbow were handy in the nook by the door. And when callers came she would darken her lashes, brush out her hair, moisten her lips before the hand-mirror, then come down the stair to meet whatever the world brought.

I see her clearly, as in life, her pale hand gripping then releasing the newel post as she crosses the hall. That afternoon's visitor is Robert Bell, come to negotiate with her 'father'. Bell's long-barrelled pistolet swings from its lanyard as his lips burn on her hand. She watches the two men go into the privy room and close the door. *This is not my family.*

Shaking at the knees, she climbs the peel-tower stair. From up here she can see the English hills, the Solway's sheen. Below, the doos croon and scold. The favoured whites stir restlessly in their special cage, yearning to fly hame. Just so did Teresa of Avila write of the soul. *My father took and loves me as his ain.*

I see her well, down to her green-embroidered kirtle, her distracted, fervent movements in those last days. But I do not see her thoughts and I do not see her inmost heart as she stands on the battlement, while out on the estuary the salt grass reishles to a shift in tide.

The days before the end-feud feast rang hard and true, the cold like a blow struck on the anvil, bare trees stock-stiff against the bluest sky. Good weather for travelling and gathering; fine nights for folk to stay warm indoors to eat and raise glasses in friendship and accord. Fine nights too for reiving, rape and murder.

At dinner Dand declared he and his wife and son would go by hired coach to Blackett House, to show they were gentry-folk of substance. The going would be good, if bumpy, and the last mile or so level ground along the newly planted avenue.

'We will ride, Dand,' Janet said firmly. 'For we are riding folk. That is how my forefaithers and yours made themselves, and that is how we will keep what we have.'

'The Irvines have bought a coach,' Dand objected. 'It is aa' painted wi' their arms, and decorated wi' . . . bonnie stuff.'

I had seen it on last my visit, nestled in its own wee house. It was fresh-painted with a landscape, part Annandale and part

Arcadia, where strangely proportioned dogs herded elephantine sheep, watched by a shepherd in a toga, crook in one hand, lyre in the other. Hideous. Helen had rolled her eyes.

'It needs no coach to make Elliots and Flemings equal to the Irvines.' Janet put her hand on his arm to soften her words.

'Aw, but Janet.'

Her hand slipped down to his wrist. Adam had looked away, but I watched with fascination her fingers gently encircle his big broken thumb.

There was no coach waiting in the courtyard on Saturday.

It had been agreed to limit the number of followers on both sides. For simplicity and to avoid alarm, it was said, but I thought economy probably came into it. Earl Angus had insisted – offered, he said, but it was not that – he personally pay for the whole affair. The heidsmen and their nearest kin would dine at Blackett, while the followers were to have all they wanted at the Scabby Duck by Ecclefechan.

Some twenty of the Fleming men gathered in the frozen courtyard. A few I recognized from the hot-trod. I confess their nods of acknowledgement pleased me. Apparently I had faked being a reiver well enough.

We were all sprushed to the gills as my mother – mither, I so nearly wrote with this cultured hand that only once in a while reverts when the heart prompts – used to say. The day before we had all washed our hair, had Marie trim away the fluff, then combed it out to be gathered and knotted at the back. Best britches, clean bunnet, clart scraped from my boots. Adam emerged in a gold-trimmed, cross-looped, green doublet with stiff high collar. He had the grace to blush when I grinned. Philby dogged his heels, and even he sported a broad new leather collar.

We were all quite the thing. As we milled around in the freezing sun, it felt like going to a wedding, as in a way we were. I understood this day would link the Flemings and Irvines in common fealty. No wonder Adam looked bright, for it would do his suit no harm. He had talked of raising it with his mother once this day was done. 'No harm trying. If that fails, we can aye run awa!' I wasn't at all sure he was joking.

Jed gripped me by the arm. As ever he wore his leather jerkin, but had shined it up, boots likewise. Clean-shaved, tangled hair tidied away under a raised felt hat.

'My, you scrub up weel,' I said.

'Wheest, cheeky-breeks.' He leaned into me and spoke low. 'You're armed?'

Only then did I register the sword on his hip, dagger on the other. None of the followers bore arms, nor the heidsmen – apart from a pouched dirk, which apparently didn't count. That was the agreement. Such meetings of long-at-feud families had gone wrong before, especially with drink taken.

'No. But you?'

'On occasions like this, one from each party bears sword. It's . . . ceremonial.' He leaned closer, his breath like old leather as he spoke urgently in my lug. 'Get it now.'

229

I excused myself and hurried to my room. I dragged long stiletto and sheath out from under the pallet, made all good under my clothes, and re-emerged into the dazzling cold with heart a-thumping.

We all mounted. Jed looked across at me, gave a brief, dark nod. Now only one was awaited.

Janet Elliot Fleming passed out her front door in a long crimson gown cut low and lace-trimmed. Her tallow hair was piled up and pinned in the old manner. Her cloak was sky-blue velvet, half-length. She wore dark gloves embroidered, and riding boots with silver spurs.

Head held high, she crossed the yard to her bay roan, put one foot on the near stirrup and swung herself up onto the saddle easy as a kite plucks a dove from the sky. She sat across the saddle like a common woman, but her assurance would make Ann Irvine in her coach look like a sparrow riding in a turnip lantern.

I saw many unco sights in the Borders that year, and men of dash and daring, but she was earth and fire, the Elliot spirit incarnate. Across near-on fifty years, in that blue cloak, boots and glinting spurs, in my mind she rides still, magnificent.

She looked to her husband as though he were in charge, but it was her nod set us on our way, our best dogs following ahint, Philby aye by his master's mare.

Blackett House was a size up from Irvine Hall. New walls with castellation and corbels pushed out beyond a central keep, yet they lacked conviction, as though their makers knew stone piled on stone could not long resist the new artillery. Dark and grace-less, it was neither castle nor comfortable family home, and the big windows in place of slits were an admission the days of such strongholds were over.

Yet we were impressed, of course. Money and power are always impressive. As always I tried to keep steady by muttering sarcasms to Jed as he rode impassively beside me, his eyes set on Adam's back as we went through the gates, bound and crossed with brass, into the thronging courtyard.

Under the eyes of their heidsmen, the Irvine and Fleming followers behaved themselves. Hands were grasped, shoulders battered in mutual admiration. Jed told me that the feud had for a generation been more one of ritual cursing and stylish spitting than real feeling. On several occasions both families had ridden together – the freeing of Shuggie Riley from Saughton, the Redeswire reiving. Our hot-trod, and the arrival of Dand as the new heidsman, had finally made the feud redundant as the old peel tower behind Blackett House.

Past the stushie of men, I saw Earl Angus emerge from the front doorway. He wore his black jerkin with gold-thread trim, scarlet gloves, and his high-heeled boots and cockaigne hat with plume were aimed to make that rather spindly man appear some-what grand. It may have been the boots, but he seemed not entirely steady.

'Yon man is never a Protestant,' Jed murmured.

Stepping out by him came my Aunt Ann, looking important in blue blousy stuff, topped with a hat like a startled partridge.

Just behind, my Uncle Will bent and swayed in gratified winds, his long pale face turning this way and that.

We unhorsed. By the stables I saw Elenora carrying bottles of wine from a cart into the kitchens. She saw me, nodded and went inside. Her brief smile seemed strained.

As Janet, Dand and Adam made through the crowd towards the Irvines, Jed and I were in tight behind. We were coming up the steps, smiling, hands outstretched, when there was a clatter and commotion ahint us. At the head of a dozen men, Robert Bell and John Rusby rode in through the gates, fresh from the hunt.

Our greetings paused, then were consummated, a little awkwardly on account of the distraction behind. Handshakes and curtsies (in the flamboyant French fashion from Aunt Ann, the more dignified Italian incline from Janet). Gallant kisses for the ladies and between them. Aunt Ann's patronizing pucker glanced off Janet Elliot's imperious cheek. Adam inclined his bare head to the Warden, then greeted more warmly the Irvines he believed might yet become his in-laws.

Bell came bounding up the steps, Rusby behind with hand resting on the hilt of his sword where it hung by his side. He must be the appointed armed man. He and Jed stared each other out till Jed shrugged and turned away as if towards something more interesting.

'*Bonjour* to all! Welcome to our house!' Bell seemed very pleased with himself. I caught a distinct whiff of scented oil in his hair as he brushed by me to greet the Earl of Angus with a near-casual shake of the hand.

I admit Bell was a fine, vigorous figure as he gave elaborate attention to a simpering Ann Irvine. As he shook with Will, his left hand firmly clasped his intended father-in-law's forearm. To some it may have seemed sincerity, to me it looked like ownership.

Then he turned to Dand and Janet. 'Welcome, both!'

I saw Janet's cheek twitch. 'Welcome to you, Master Bell,' she said, and held out her gloved hand. He had no option but to incline his head and kiss her glove.

Bell to Dand was straightforward, the strong handshake, the forearm clutch. Then the black cockerel, long curly locks perfuming the noon air, turned to Adam.

'Fleming.'

'Bell.'

The handshake was brief, firm and equal. Bell turned away with a hint of a smirk just as Helen emerged from the inner hallway.

She paused a moment in the winter sunlight, green cloak over one arm. In an unadorned pure yellow linen kirtle, bare-headed with her fair hair wound up above her long neck, she seemed a hesitant flame. I swear the rough men in the courtyard fell silent, looking her way as though at some eternally desirable, eternally unapproachable end.

She was equidistant between Adam and Bell. She would have to greet one first. Then she saw me off to the side, and with a smile that lit the day stepped over to hug her cousin. No one could object to that.

Her breath was warm in my ear as she whispered, 'Find me later.'

When she released me, she was now nearest Adam. She took one step towards him, he took two to her. I thought one would have to be blind not to see the gladness that ran between them. He smiled, took her bare hand, kissed it tenderly. They said brief things I could not hear, their heads close.

Robert Bell stood behind, not a happy heidsman.

As she came to him, she held out her hand. Bell had no choice but to take it. Then his other arm dipped round her waist in an unmistakably possessive gesture. She smiled modestly, then turned to greet Janet and Dand, and that turn freed her naturally from Bell's hand.

I thought I saw a pucker by the corner of Janet Elliot's lips as the heid ones turned to go within. Will Irvine stretched out his arm to the woman who was and was not his daughter, and looked on her proudly as she came to him. Helen glanced briefly up into his eyes, then smiled and took his arm. The rest of us began to follow in due order.

John Rusby thumped into my shoulder. I looked close at the man I believed had poisoned Adam, and tried to have me killed in Langholm. He was tall, heavyset, pockmarked. His nose had been laid to the left. His eyes—

'Who you looking at, cunt?'

I had played this scene a hundred times in the city closes.

'A fellow guest, *mon ami*,' I said innocently. 'A fellow diner at the banquet of life.' (Horace, I think.) Rusby's eyes were

234

brown, wide and entirely without light. Whatever had once lived within had long left.

'I'll see your arse stuffed, wassock.'

I leaned closer to him. 'I shall count the hours.'

I left him struggling to untangle that, and made to enter the main hall on only slightly shaky legs. I would say that man's eyes were empty, but it was more that whatever they looked on for him was void.

'Nae dugs,' Rusby snarled. His kick caught the sniffing Philby in the ribs. His shriek brought Adam's head round, but his dog had already slunk away. In the courtyard the lesser family, followers and retainers began to set off for the Scabby Duck and the entertainments there, and those of us who were neither high nor low followed the heidsmen into the place of peace.

Warden Angus had laid on both priest and minister, to be on the safe side, just as at the Armstrong wedding that seemed an age ago. The priest was still lean and anxious; the minister was comfortably round. In St Andrews the last priest to officiate at a wedding had sizzled in his own fat.

At least we were to have music: a tall bald piper and a fair young fiddler lurked in the shadows. Rosining his bow with slow, sensuous hand stroked up and down the horsehair, he winked at me, the tart.

We sat down to dine. William Douglas, Earl of Angus, as host and Warden took one end of the high table, with Will and Dand on either side, their wives beside them, smiling falsely at each other. At the far end of the table, Robert Bell ruled. Jed murmured that Angus's young wife had died some years back, as spouses do, and he had never got round to replacing her. Broken-hearted, some said. Too busy scheming and changing religions, others said.

Sitting at the low table, I asked Jed to fill me in on the others. The black-haired, slightly frantic man with gap teeth two places up from Robert Bell was his younger brother. They cried him Ding-Dong or Clapper. He was an unconvincing copy of his brother, his shoulders less strong, his swagger somewhat hollow. He was plying his charms with a round-faced sonsie lass with nice eyes and a puggy nose.

'Yon's Maggie Douglas,' Jen whispered. 'Youngest daughter.'

'Married?'

'Na.'

'But Douglas has sons?'

'He lost baith.'

'Ah.'

I felt for the man. Such were the times, but that did not make it easier to thole. Though aristocratic in French finery, William Douglas today looked grey and hollowed-out as a wasps' nest when winter comes.

I toyed with my mutton broth, keeking over my spoon to watch Clapper Bell close in on his future. With big brother Robert commanding at the far end of the table, his eyes fixed hungrily on fair Helen, for the first time I glimpsed why Walter Scott of Branxholme and Buccleuch might take an interest in the goings-on in these parts. Add Irvine to Bell, have Clapper Bell become heidsman by marriage to the Douglas family, why then there would be some power indeed.

What I could not jalouse was the end Buccleuch worked towards. I ate little, drank less, staying alert, watching and thinking. I noted the venison stew was unusually tender, the claret full, rewarding, then dry at the finish. I sipped and inwardly toasted Elenora Jarvis and her wine. A big day for her, supplying this lot. She too had her protector.

Then when fruit, tarts and cheeses came, and the company was mellow, Earl Angus scraped back his chair and stood up. His gloved hand tightened on the table as he spoke of old feud laid aside, and the joy this gave him not only as King's Warden but also as a Borders man. (Many would dispute that under their breath.)

'We aa' maun ride thegither,' he cried, his tongue broadening with feeling. 'Then nane daur stand agin us!'

I wouldn't be too sure of that, I thought. The English Queen is a corpse in finery and slap, Jamie Saxt is waiting cannily as he has for thirty years, men like Dowie Fairfax scurry to and fro between the Courts. Each week brought news of more banditry, both sides of the border, as though all were grabbing what they could while it lasted. Pigs at the trough, heedless of the butcher waiting in the wings.

Meanwhile, our Warden spoke of honour and courage, family and fealty, the ancient virtues that made us Borderers. He brought Will Irvine and Dand Fleming to their feet, witnessed the shaking of hands, the pledge of mutual accord, then that of fealty to his office and thus the King. The thin, weary priest blessed the day on behalf of the True Church, the wee fat minister spoke fervently of the Blood of the Lamb.

We all stood. As the toast to loyalty and amity was given by Robert Bell, Helen glanced my way. Behind her smile, she looked forsaken yet resolved. We raised our glasses, cried *Aye!* and drank. The music struck up, the kind that raises the spirits for the first few minutes, then becomes noise to talk above.

And I thought that would be the entertainment for the day.

Will Irvine clapped his hands, but most folk just talked louder. Then beside him Robert Bell's palms struck like pistol shots, twice. The pipes gurgled and died wheezily.

Will stood by the ingle, swaying slightly. His face was pale and moist. Queer that a man can go through many a bloody battle – and Will Irvine was known to be handy indeed – yet be overcome at the prospect of making a speech. Beside him Helen looked anxious, with embarrassment I fancied, as he glanced at a slip of paper then thrust it into his pocket.

'Dearest friends,' he began. Then shied away from that line like a horse refusing a hedge. 'My dear Lord – sorry, Earl,' he began again, looking to Angus, 'My strongest gratitude – I wish to thank you . . . for –' he looked around helplessly at the flushed faces, the table a wreckage of plates and food and fruit – 'this. It is . . . just grand.' Cheers, glasses raised to our Warden, who was paying for the whole clamjamfry. 'It is a happy . . . thing . . . when ancient feuds are finally buried, never to be . . . disinterred?' Helen bit her lip, looked down at the flagstones. Aunt Ann stood just behind her husband, fair bursting with pride.

Will raised his glass to Dand. 'Friend, we have ridden together and fought together. Now may our families always ride together in peace too. I honour you – oh, and Janet as well!'

Dand and Janet raised their glasses in response and we all drank deep. More of this sweet, inept speechifying and we'd be horizontal with goodwill.

But Will had not finished. 'And while we are all gathered here, it behooves . . .' He paused, distracted perhaps by the word's equine implications. 'What I want to say is it gives me, and my fair lady wife, great pleasure to . . .' He took a breath, saw the finishing line up ahead and bolted for it. 'To announce the engagement of our daughter Helen to heidsman Robert Bell.'

Bell grabbed Helen's hand, raised his other high in some kind of salute. At his side she lifted her gaze from the floor to stare blankly over the company, the cheering and the silent.

I slipped away from the loud press and followed Helen and her attendant down the passageway, up a stair, along a corridor. They hurried through a door on the right, closed it behind.

She had pleaded a headache, I think. Or fatigue. The girl-child I had known never tired and there was nothing wrong with her head. Her eyes had caught mine, just the merest flicker and turn of the head before she left the Great Hall. I knew the signal of old.

I chapped on the door. Chapped again.

'It is Harry Langton!'

Muttered voices within, some argument, then the bar slid back. Door opened a keek.

'Go awa. She disna want to see anyone.'

Alysoun's hair was pulled back and parted harder than a landlord's heart. Two hectic spots high on her cheeks and a fine scowl that might discourage a gardener's boy, but I was not that boy.

'I am no anyone, lass.'

Helen's voice called from within.

'Why should I not talk with my cousin in my own house?'

'Because my lady has forbidden private audience. She pays my way.'

'Look,' I said gently. 'It is hard to serve more than one.' (Who knew that better than I?) 'Hard too to put much aside for a trousseau.'

I let her hear my purse clink. Her eyes wavered, but still she barred the way. I imagined my aunt was not to be crossed lightly. No one cared to be thrown out to the road.

'No private audience,' she repeated.

'If you remain with us, it will not be private.'

She hesitated, then stood aside.

It was a small workroom looking onto the wash-house and yard. When we greeted each other, Helen rested her head on my shoulder a moment and I smelled lily on her. Then her back stiffened and she moved to the window. Her eyes darted to me like the kingfisher heading downstream and away.

'Congratulations,' I said. 'So you preferred the tarter berry.'

She near-smiled, then looked away. Against the light outside, her head trembled minutely. I had never seen my cousin ashamed. No, too strong a word. Apologetic. And proud.

'They last longer,' she murmured. 'Reason must allow.' Her hand gripped the window rail. 'You are a great man for reason, Harry.'

'At the service of worthy emotion, yes.'

She glared at me. Alysoun stood but feet away. We could not carry on speaking in obliquities.

Helen pointed at the spinning wheel in the far corner.

'Alysoun, finish off yon spindle. Please,' she added.

Her attendant–gaoler looked at us both. After all, what harm could we do? No one could mistake me for a suitor. She sat down on the stool, turned her back and began to pedal. The wheel spun, whirred, creaked.

Helen and I moved closer by the window.

'Emotion!' she hissed low. 'What would you know of it? Our family will advance greatly. That cannot be gainsaid. And then Adam—'

'Yes,' I said. 'And Adam, what?'

'Will be safe.' She looked down and abruptly clasped my hand. Her fingers were chill as death. 'I understand there are those who would kill him if he went wi' me.'

'There are. But who told you that? Adam? Bell?'

'No.' She looked startled. 'Warden Angus. He has promised to keep my . . . dear laddie . . . safe. We have talked in confidence.'

'Ah.'

The spinning wheel clacked and birled, my thoughts likewise. Helen squeezed my hand hard till I had to look at her, so close to, one might have mistaken us for lovers.

'Will you explain to him, Harry?'

'Is this what you want?'

'My faither—'

'But he is not that.'

She looked right at me then. 'So I owe him all the more.'

'What do you want for yourself?'

She looked as if I had asked her to walk with me to Byzantium or some other improbable fabled place.

'I want what must be,' she said at last. She let go my hand, stepped back. Still she spoke low. 'Rob is a strong heidsman. He is bold and resolute. He adores me.'

'And you love him?'

'Love?' She seemed doubtful.

'Aye, love. When another means more than yersel. Meeting of two souls, time abolished, that divine sympathy poets write of. You have known it, surely.' I pulled her round to look at me again, close to. This time the pale flecks in her eyes held steady.

'We have been there, Harry,' she said sae saft. 'But nane can bide there lang.'

As I blinked at that, she pulled away.

'Explain to Adam as best you can.'

'You must do that,' I said. 'You owe him as much.'

To live without family would be like living without God is for some: unthinkable. Add that to Earl Angus's offer of protection for Adam . . . Though she would break my friend's heart, it was not lightly nor selfishly done.

'I will let him know when we may tryst,' she said at last. The room was quiet. Only then did I realize the wheel had stopped. 'In the usual way. On you go, coz.'

As I took my leave, exchanged kisses, she gripped my arm, looked me full on. Something blazed in her, or in me, God knows.

'You alone want nothing of me,' she said soft. 'You alone kenned me true.'

Blinking and half blinded, I closed the door ahint me. Then remembered. Chapped on the door again.

'One Fate spins, but it is another bears the scissors, Alysoun,' I said, handed her coin. 'Keep this to yourself,' and hurried awa.

THE SCABBY DUCK

Helen, fair Helen, the ballad bears her name, yet what did anyone know of her other than that she was fair? What did I? Perhaps Adam truly knew her, though I jalouse he was too dazzled to see more than her outline.

Even in memory she remains shut away, visible but untouchable as a glassed-in reliquary one kneels by at a shrine.

The truth is I knew her as a child, and saw but little of her grown-up, when our time together was constrained. I can say Helen Irvine was by-ordinar bonnie, yet plain enough when her eyes and nose streamed at May blossom time. She was calm and fervent, frank and evasive, cunning and honest. I believe that without knowing it, she was true to something beyond saying.

She had a power, most surely. That dawn we raised the hot-trod, when she appeared on the steps of Bonshaw, an entire courtyard full of fired-up fighting men fell silent at the sight of her. Her effect was far more than carnal. Even Robert Bell was tamed, uplifted.

I think on the time we walked round and round the garden together, talking in riddles, our eyes meeting as we bent over the last roses – the light that shone that day from her walk, her gestures, voice and eyes, was not truly hers.

I have heard the unprepossessing, half cut makar Montgomerie speak his verse and strike a smoky, worldly room dumb. And in Firenze an ordinary venal youth summoned the entire angelic order as he sang his solo, then ten minutes later I saw him pick his nose, bored, spotty and plain, as he sat again among the choir.

So it was with fair Helen and her beauty. She did not own it any more than the singer owns the song, or the makar owns the poem. She was but its vessel. I believe she was scunnered by it, at the effect it had on others, who failed to see her, being dazzled by the light that poured through her.

Yet she said I knew her, and I took her word.

Many were still clustered round Warden Angus and Robert Bell, as wasps round jam, and as like to come to a sticky end, if my patron had his way. He would not be best pleased at this development.

Janet Elliot grasped my arm among the crowded hall.

'It was a bonnie notion, Harry, but never likely.'

'Adam will be broken-hearted.'

She shrugged. 'Never fear but he'll soon find another.' She smiled and went on her way towards the press around Bell and Angus, Will and Dand.

I found Adam in shadow behind a pillar, deep in talk with Jed.

'Leave you to it,' Jed said, put his hand on Adam's shoulder and moved off.

I had thought to find my friend crushed, but even in poor light his eyes blazed.

'That's that, then,' I said. 'I am right sorry.'

He gave a queer grin.

'They're no married yet.'

I shook my head at this foolishness. 'You think to run off wi' her?'

'Will she see me?'

'She says she will tryst one more time.'

'Good!' He slapped the pillar. His lean frame was quivering. 'Did she say where and when?'

'She said she would send a message, in the usual way. Whatever that is.' I paused, but he said nothing. 'She said she needed to explain herself to you.'

Adam seized my damaged hand so hard I yelped.

'Why would she want to marry Rob Bell? Man, he's thick as the walls of Berwick!'

'He is a powerful heidsman whom many follow. The family have some wealth and lands. He is close to the Douglases. The match is unco good for the Irvines to resist.'

'She told me many a time she loves me, and given many proofs!'

'I do not doubt it,' I said. I saw them again, at it on the horse blankets. You could ignite a sodden forest from that fire.

'It is not what she wants,' he insisted.

'But it is what she has decided.' I hesitated. Was it my well-wishing for them, or my fear of Buccleuch that loosed my tongue then? 'It is also for your sake, that you might live longer.'

His eyes were an auger screwing into my soul.

'Ah,' he breathed. 'I understand ye.' His smile was not canny. 'Of course, should Rob Bell ding his last, there will be no wedding.' He slapped the pillar once more. 'I'll bide for you outside,' he said.

His hectic cheer was far more worrying than his gloom.

It was decided the company, many already bleezin' fou, should continue the celebrations and join their followers in Ecclefechan at the Scabby Duck. I watched and pondered as the heid yins swept by me into bright day.

'Congratulations, Aunt Annie,' I said.

'It's *Ann*, as you well know.' Still, she smiled. 'A fine day, is it not? The Bell heidsman! Your mother would never have thought it. I expect you'll be back to Embra soon?'

With that she swirled away triumphantly. I could see her point: it seemed my time in the Borders was near done. But she had not said *your mother* with any kindness, and that was hard to forgive. Once Helen's wedding was by with, I would be free, a man of no allegiance.

★

We rode to Ecclefechan on the old road. In the low winter sun its ruts and puddles set hard and glittering as chain mail. Adam was silent up ahead, Philby loped by the mare's rear heels, Jed and I were tight in behind.

'So now life can go back to normal,' I said.

Jed looked at me. 'Normal? In these parts?'

But the company around us were in high good humour, with drink taken and the prospect of more to come. Free drink, foreby, for Rob Bell had called that he would pay for all.

At the last moment, Earl Angus had stayed behind with the women, saying he had other business to attend. It was clear enough to all that he was a sick man, and I understood better his grey peevishness, his wasted hands without gloves. Will Irvine and Dand Fleming said they would follow on soon and waved us off before closing on their superior.

If Clapper pressed on with his suit and married the Earl Angus's daughter before the father died, it would not be long before the Bells were a leading force in the Western March. Perhaps *the* leading force, if they could make alliance with the Johnstones. Lord Maxwell was still but a boy, could be disposed of . . .

They had infected me. Time to go home.

The sun was low in our eyes as we dismounted below the clumsily painted sign of the White Swan. Even in kindly, red-going light, the Scabby Duck (as all cried it) was a low and malodorous hostelry. The men who jostled in the courtyard were not otherwise. Many I did not recognize from earlier, and

I noticed some wore daggers at their hips. Here and there a sword glinted in its hanger. The word of free drink spreads faster than balefires.

Lads poured wine from jugs. I drank cannily, for that wine would strip rust from an ailing gate. I signed to Jed I was going inside to find something better. He nodded and never took his eyes off John Rusby, lounging at the top of the steps by the doorway, one hand on sword hilt, the other thrown wide, grasping the hitching rail. As I passed him, I was awarded a glance from his void eyes, then he went back to studying the courtyard.

At the bar I found a man with a barrel he claimed came from the Highlands. I sampled a faintly piss-yellow *uisge beatha*, which in fact came from a rough corner of the Place Below. I was asking after brandy when I heard an oath, then a sharp yelp and snarl from Philby.

A couple of Bells were laughing as they kicked him towards the door. *Thud* on one flank, *bang* on the other. The grey lurcher staggered, then fled for the door. I followed on, with several behind me.

It happened very quick, as it was meant to. John Rusby stepped from the rail into the doorway, drew his short sword, slashed and laid bare Philby's hindquarters. The dog screamed, fell over bleeding in the dirt, tried to struggle to its feet.

Adam ran cursing up the steps and grabbed Rusby by the throat. With his other hand he pinned down the sword arm. Rusby leaned back easily, looking past Adam to the crowd, to

Robert Bell who stood unarmed beside his brother, calmly watching. Philby was trying to drag himself away, bleeding and screaming. Without thinking I pushed forward, reaching inside my jerkin, then had my arms clamped from behind. Another Bell put his dirk to my side.

'Dinna fuckin move, son.'

The crowd made some vague roar like the sea as John Rusby's free hand reached for his dagger. Though Adam was unarmed, self-defence would be the plea.

A force surged up the steps, smashed Rusby across the head, sent Adam spinning away along the hitching rail. Jed drew his sword and advanced on Rusby.

'A square go, whoreface.'

'My fight!' Adam yelled, but two of his family held him back, and more closed round him. Philby staggered by me, his grey flank hanging open, blood streaming. I saw Rob Bell hesitate, and then behind him more men rode into the yard, armed all. Troopers, yelling for order. By their yellow flashes, they were Buccleuch's men, charged by the Keeper to keep order in Liddesdale. Behind them rode Will and Dand.

But nothing was going to stop Jed and Rusby. They slashed, parried, jumped back. This was not a pretty bout learned in schools, but expert, dirty and desperate. They clashed again, Rusby's sword arm was forced high. His other hand came up with the dagger. Jed whirled, broke the grip just as the dagger slashed open his leather jerkin, showing pale stuffing, then darkening. His sword point dropped, he staggered to the right. Rusby rushed him, Jed's sword came up and buried itself in the man's groin. One scream, then Jed finished him off.

Neck near-severed, Rusby's sightless eyes turned towards me, then he dropped.

The dismounted troopers were on Jed. Three made to lead him away, blood running out through his jerkin, but armed Bells blocked their passage. Rob Bell pushed through to confront the Captain.

'Give us this man!'

'What do you propose to do wi' him?'

Bell hesitated. 'Protective custody.'

The Captain looked down from his horse, pistol casually in one hand.

'I wonder how long he would live.'

'We are acting for the Warden and the King's Peace.'

The Captain was lean and so hardened that when he smiled you could strop a blade on his cheekbones.

'Aye well, we are come on the Keeper's authority, and Eccle-fechan is his ground. We will take him. Anyone who resists will be arrested.'

Bell glanced at Clapper, at his own supporters. They were plenty and their blood was up, but only some were armed, and most were stuffed to the thrapple, and clumsy-fou. Fine for a hanging mob, but poor match for a dozen mounted troopers.

Yet he was Robert Bell, and none crossed him. Had he sword or pistol to hand, I believe he would have taken down that

Captain, but he had made a point of being unarmed, an innocent spectator.

'We will hae justice done syne!' he cried, then went inside with his gang, a face on him like the Deil's punchbowl.

Adam seemed dazed and his head bled where it had banged the rail. Dand pushed through and clasped his arms round him.

'We'd best awa, son,' Dand said. 'Here is no safe. I'll get our men.'

Jed was swaying yet still standing as they bound his hands and tied him to a horse. He raised his head, nodded to us, then turned away with the Keeper's men.

It was then, at the corner of the courtyard, under the stables' overhang, I saw a face I knew. Obscured under a bunnet, wearing drab grey, but even in failing light I could not miss the long jaw fringed with a tight English beard. Dowie Fairfax seemed intrigued but not dissatisfied as he turned away.

Laughter came from inside, laughter hard as millstones. Then a scream that rose, faltered, regained and was crushed under more laughter. I pushed inside. The logs glowed red in the wide hearth, and on them something long and grey and four-legged writhed, tongues of flame rising from its flanks, muzzle and ears streaming fire. Then the body flopped, the fat ignited and the corpse was mercifully wrapped in flame.

Outside in the freezing twilight it took a lot of vomit to banish that smell, that taste polluting the roof of my mouth all the way down to my soul.

*

My hand shakes as I write, and it is not my age. Some scenes are so rank they besmirch even the innocent onlooker.

When the minister talks of Hell (as he does most Sundays, trying to scare us into Heaven), that is what I see — the last moments of Philby, the stench of burning hair and melting flesh, the laughter of men turned to demons.

We have done these same things to men and women in my time in the name of true religion, but I have seen no end more obscene and pitiable than that of the harmless, faithful lurcher, dying in agony amid the laughter.

I can write no more today.

THE CYPRESSE GROVE

Last night Drummond and I sat up late in his study, a prime ash log settling in the grate and the brandy well-rounded. Once in a while neither of us can bear our solitude – his amid his busy family life and letters, mine at my table, wandering in the garden and fields, everywhere alone.

He is half a generation younger than I, in his late middle years, and I like to say things that will shock him out of his patient deference to my age. I sometimes think he rather enjoys being scandalized, to hear uttered what he would not let himself think.

In dowie mood and heavy heart, I said rude things about our present King Charles, ruling the Kingdoms from the South, discarding Parliament, set on heading the Church just as the Auld Hag had. But he was not Elizabeth. He was not even that clumsy, cunning Jamie Saxt that lived to marry the Kingdoms and put an end to the Borderlands of my youth.

Drummond protested all monarchs are God-appointed, and to be spoken of respectfully.

'Some awfy poor appointments,' I murmured into my fiery glass. 'And it seems He keeps changing his mind about what faith each should follow.'

'There is but one Faith,' Drummond said hotly. 'It is the Church that lost its way and needed reformed, not the Creator. Your beliefs are of their time, Harry, and that time is gone.'

He likes to think in my heart I still follow the Old True Church. He imagines me slipping away in early hours to secret places where recusant priests still intone the Mass, and heretical women kneel to kiss the feet of the Virgin. Drummond is a poet, and thus a romantic. And because I am his long-term guest, I just smile enigmatically.

'I honour the Reform for its aim that each reads and thinks for himself,' I admitted.

'Indeed!'

'And now all must think the same, and follow the same Prayer Book.' Drummond made no reply. I knew he was unhappy with the fervour in our land, though he took the King's party. 'Reform may have banished corruption,' I continued. 'It would also banish wit and laughter, music and dance and kindliness.' And fornication, I did not add.

Drummond was about to chide me, but drank deep and lay back in his seat, dazed. He stared at the fire, his mood changing. Excess drink did not take him well. The ash log shifted, burning slow and pure.

'I love my good wife and children,' he said. He paused. The candle glittered in his eyes. 'But aince I loved more.'

'I know,' I said. Once or twice a year we strayed this way, especially in the month of her dying. 'You wrote about it most beautifully.'

'*The Cypresse Grove*,' he said. He was pleased I remembered, then his mouth shaped bitter. 'I would burn it all to have her with me now.'

'I do not doubt it, *mon cher*,' I replied. I knew exactly what he meant. I said the same myself inwardly each morning when I sat down at my table. 'But the work remains, and will outlast us all,' I said.

He grunted. It's no consolation, I know.

The fire whispered within the log. His Bruges timepiece clicked on the mantel shelf. Words I had not anticipated came to my mouth.

'Drummond, I am not long for this world.' He began to protest, I raised my hand. 'These past months I have been writing my best recall of those events at Kirkconnel forty year syne.'

'A true history of Fair Helen!' he said eagerly.

'Scarcely that! It contains remarks and asides of a personal and philosophical nature you might find offensive, for it is written in the spirit of Montaigne and Lucretius, not Tacitus. I have written it for myself, but now I find . . .'

I could not say it, appalled by my own vanity at this late stage. His hand fell on my arm.

'Old friend, I shall read with one eye open and one closed to your foibles.'

'Not now,' I said. 'Later. When I am not.'

And so it was agreed these pages, together with my few books, and my oft-resumed, never-completed translation of *De Rerum Natura* into English pentameters that for forty years have stubbornly refused to flex for me, will be for him to execute as he may choose. May those shy beasts disappear into the deep forest of his library, and dwell there undisturbed!

I woke this dawning to find myself alone in the study, with grey ash in the grate, and a blanket happed about my shoulders.

Now once more I am at my table, full and warm enough, though my breathing labours and I cannot clear my chest. The end will come soon. I have been wrong before, but this time I think not.

Truly, I do not deserve William Drummond of Hawthornden. I must finish this for both of us.

FLITTING

'For sure I will kill him!'

Adam prowled around his bolthole in the peel tower, sack in one hand. Into it he had been throwing old bones, tennis balls, a rug, a chain collar, anything that had been his dog's.

'Bit late for that,' I said.

He stared at me. 'Rusby? No – his master. Rob Bell will ding no more.'

I began folding blankets. Adam had announced his intention of moving back into the house. Dand's raw anguish and concern as he shepherded us out of that awful place had been undeniable. He had acted like a father, not a usurper.

'I am not sure this was Bell's doing,' I said.

'Why, man, he stood and smiled! Did nothing to stop the fight!'

It was true. All night I had replayed the sequence of events from our arriving at Blackett House to our hasty flight from the horrors of the Scabby Duck. Like Adam, I had at first assumed a conspiracy on the part of Bell, perhaps with the Warden. Certainly

Rob Bell had been conspicuously unarmed. Earl Angus had called off coming with the party in Langholm, keeping back Dand and others who might have protected us.

'Rob Bell is headstrong and fearless,' I said. 'He may be sly, but he is not subtle. And who could have controlled and foreseen that outcome?'

'They meant to have me killed, and then plead self-defence!'

That had been my first and second thought. But Jed had been armed, and all knew he was Adam's guard. Surely they would have foreseen he would have intervened?

'*Cui bono?*' I murmured, picking up an old muzzle and leash and dropping them in the sack. 'Remember our legal studies, old friend. Rusby is dead, and Jed is in gaol and will come to trial in due time. Who benefits from that?'

He stared out the window slit. He looked stricken, old before his time.

'None that I can see.'

'Nor I,' I admitted.

Perhaps it was just another pointless fight and death that had no meaning or cunning plan behind it. Things happen. Men carry swords, get drunk, clash and react. It was said the great Maxwell–Kerr feud had begun over the theft of a sow.

Adam stood helpless with the sack in his hand.

'My dog is deid,' he said.

'Yes,' I said. 'I asked that they quickly cremate him. He was not a bonnie sight.'

The tears bobbled and ran till his tongue licked them from the side of his lips. I stood at his side with my own griefs.

'Mind this,' I said. 'If the Keeper's troopers had not intervened, the Bells would have strung up Jed for sure.'

'You still think I should ally with Buccleuch?'

I held up my hands. 'I am just saying.'

'And I am just the son,' he said. 'In any case, my mother would never have it.' He brushed his hand across his face, gave me a queer smile. 'May be I'll no bide in these parts long.'

Better marry than burn, the severe saint wrote (the translation in the King's Bible is crisp but slightly skew-whiff). As I took my leave I thought: *Better elope than kill.*

I met Snood in the doorway, grappling with a bundle of brooms and staves and firewood.

'Give you a hand,' I said.

'Aye.'

I took a load and followed him up to the roof. I minded stepping through that doorway to see Adam stotting his tennis ball and playing the drunken daftie. That seemed long syne, though it had been but weeks.

At that moment, with the fresh Border wind shaking my hair, I yearned for the clash and stour and stink of the city. I wanted days of scrivening, drafting and copying, and nights spent on the town among my own kind, those not-quite folk who live by their wits and wit, flirting, singing, flyting to the midnight bell. Or in my smoky room toying with *The Nature of Things*, trying to make the metre run both regular and pleasingly various. Which is as hard as trying to understand the hearts of men and women . . .

I turned, startled by the clap of wings. Three doos swooped and fought for the seed Snood scattered. They were pure white, streamlined, alert and very hungry.

'Homers,' Snood grunted.

The blind bard kept pigeons? These their descendants?

'Sorry?'

Like many country folk, he looked at me as if I were the daftie.

'You tak them to whcrever, then they fly hame. Here. For guid com.'

He was quite the blether today.

'These are not for the table?'

'Na. Jist sport. Himself attends them.'

First I'd heard of it. Pigeons for sport. What next – tomcats trained for choirs?

'How long has Himself – Adam – been doing this?'

Snood shrugged, all his brain power concentrated on the birds at his feet.

'A whilie.'

I left him to it.

ALFORNOUGHT HILL

What memories cling yet, like a bairn that won't let go its mam? The wintry chittering of pea-sticks in the Bonshaw garden, the blood-dark of haw berries among thorns shook in the wind, glister of burns as light drained from the haugh, the slow march of flat clouds over Tinnis Hill. Above all, fair Annandale seen from Alfornought, the dale below wide and fecund as a green lover's thighs sprawled on a hillside, offering all that men want, fight for and cannot keep.

The morn after the end-feud feast I happed up well and went for a long ponder-daunder upstream, among the knowes and denes. I needed to be away, outside and walking. The day was grey but bright, the wind snell but in at the back of it a hint of growing things. It sieved through the gorse, went rattling through the trees. I grasped down a twig, put my thumb to the first buds. Not sticky yet, the sap safe deep down. It would rise in due time and nothing could stop the light returning. And retreating again.

I let the twig spring back to its own devices and followed the burn up the brae, across a dene, into a narrow cleuch, the land rising. Over a pass and into a desolate glen. In the distance, the hill of Alfornought. From up there one would get an overview of Annandale, and an overview is what I sought.

Crops and good pasture yielded to scrub, then rough pasture to heather, low and blasted. I gained a high sheep path that wound and mounted, dipped across scree and finally into a burn-cleft not far under the summit.

I sheltered a while there, watching bog ooze into its beginning as burn, the buzzard holding steady in the wind with tiny adjustment of wings. At my back, twa–three days' ride off, was Embra, where my parents lay in Blackfriars and I lived by translating men's thoughts and desires into fair hand. Before me spread Annandale's long slopes of green, gatherings of woodland, burns, smoke rising from the farms. Liddesdale to the left, black-avised and secretive. Away to the right, Nithsdale, where Maxwells and Johnstones fought to the end.

When I lifted my eyes just a little from tracing the Kirtle, there was the Solway, and above that not massed clouds but the misty hills of the English Western March.

I turned, looked behind me. No distance at all, the great hills piled up above Moffat, the Devil's Beeftub, then on to Crichton Castle and Embra.

Between these kingdoms lay the low green corridor of Annandale.

I shivered and dug in my pooch for oatcakes and cheese lifted from Mrs Smeaton's kitchen. Far over the southern horizon, beyond where the grey and blue were most pale, lived all Adam and I had talked of when we were young – the Continent, haven of painters, poets, players, high music and free-thinkers, warm days and wine of quality. I had already seen enough to know this not entirely true, that it could rain and free-thinkers were persecuted, but still it held out promise of a better, sweeter life.

Here all about lay Scotland, dark and dreich and dear. Cloud-shadow scurrying over hill and burn, cold wind and dry branch, our hard humour and hidden hurts. Here affection came wrapped in insult as sweet fruit is in burnt pie-crust, tenderness was hidden under armoured jacks, with only keening pipes and fiddle and human voice to tell the heart's ways.

How could I stay in such a place? How could I leave it?

Then of itself my mind cleared, as though upon this height I was above the cloud and could see what had been going on down there.

After all, *Cui bono?*

Rusby was dead and Jed in the gaol. Rob Bell's best swordsman, and Adam's shield, were both off the chessboard spread out below me.

Who benefits? One who wishes neither man well.

What has changed? Neither is now close-guarded.

To what end? That both should come to harm.

By what means? What indeed?

Or perhaps it meant nothing, for who could have foreseen

264

how that scene on the steps of the Scabby Duck would play out? There had been too many uncertainties to control the outcome.

Rob Bell had no need to kill Adam, apart from not liking him, which for Bell might be reason enough. But he had already won Helen. He was in tight with Earl Angus. He would be joined with the Irvines. The Irvines had ended their blood feud with the Flemings, who for now at least remained sworn to Lord Maxwell. How would any of these gain by Adam's death, or Jed's?

Who had set John Rusby on, by what means, to what purpose?

I ran through the folk at the feast, all the faces. Will, Dand, William Douglas. Rusby off to the side, glaring at Jed who stared him back. Crosier the saddler – what was he doing there? – unloading provisions, managing the carts and harness for Elenora, who had been too rushed to look at me straight, her hands quick and deft among bottles and cheeses. Dowie Fairfax in the shadow of the courtyard eaves when it was done, intrigued, not displeased. *Who benefits?*

Once you discern the shape among the shrubbery, it is clear what manner of beast you have been looking at all the while. I set off back at a fair lick, all the way to Kirtlebridge.

I found her alone in the yard, staring at a muckle heap of empty bottles.

'Mistress mine.'

She turned and tried to look at me, but her eyes were weighted to the ground.

'You must be right glad to see John Rusby dead,' I said. 'He was more of a thorn than you let on.'

The wind dunted her bonnic yellow headpiece as she nodded.

'How did you do it? Why?'

She tried to stare me out, but her head kept turning away.

'Best come awa in, my lad,' she said at last.

'Is it safe in there?' Her head came up then. I swear her hand flexed to strike me, and I stood back a pace. 'Just asking.'

We went to her back room. She barred the door, but there would be nae houghmagandie, no bareback carry-on this time.

'Who directed you, Elenora? Was it Fairfax?'

She turned away from the window that looked onto the road.

'Not everything is a plot, Harry. Some things just . . . occur.'

I acquiesced. Then pressed the point.

'So what just occurred?'

As she looked at me, into the silence came hooves. She jerked round, looked out. A lone horseman came slowly by on the Lockerbie road. I did not know him. He rode on by, singing.

> *It came about the Lammas-tide*
> *When night are lang and mirk.*
> *Her three sons came to the door*
> *And their hats were o' the birk . . .*

Her shoulders dropped and she turned back to me.

'I set Rusby on,' she said. 'He was pressing me sair. I said he couldna have me. He said, *Why for no?*' She paused, and for the first time she looked me in the eye. 'I tellt him, *Master Horsburgh is why for no.*'

'Why name Jed?'

She glanced again to the window. I wondered whom she was expecting, or dreading.

'I didn't want you hurt. Anyhow, he wouldna hae taken you seriously.'

I was hurt, but she had a point.

'So you set Rusby on Jed?'

'I wanted that man aff me! Canna bear him.'

'Well, you'll not have to now.'

She nodded sombrely. 'I thocht Jed could look after himself.'

'Rusby near killed Adam while he was at it.'

'So I heard, and I am sorry at that.'

It had been a desperate woman improvising, no conspiracy. I put my arm about her shoulder, more brother than lover.

'And Fairfax?'

I felt the shake pass through her again.

'He must hae his share of me.'

A LANG-WAKE LITANY

I lay long awake last night, disturbed by the day's writing. The creusie flickered, yet but made darkness more apparent. I did as I often do on such *nuits blanches*, and took the ride from Embra to Nether Albie as I once knew it lang syne, seeing in turn each burn, brig and carlin' crossroad, and murmured aloud to the dark a prayer of sorts: *Blackford, Gilmerton, dell of Auchendinny, then by Howgate, Milton, the Leadburn Inn. A dank nameless wood, then Mendick muir, grey Wether Law. The Lamancha bogs, the brigs at Romanno, Lynn, fair Blyth. Saddle sore to Broughton, good wine, poor food, sleep waits there.*

Not asleep yet?

O'er cleuch and dene, brig and ford, brae and dell, knowe, gill and haugh. Kestrel and peewit, dire hoodie craw. Tweedsmuir aye in rain. The climb to Crook where a chiel once brought me milk and oatcake. Linkumdoddie, that lonely shieling. Hard going, then all Annandale spread green to Solway, faint massed Lakeland hills. On by shieling, smithy, cot and inn, by broken tower, burnt manor, to pasture of gimmer, cob and kye.

Who truly wants to sleep, minding o' this?

Moffat, the Dryfe Water, Willie's Cleuch and Kitty's Cairn. Across Winterhope, Setthorns and Kirtleton, and now familiar lands, the high woods above the Kirtle, disused mill by Drowncowsike, then last ford afore Between the Waters. Up the cleuch, woodsmoke, peel tower, then beat upon the gates of Nether Albie.

And should I get to the end still awake, there are loved faces waiting there.

STRONG BOX

I rode through the gate of Nether Albie, by habit checking for Jed coming from his hut with an insult and hint of smile in that battered face. When I stalled Handsome Jenny, there was no sly Watt in the shadows.

I crossed the yard, wondering if Janet Elliot was watching, and found the peel-tower door unbarred for the first time since my arrival. I went up the dark grey twist of stair, for once not stumbling on the trip-step. The door was open onto an empty room. No pallet-bed, no lurcher, no moody heir nursing dark thoughts, only an odour of man and dog and sweat. Someone had taken a beesom to the floor, and the room was clean and empty save for a row of shiny-tipped pikes held in brackets on the far wall.

I went to the door, had a listen and keek up the stair. Only the genteel murmur of the cushie doos in the pigeon loft. So I knelt at the pillar-bulge, and with a pike-blade prised out the stone third up from the floor.

The hidey-hole was empty. Adam had moved his strong box.

I replaced the stone, checked its alignment, dusted down my hands and left the tower.

At the kitchen table I scoffed dried-out pheasant pie left from dinner. Mrs Smeaton had put her feet up and was snoring in her chair in the neuk. Alec and Marie giggled and nudged as they finished cleaning up, then they slipped off into the scullery to carry on. I heard the lock turn over very quietly.

So life birls on.

I licked my fingers, dabbed up the last of the pastry crumbs while picking over leftover fragments of conversations. I remembered Buccleuch asking how come Dand had survived the hot-trod ambush, how he had reclasped his hands before looking up and asking me to continue my account. Was that when he recast his plans? At the time I had been too preoccupied with getting out of my interview alive, but now I believed something had shifted at that moment.

I thought too on Mistress Jarvis and what she was prepared to do to stay siccar. Rusby she disliked, detested maybe, but Dowie Fairfax brought a look to her I had not seen before. The way she shrank then yielded when his arm came round her, her false smile when she bade him farewell and come-by-soon.

He alone frightened her. She would oblige him if he had asked for the clash and gossip of the district, for instance the trysting of Fair Helen. And that information could have passed to Robert Bell, and thus their assault on me that first night. But

Fairfax was the servant of many masters, and I had glimpsed him at Crichton . . .

Like a hen, I fixed my eyes on nothing and tried to pick it up. I sensed I was near getting it.

I could rely on Elenora to do whatever she felt she had to. Which of us does not? She had more brains and smeddum than most, and her necessities, which might include betraying her gossip-merchant, sparring partner and occasional bed-companion, *moi*.

I got up, sighed as an old man does at having changed position. I looked round that warm kitchen, the hanging brass and iron, ashets and bowls, jugs and scrubbed surfaces. Mrs Smeaton with mouth open and big red hands open wearily on her lap. This was the one place I felt at ease in that household, and I would soon be leaving.

I closed the door quietly behind me and went on up the stair to find my friend, that I might better know his heart and better report on him.

What is to be done wi' the likes of us, shoogling along atween muir and sky, trying to be true while fighting to stay alive a day longer?

I found Adam in his room, writing at the table. He looked up, blotted, then quickly folded the paper to a mail packet. Two other letters lay on the desk, sealed with his stamp. I noted one had an address in Carlisle, the other London.

I looked at him; he looked me back. Gave a wee smile then

scooped the three letters into his coat pocket. I could feel his high spirits, animated as a sleuth-hound on its scent, all lounging and scratching done.

'I maun go see our Jed in the gaol the morn,' he said. 'You want to come?'

I hesitated, for I had a report to write and pass to Crosier.

'Of course. Jed would not want you to ride alone, so you can make do wi' me.'

He laughed. 'I feel siccar wi' you at my back. You've turned into a right wee thug.'

He grasped my shoulder, looked into my eye. His were shining. He was filled to bursting.

'Thank you for everything,' he said, and turned for the door.

'It has been an education,' I said, and followed after. He wasn't going to tell me his plans, and I couldn't blame him. Such were the times, that left each man and woman imprisoned in their own stockade.

GAOL

When I have stood before painted scenes of the wealthy and great — their sport, amours, parley and conference, my eyes always pass from the grandees to the one who attends a pace or two behind, eyes lowered.

Friend, confessor, adviser, amanuensis, conscience, betrayer, he may be any or all of these things. He is there in the scene, but he is not of equal rank, that much one can tell by his plainer dress, the humble stance. He is at Medici's elbow, or standing in the wings with the melancholy Prince. He is there with blotting paper when great generals sign the peace, and on the smaller, second horse carrying spare arrows when the Duke goes hunting. At the marriage he stands behind the groom looking doubtful, or sharing a low joke with the bride's attendant.

In all these scenes I search for him, the overlooked, the witness, the hero's stolid, stalwart chum, and when I locate him I ask myself two questions. *What does he make of this? Who is paying him?*

*

Next morn we set out for Dumfries to see Jed in gaol. It would be the last journey of any length we made together.

In my pack I carried for Jed sweetmeats and a game pie from Mrs Smeaton. Adam had a couple of bottles of brandy, his mother's salve for wounds, and – to my surprise – a small Bible he said Jed had asked for. I hoped that unruly man wasn't intending to make peace with his soul quite yet.

Prisons in the Border Marches were not as elsewhere. People frequently escaped or were freed, and as often they mysteriously died in them. Much depended on the gaoler, more on whatever guards there might be, and most turned on which Warden or Keeper instructed those guards. Sometimes gaol was the safest place to be, at others it was as good as a death sentence.

The clatter of arms drowns the voice of the law, Montaigne observes.

Armed and armoured, we rode cannily around Bell lands, then rejoined the Dumfries road. We were now in Johnstone lands. The greater hills subsided and the land smoothed out. We left behind the secret glens for hiding kye, and the fords where one might expect ambush. This was country that hid its darker intentions under a more amiable face.

For the most part we rode in silence. My friend sat high, humming to himself, a wee smile on his lips. He seemed older, yet unburdened. His steel bonnet bounced from its strap, his sword from its hanger. No one would mistake him for a student now. There had been a fine hardening and new resolve.

'Good to see you back living in the house,' I said.

'A damn sight warmer!'

'You no longer think Dand wishes to kill you?'

He had the grace to look embarrassed. 'I was dishevelled in dress and mind. My faither's death, and John's afore him, and my mother's marriage to that lascivious clown . . .' His face darkened, then he let it go. Almost smiled. 'Still, many of us would make matches few others approve.'

'Indeed,' I said.

We rode on briskly. Though the days were drawing out a little, afternoon was well advanced, and we needed to get off the road before dark.

'If Rob Bell were to die . . .' he said to the general air.

'. . . You would be arrested. And the Bells would see you hanged.'

'If he died unwitnessed—'

'You would never get him alone. In any case, I doubt you are a match for him.'

That took the smile from his face.

'I would hack him to pieces.'

'Difficult if he has already shot you.'

He huffed at that, but was silent for a while.

'If another were to get close and kill him . . .' he mused.

'. . . You would be as bad as he.'

'Ach, forget I said that.'

'Said what?'

We rode on. It was strange to look down and not see Philby louping by the horse's heels. I winced, did not say.

'So you must accept this match, or run away with Helen. If you can change her mind, which seems improbable.'

'You do not know her as I do, Harry.'

'I should think not. Yet I know her.'

He frowned but said nothing more.

At last, sore-arsed and stiff-backed, at dusk we picked up the river and followed it on to Dumfries. Toll gate, the guards, name and business stated, packs checked. They stepped back and stared as we rode into the safety of the town in whose narrow wynds just five years back the Johnstones had hacked down hundreds of Maxwell men. They said the streets ran with blood, though in my experience spattered, oozed, seeped and dried would be more like it.

We found a lodging and there ate salt cod washed down with clear fiery spirit all the way from the Baltic. The folk there were easy enough, yet still we barred the door to our room when we retired. Adam did not talk further of his plans, nor I of mine, and so we had barred our doors to each other long afore we slept.

The gaol was hard by the river, little more than a big cellar off the tollbooth. The gaoler was a short, heavy man with a few red hairs clinging about his grizzled head. The only guard was a gangling youth with a skelly eye who seemed weighed down by his o'er-long English rapier.

Adam and I looked at each other. This was at once more casual and more dangerous than we had reckoned on. Rob and

Clapper Bell alone could take this place and dispense what they cried justice.

The gaoler refused to let us see the sole prisoner.

'Ye'll hae to await the Maister.'

We heard horses, clattering fast and crisp on the cobbled yard road outside. Six troopers with yellow flashes, among them the Captain I recognized from the Scabby Duck. At their head, slipping down easily from his tall bay, my Lord Buccleuch.

'Fine morn, Fleming!'

'It is indeed, sir.'

Adam hesitated then removed his cap before shaking hands. Walter Scott looked at me with mild interest.

'Ah, the crystal-ball mannie! What does it show you lately?'

'Alas, my lord, it fell from a high place and is shattered.'

He smiled at that, but did not proffer his hand before he led us into the gaoler's room. Plain table, three stools. He sent the gaoler and his man out with a flap of the hand, as one would dismiss a wasp, then asked us to sit.

It was quiet in there. Through the window slits on one side I could hear the river coursing. On the other, the troopers' horses panting, the creak of their harness.

'You come without followers, I see,' Buccleuch observed.

'We came only to bring succour to my man,' Adam replied. 'We felt ourselves safe within your domain.'

Buccleuch inclined his head at the compliment.

'Unfortunately, though I have lands here, Dumfries is outwith my writ as Keeper of Liddesdale. The Warden holds sway here, though Johnstone might dispute that. Willie Douglas of Angus would have care of the prisoner. I tell him your man Horsburgh was arrested in Liddesdale, so should remain in my care. It is a fine point, eh? Quite hard to hold the line.'

Adam went pale, but managed to keep his voice steady.

'If Earl Angus has Jed, he will give him to the Bells.'

'I expect he would,' Buccleuch said mildly. 'Yet your family favours Maxwell, so perhaps all will be well.'

Silence. River tummle and horse pant. I understood we were negotiating for our friend's life. Perhaps our own lives too.

Adam looked Buccleuch in the eye. Not for so long as to be challenge, but at that moment, his head held high, voice firm and formal, he had a dignity and presence I could never attain. He had a family. He spoke for them. He *was* them.

'My Lord, I would gladly give my loyalty to you, and that of my followers and family to come.'

Buccleuch inclined his head, like a man at a card table modestly scooping up his winnings.

'Yours is an old and worthy family. Unfortunately, I do not think your mother will ever agree.'

'My stepfather—'

'Will aye agree with her. I believe he values the prisoner, but he values his wife more. And she remains mired in old feuds, old hatreds, old loyalties. Such constancy in changing times is most admirable.' He shook his head. 'Most admirable.'

It might as well have been a death sentence.

'When I am Fleming heidsman, I shall have my way.' Below

279

the table, Adam's hand was gripping his thigh in the effort to control himself. 'And damn my mother!'

Buccleuch looked at him with interest.

'Yon's no way to speak o' your mither,' he said mildly.

I noted the shift of register, thought it perhaps good. Certainly he was considering something.

'I mean, sir, my mother is at heart an Elliot, and I am not. I hope much will soon change in the Borderlands, for we cannot go on as before.'

'And we will not. Ask your friend here.' For the first time he looked at me. Up to that point I had been the mute and un-acknowledged witness of these negotiations. 'The smallest shard of his broken ball will say as much.'

'It does,' I said. My voice sounded thin. After all, I spoke for no one but myself. 'Our hope is that in a new settlement the times will become more peaceable, enlightened and more kind. And more prosperous for all,' I added.

'Amen to that,' Adam said quietly. My speech had been short, but it was the distillation of our student days.

Buccleuch regarded us steadily, first one and then the other, then both together.

'A new settlement . . .' he said at last. 'And prosperity. A renaissance, even. Who can argue wi' that? You have missed your calling, Master Langton!' He stood up, his stool scraping loud on the flagged floor. 'You may see the prisoner now.'

He called on the squat gaoler. I made to pick up my pack for Jed.

'Na, na,' Buccleuch said. 'Just one visitor. We will wait for you outside, Fleming. No hurry.'

Adam picked up both packs and with a backward glance – plea? warning? – stooped to follow the gaoler down the low passageway.

Walter Scott and I walked alone by the scurrying river. The day was fresh, the first flowers bent their lowly, enduring heads in the wind. Three grey ducks were carried off downriver, bobbing over the rapids looking very pleased with themselves. An otter turned brown eyes on us, shrugged its back and was gone.

Scott was silent, looking about him with keen interest. Impossible to say whether he was assessing the beauty or the strategic value of our surroundings. Hands lightly clasped behind his back, slight smile on his broad lips, he was so ostentatiously relaxed that I realized he was not. This apparent gentleman of leisure on his morning stroll was a whirr of calculation.

'You ken them both well – do you think Master Fleming would outface his mother?'

The question was lobbed casually into the air, like a man tossing the ball for service at *tennez royale*.

I considered what I had glimpsed of love and repulsion, ownership, adulation and resistance, between those two. Their recent rapprochement. How she would dandle her arm over his as they sat now at dinner, how he looked at her with gladness, how they shared the same humour. His new poise and calm.

'Yes,' I said. 'He knows in time he must be the Fleming heidsman, not his mother.'

Buccleuch nodded, flexed his arms. 'Yet it may be many years till that comes about, for Dand Fleming seems both healthy and unco lucky.'

The corner of his mouth twitched. I understood then, clear as if I had heard the low instruction, seen the purse offered and palmed, that Dand had been meant to die at the hand of the Kerrs at Jarrall Burn. His survival, and that of Robert Bell, had been a setback. That was when Buccleuch had began to develop other plans.

He stopped and regarded a pair of swans nestled on the muddy bank. I stood by him and we watched the male entwine his long neck over the female's, and her undulate elegantly free, and his fresh white wooing renewed.

'How can they stay sae fresh and fair amid this clart and glaur? What think you, Langton?'

The man never ceased to leave me a-gaping at his sudden shifts.

'I think they have an oil in their throats,' I replied. 'Such that the dirt does not stick to their feathers. They spend much time preening.'

He nodded. 'Very like, very like.'

As we stood together watching the courtship, he began to quiz me. Young Fleming's intentions? I said I believed he was making plans to elope and marry in Carlisle, take what money he had and live abroad with his wife until such time as it was safe to return.

'Carlisle! How very fine and romantic. And would she agree to go with him?'

'My cousin has a strong will and mind,' I said. 'But her heart is not open to me.'

'Do not elude me, laddie. *Will she go?*'

I made myself look into his eyes.

'Truly, sir, I do not know, though we spoke privately after the announcement.'

I had his interest there, I could tell by how casual he became. I told him of my brief interview with Helen. That I sensed her to be decided on Bell, not out of weakness but out of strength. Yet she would see Adam one more time. To explain herself.

'Or be dissuaded? Is that what she in part hopes?'

'It could be,' I allowed.

'One more tryst. Very good.'

Across the river, the female had tired of the courtship. With a hiss she slid into the water, the male waddling after her. Then with a long clatter of wings they took off and flew, he still in pursuit.

'I wish you to encourage him in this,' Buccleuch announced. 'I will give what protection I can.'

'It is kindly of you, my lord, to take such interest. May I ask why?'

From his glare, I saw I had gone too far. I would have backed away, but my heels were already at the riverbank. He stepped forward, eyes glittering steel.

'Can you swim, Langton?'

'No,' I stammered.

He slowly put his left hand to my chest. His right lay on his sword hilt.

'Then you must take care to never get out of your depth.'

'I am truly one for the shallows, sir.'

He pushed, very gently, never took his eyes off mine. I felt the river rushing by my back and waited for its snell embrace.

'Perhaps I am a romantic, Langton,' he said. 'I like to see true love win out.' He chuckled as he stepped back. 'Besides, I would rather like to jerk the Bell-rope and hear that cocksure gallant ding out his alarum.'

That at least I could believe. He turned, and with a jerk of his head bade me follow on back toward the tollbooth. I did so, obedient as Philby had lately been.

My instructions were to learn of that last tryst, by whatever means, and inform Crosier without delay. I was not to accompany Adam Fleming on his meeting, but I must find out its upshot, whether Helen Irvine chose to stay or leave the Borders. If the lovers planned to flee, I should jalouse when they would go, and to where. This was vital so that they might be aided and protected.

We stood outside the tollbooth. The Captain of the troopers glanced to his master, who nodded once. Two of the troopers went within.

Buccleuch clapped me heartily on the shoulder as though we were both friends and fine fellows.

'Then your work here will be done, my trusty feir. Go home to your Justice, who says he is lost without you. After that, you might do well to go abroad for a spell. Rome is pleasant outwith high summer, and the Old Church has need of such as you. I have contacts, when the time comes.'

I took his instruction and his purse, but hugged my one small consoling secret to myself. For I could swim perfectly well, having been taught by no other than Cousin Helen, when we were children in the wide, sky-enlarging pools of fair Annan Water.

When Adam emerged from the cell he looked as though he had been to confession.

'Jed asks to see you.'

The cell was dim and smelled as they do, of stone and piss, death and sweat. That apart, I have seen worse. Jed was sitting on a long bench, back against the wall, arms round his knees. In the grey stone-light, his pockmarked face was pale but calm as he greeted me.

I gave him Mrs Smeaton's goodies, which he added to the windowledge. The small black Bible sat on a wee table.

'I see they gave you a chair,' I said. 'And candles.'

'Aye,' he said. 'They look after me right well. Keep my wound clean and all. My ain personal bodyguard without. And now this food and drink.' He chuckled. 'I feel like a pheasant being fattened in the coop.'

I did not like the image, but said he had Buccleuch to thank for keeping the Bells at bay. We talked but for a short while. He said his wife was coming to visit, and perhaps his grown-up children. He said I should have a wife and children, and leave something behind that was better than myself.

I said I would do my best. He cleared his throat.

'Had a friend once,' he said, looking at the dirt floor. 'My brither, as it happens. When he was sentenced, he asked that I be his hanger-on. Tae shorten things, like.'

In childhood I had seen and turned away from enough hangings. I knew how long it took a man to kick and choke and pish for the onlookers' entertainment.

'That's a terrible thing to have asked of you,' I said.

'Aye.'

Silence in that place of stone, the river sweeping by outside.

'Did you do it?' I said at last.

'We bribed the hangman to let me and my cousin haud a leg each and pull.' Our eyes met. I felt myself a priest taking final confession. 'You see, I had given my word,' he said.

He looked down at his battered hands, as though still dumfountert at what they had done in their time. Then he whistled saft atween his teeth, sat back and asked how Adam was taking the Bell engagement. I hesitated, then said he was looking for one last tryst with Helen.

'Aye,' he said. 'Of course.' He studied his knees for a while. 'You will watch his back.'

I did not say Buccleuch had forbidden me to guard the tryst.

286

I did say that with Rusby dead and the engagement announced, Adam should not be in danger.

Jed lay back on the bench. He looked worn out.

'Mind what I tellt ye,' he said. 'Watch the eyes, no the hand.'

The gaoler thumped the door, bawled it was time up. I stood by, wanting to embrace. I had not understood how much I cared for the man.

'See you again soon,' I said. 'At the Assizes, if not before.'

'Aye, maybe.' Jed looked back up at me calmly, then held out his big muckle paw. 'God be wi' ye.'

We shook on that. As I turned to go, he said, 'Thank you for coming to see me,' and it sounded more final than any goodbye.

We rode homeward with three troopers at our back as an escort. Buccleuch had insisted. After all, he said, Jed Horsburgh was Adam's man and Rusby had been of the Bells, so Master Rob might be looking for revenge.

'Though doubtless he will have other things on his mind!' Buccleuch had concluded with a smile, then waved us off.

'Scott of Buccleuch is a sound man!' Adam enthused as we rode for Lockerbie. 'He assured me he will bring Jed to the Assizes. Earl Angus expects to have his cousin Edward for Judge, but Buccleuch plans to have him recalled to Embra, and one of the Scotts installed in place.'

I said I was glad to hear it. Justice in the Borderlands was even more partial than in the capital.

'Then we talked of chess, and Marlowe as against Jonson, and brandy over Armagnac, and how the Reform has killed what little music and playing we had in this benighted country!'

I glanced behind. The troopers rode a hundred paces back, looking hard about. They were not honorific or ornamental. Had they been instructed to kill us, they would have done it by now.

'He is a charming man, no doubt,' I said. 'He has killed many, though I think lately he gets others to do it for him.'

'So I'm glad he is on our side.'

'It doesn't work like that. We are on *his* side, at best.'

'When I am heidsman . . .'

'So you have come around to the idea, taking charge?'

'With the right woman at my side, I can undertake anything, even making our Borderlands a place of peace and renaissance.'

I looked at him. The man was glowing, in his early prime, resolved and exuberant, fair hair loose in the chill wind, cheekbones like the blade of the adze. Perhaps he could persuade Helen. Perhaps they would marry, go abroad, and return in due time, once Rob Bell had conveniently died in whatever incident my patron was doubtless preparing for him.

We bypassed Lockerbie to the south and pushed on for home in the hard, clear Borders sunlight. The wind was cool, but all around the birds were coming back to song, and the first lambs and whaups were crying from the greening fields.

All might yet be well.

*

We got home to Nether Albie round dusk and left the troopers at the gate. We watched them wordlessly ride away, then stabled our wabbit cobs.

I was minded to wash and eat, but Adam lingered a moment in the yard, looking up at the first stars. A slim young moon lay on her back and the air was fine-smelling with horse and beech-wood smoke. On the long ride I had thought myself to a stupor, a dwam, and now was one of those moments, especially at dawnin' and gloamin', when the world stops long enough to be bonnie beyond words.

'You have never been in love, Harry.' It was a statement, not a question. 'When you are, you keek into anither's soul, and so ken your ain for the first time.' He was speaking low, in his heart's tongue. 'Your hairt rins wi'oot stop, like a broken spicket in the yard. The hail world . . .'

He tailed off, looking up into the oncoming night. He came back down, smiled and put his hand on my shoulder.

'Harry, even gin I losc all, it will hae been worth it. I have kenned her love. There'll be nae after-stang.'

I watched him hasten to the peel tower and go within. No regret, no after-sting indeed. I was right glad for him, then and now, though I fear enlightenment in these lands will be a long time coming.

DOOS

An ill wind blows through our house, and it sprang up at morning service. We were all seated there, Drummond, wife, family, servants, faithful retainers (*moi*), honoured guests (ditto), relatives, and the farming people and free men from the estate. Within minutes, it became clear the minister was using the new Book of Common Prayer to lead our service.

Low muttering from the back. The minister coughed and glared, Drummond looked uneasy, torn between his natural desire to please all, and his loyal royalism (after all, he and his father owed everything to the Stuart court). The minister began again. More stirring and muttering. I think someone spat, or else like me had a bad cold.

The minister looked to Drummond, seemed to see some support there.

'Ye'll haud yer tongues, you rogues, and hear the King's service.'

At that, Drummond's eldest lad John stood up in our pew and walked out the kirk. Followed, after a hesitation and slight scuffle, by his brother Charlie. Wee Edward began to shuffle, but was grabbed and held firmly by his mother. At his heels the miller and the weavers left, with their wives and children. The tenants stayed but most looked uneasy. The smith, a huge man with hands the size of cabbages, stood up behind us, glared at the preacher whose face had gone the colour of fresh liver.

'It is no the King's service we are here for, but God's.' His grand simplicity was spoiled a wheen when he added, 'Ya daft wee haivering pollock,' then walked out.

The dominie of course stayed, being paid out of Drummond's purse. As did I, for the same reason. Fact was, for a long time it had made little difference to me. I usually sat through these services inwardly reciting the grand opening verses of *De Rerum Natura*, or mumbling Montaigne's '*Oh, senseless man, who cannot possibly make a worm or a flea and yet will create Gods by the dozen*' during prayers, with an outward look of extreme devoutness.

The service continued with what remained. Since then, Hawthornden has been rife with quarrelling. Doors bang, muffled shouting, motherly tears and pleas. It seems the eldest boy will leave the household. Thinking of the exit of the weavers, the miller, the massive and eloquent smith, the privileged son, I think there will be a much greater stushie to come.

And I will not be here to see it. Each morn my chest fills more, my heart labours and misses, this hand tires and shakes. I wish only to finish memorializing my friends and enemies, to free them from ballad-myth and folk tale – a doomed project, for all that is put into words distorts the world, as though it were seen through swollen raindrops strung along a black wintry twig.

After visiting Jed in Dumfries gaol, we waited. Or rather, Adam waited for a tryst-message from Helen, and I marked him as closely as I could, while resisting hints from Janet Elliot it was time for me to go home. Though he had cleared out of the tower, he still went over there several times a day, as if by old habit, usually to emerge on the battlement. He would pace around, then stand and stare out southward.

Curious, I went up there alone and had a good look. It was quite impossible to see Bonshaw, for the Irvines were some eight miles down the twisting Kirtle valley, well beyond Kirkconnel and hidden by braes. *The usual way*, she had said. Not by flags or smoke or secret messenger. How did they do it?

All I could do was wait and watch. Adam spent much time with his mother, low-voiced in discussion, then loud in laughter. One afternoon he even went hawking with Dand, just the two of them and Perrin, the new stable boy, carrying the gear and a sack. I was not invited.

I began to fear I had missed something, and would soon find Adam gone. So on the third morning I sought him out. I found him in the old tack room, lying stretched out on an ancient Italianate couch, feet dangling over the end, reading *The Faerie Queene*.

'Still looking for the naughty bits?'

'In vain.' He laid the volume on the floor. 'I thought it time to better understand the English Court and mind.'

'So you intend London?'

'Perhaps.'

A small grin on his lips as he waited for me to continue my questioning. There was no point in hiding my mission.

'So,' I said cheerily, 'any news of the tryst?'

'Kind of you to take such an interest, *mon cher*.'

'You asked me – implored me – to come down to this scrawny, violent neck of the March.'

'Why should I tell you when we tryst?'

I was flummoxed and not a little peeved. I waved my arms around.

'You need protection! Jed is in the gaol, so I should shadow you.'

He sat up and looked at me, all flippancy gone.

'Harry, I do not want you to be there.'

'Why for no?'

He ticked the points off on his fingers, an aggravating habit.

'First head: Bell has secured his engagement, so he thinks. We are all happy families now, united in fealty to our Warden Earl of Angus – and long may he live. Second head: It appears my stepfather is not trying to do me away. And yon turd John Rusby is in the ground.' He shrugged. 'No protection required.'

I disagreed, though could not say why. 'Third head?'

'I don't want you in harm's way.'

'You said there will be no harm!'

'Then you don't need to be there.'

'Smart clerk!' I sat on the other end of the settee, held out my hands in appeal. 'I just want to help,' I said.

We looked at each other. The kitchen girl singing in the yard just made the room more silent.

'Harry,' he said softly, 'your head at the window altered the light within.' Then he chuckled. 'It was not unstimulating. But out of respect for Helen, I think not again.'

I was on my feet. Could not look at him. Felt I could never look him straight again.

'I would die rather than follow you again!' I cried, and fled the room.

The pain of that moment has lasted longer than that from my broken nose or this ruined hand, though how are we to know this world, if not by clear witnessing? But he knew I had seen them at it, and that humiliated me beyond measure.

Still, I had meant what I had exclaimed on fleeing, and he knew it. Perhaps that was why he told me just enough when the time came.

The next morn I lay up among the hay in the stable loft. It was warm up there, and the horse-reek brought comfort. I could think there, and there was much to think about. The position also afforded a clear outlook over the stockade fence, and the side of the house, the courtyard and the peel tower.

I was feeling again my faither's muckle paw on my shoulder

as he took me on his business through the warehouses of Leith. How these things linger, the imprint of his strong fingers when his voice is lost to me save in dreams.

The usual grey doos flew out of the peel, made their short circuit, then hastened in again. And then a white one appeared against blue sky, higher up. I had not seen it leave the tower. It flew past the battlement, then banked, circled back swift and agile, then swooped inside.

I crouched in the dimness under the roof and watched. Soon Snood emerged from the peel, and plodded across the courtyard into the house. Moments later Adam hurried from the house, made straight for the tower, went within. Snood did not reappear.

It was my moment. I scrambled down the ladder and ran across the yard. I found him at the window slit in the doo-cot storey, holding a scrap of paper to the light. He looked round, alarmed. Then he laughed.

'So you worked it out,' he said.

'And you have your tryst.'

'Aye!' He was lit up with it.

'Today?' He made no answer, but I had studied him when he was young and unformed. 'So it is the morn's morn.' His eyes shifted. 'The morn's afternoon,' I amended.

He couldn't help grinning. Tomorrow afternoon it was.

'Best shake out the horse blankets,' I said.

'If you—'

I held up my hand. 'No,' I said. 'Promise. You'll be on your own.'

He held my eyes. He had likewise known me when I was young and unformed. So he laughed, folded the scrap of paper away in his britches.

'Wish me luck,' he said.

'With all my heart,' I said. 'Should you win her, let me know afore ye go, that I might say goodbye.'

'If there is time. If not, come and visit us in Carlisle or Constantinople!'

He was already heading out the door. '*Things to do, plans to lay, night is night and day is day*,' he chanted.

I stood at the slit and watched him hurry across the yard into the house. No doubt he had a letter or two to pen, money and gear to bundle and lay by. Carlisle, then the Continent. I whispered a plea to a Power – to whom I suspected all the doings of our time were less than the mild throb from my right palm, something noticed and then forgot – and went up the winding stair.

In the doo-cot all was cooing gossip and warm, sharp birdstink. That we made gunpowder from the excreta of these! In the near corner, in a crate apart from the other birds, the white pigeon was still stuffing itself with grain, its job done.

I like a puzzle solved. I watched the bird for a while, then made my way down the stairs and out towards my little room. I too had a short note to write, and all the while as I scratched it out with my left, I did not for a moment register the itch of healing beneath the bandage on my right hand.

*

I rode to Kirtlebridge where Crosier took my sealed note and dropped it in his leather apron pouch. He looked at me; I looked at him. I gave him small coin; he nodded and I left. I walked out into the spitting grey, my work here done. It was out of my hands. Helen, Adam, Buccleuch, Bell could work out their fates without me.

I rode on to the Fortune Rigg. I yearned now for Embra, to be again in warm chambers, sleeping without watchfires waiting on the roof, spending my days among languages, translating the thoughts and desires of others into clear and lasting words, to be paid but not enmeshed. No more sweating horses and saddle sores, no concealed weapon under my jerkin.

And yet, even as I handed the reins to the cheeky stable lad, I knew I would miss this, the one great adventure of my life. In even its darkest moments, I had felt myself extended, fully alert in body and spirit. There had been terrors and terrible things done – that flurry in the pend, the feeling of my dagger entering another's heart, a boy lifted clean off his horse by a lance through his chest, Philby twitching on the fire.

But I was young, and there had been joys too. I had ridden hot-trod across the Border in fierce company, had that intimate walk and talk in code with Helen in the walled garden, known her silent midnight visitation. I had taken fighting lessons from Jed, then washed the dust away and gone in to eat with great appetite. I had killed a man. Yon drunken, despairing, hilarious night Adam and I had spent reciting King Jamie's *Daemonologie*. And that evening among the players, musicians and servants, with my own people who lived by music, playing roles, wit and laughter, knowing it all a make-believe, a feverish dream. Pleasures too with my witty innkeeper, whom I hoped now to see one more time, to say farewell and see if she required anything of me.

But the Fortune Rigg was stowed out. It was market day, the fire was piled high, the windows rattled with shouting. In one corner several of the Keeper Buccleuch's troopers were filling their faces, and at the other side of the room three men who on their shoulders bore the red flashes of the Warden Angus' riders. Some nodded, the younger ones glared at me, but nothing more.

I made myself known at the bar, then found a stool by the pillar and waited. I thought of Jed, and prayed my patron still held the line against Bell and Earl Angus. Buccleuch had seemed set on keeping Jed alive, though the incarceration left Adam unattended. As Rusby's death had exposed Robert Bell . . .

Cui bono? I was sitting hunched over, thinking hard, when Elenora tapped me on the shoulder, then thrust a cup at me.

'On the house,' she said. 'All the way frae Langue d'Oc'.

She was smiling, but her coif was askew and she seemed uneasy. She spoke quickly and her eyes were shifting round the room. Perhaps the rival troopers bothered her.

She asked after Jed. I reported our visit, said I thought him well guarded. If Justice still existed in the Borderlands, the Assizes would find for defence of his heidsman. His wound was being well attended.

A bray of laughter from the Warden's men. She flinched and turned back to me. She seemed little reassured.

'You'll be awa soon – wi' the engagement announced?'

I hesitated. 'It seems yon way.'

For a moment she gave me her full scrutiny. I swear that woman could read me better than any.

'I would fit you in afore you go,' she said, 'but as you see I'm right busy.'

I said I could see that. Still she seemed uneasy.

'I thought that with Rusby dead . . .'

Her breath was shallow, her eyes scarce meeting mine. 'Best finish yon wine and go,' she said. 'Some here have no cause to like you.'

I nodded, said I would try to call in before going back to the city. She said maybe next time she was in Leith on business . . . We both knew it would not happen. She squeezed my arm, put her head down close to mine.

'Tak tent,' she said quietly. 'Awa hame wi' ye.' Into my hand she slipped a sealed note, folded small. 'Sew this away in your jerkin. One day you may have need of it.'

She left me there in the poor light by the pillar, hurried back toward the servery, glancing at the tables, even up the stair, before disappearing into the kitchens. I checked at the note. It was addressed to Captain Jan Wandhaver of the *Sonsie Quine*, Port of Leith.

I drank down my wine, though it did not taste as good as before. As I made casually for the door, head down, one of the

Buccleuch troopers stood in my way. I don't know what they put in these men's oats that makes them so tall.

He stared down at me. I recognized him from Dumfries, the Captain's second.

'Stay well out of this, laddie,' he said.

'I intend to,' I replied, 'if you'll let me by.'

He stepped aside. I went to get Handsome Jenny, wondering what *this* was that I should stay out of.

I rode home the short way, unmolested. Whatever happened now was no affair of mine.

CLOCKWORK

The dark timepiece in Nether Albie hallway struck noon. Of late many favoured the pendulum and gears because they took the guesswork out of life, the look at the sky for the obscured sun. I mused that for Lucretius the energy that drives all is quite impersonal, yet not mechanical. For on account of the *swerve*, nothing is predictable, and any History great or tiny may take a new, unguessable turn. That is the difference atween Life and clockwork.

I loitered in the hall as the chimes struck and faded. New-made in Leith, bought a week earlier in clear imitation of the Irvines, this piece was Dand's joy. He had already shown me three times how it presented the phases of the moon. He loved to wind it, humming to himself as he turned the handle. I thought it like a man enjoying winding up his own gallows.

'That's me awa, then!'

Adam had been closeted with his mother, then in his own room, all morning. Now he was sprush, shaven and trimmed. Britches in heavy dark cloth, doublet with leather trim – not fancy clothes, but good gear for hard travelling.

'Interesting salve,' I said. 'Essence of dead cat? With a hint of ox-bollocks?'

I ducked his cuff.

'Musk,' he said. 'Never fails to turn a lady's head.'

'Aye, but which way?'

'You wouldn't understand,' he said.

He was fair fizzing. I have seen alchemists' fires that spat and flared so. Mind you, they never yet made gold. I glanced around. We seemed to be alone.

'Good luck wi' her.'

He reached out, clasped his palm round the back of my neck and looked into my eyes.

'Thank you,' he said softly. 'Promise you won't . . . ?'

'Na,' I said. 'You'll be alone.'

'I have told my mother and Dand I'm to Langholm all day on business. We have parted on good terms. Mind you ken nothing about this, so it will not fall ill on you.'

He was brisk now, ready to find out which would prevail, the prompting of the heart, or family loyalty and advantage.

'See you this evening, next century, or in a better life,' he said. And with that line (which he must have been saving a while till it gained interest) he was gone.

For this last hour I have done nothing but sit at the table by the window, dumfountert. The pulse in my neck, the numbness in my arse-bane, the pigeon that kinks its wings and is gone, these are all I know.

The rain comes down in ropes of murky horse-piss.

I am scarcely breathing now. It is as if I have snuck up on something so omnipresent we do not see it. There is no mention of it in Lucretius. I am of Nature, yes, yes. And yet I sit here aware of it, and that is of another order.

'*You have astounded yourself at your own existence,*' a voice whispers. '*You are making ready to die.*'

Then again, who is not? I sit, watching ink dull as it dries.

THE SHOT

Right up to the end I told myself that were I canny enough, it would yet be possible to square my own interests, those of my dearest friends, and the demands of the heid yins of the world. I let myself believe it would not come down to a choice atween them.

But it did, as in the end it must.

I came out onto the peel-tower roof and watched Adam dwindle on the upper road. Usually he went on foot to meet her, down through the woods to the burn, then following it to the old brig, crossing it and taking the wide track by the great beech and oak that led to the graveyard, the kirk, the Lea. That was the way we had gone the first time, on the day of my arrival.

But today he rode, his horse side-packed, panniers bulging. Perhaps they had changed the tryst? The day drove smirrs of rain through the dale and I shivered on the battlement. No, he would take the road beyond Kirkconnel, tether the cob in the woods and come down to the kirk where they would meet indoors, as planned. The horse was to keep his options open. I suspected he carried coin, clothing, a few *lares et penates* – a book, a portrait, a keepsake, whatever scraps and mementoes mark this is where we live now.

He truly believed Helen might on impulse of the heart go with him, to take the byways across the Border before dusk, sleep in some remote inn before Carlisle. A quick marriage, a boat South, then whatever employment or shelter his letters had sought. They must have talked about it before. And perhaps she would go. What did I ken of any heart other than mine own, when even that baffled me?

I stared the way he had gone till my eyes watered.

The rider from the West rode fast and alone. Neither was common in our valley. Even less common was the yellow coif she wore. I ran down the staircase, across the yard to catch Elenora outside the gates, where we would not be overlooked.

She slid down from her horse, her face pale as a revenant in a ghost-ballad.

'Thank the Christ you're still here,' she said. 'Dowie Fairfax!'

'Where?'

'He was at the inn yestreen and . . . stayed the night.' She shivered. I understood now her nervy way when I had come by. I was not entirely surprised. I understood now that where Buccleuch was scheming, Fairfax would be not far off.

'And?'

When she raised her head I saw a soul torn.

305

'He was in high humour this morn.' I let that pass without comment. She looked at me. 'Harry, he will kill me if I clype on him. But if I do not . . .'

'What has happened?'

She looked away, around, at the hills draped in rain as though help were hidden there. She breathed deep and decided her fate, and mine.

'This morn Rob Bell came by, alone.'

'Bell?'

It made no sense. Fairfax was surely Buccleuch's man. What would Bell want with him? Jamie Saxt himself would have been more likely.

'They have ridden thegither for Kirkconnel. A short while after, the Keeper's troopers went also, in two groups. Whaur is Fleming?'

'Gone trysting to Kirkconnel.'

The small rain glistered her face in a fine web, and o'er-late the blind began to see.

There must have been a decision made, the kind I wrote of earlier, between conflicting interests, yet I have no mind of making it. One last wild look atween us, and then she rode back to the inn. I ran indoors, armed myself, and plunged down into the woods towards the brig.

Cui bono? Wet branches whipped face and arms, scourging my stupidity. I could not see all, but glimpsed enough. Jed in prison, Rusby dead, Buccleuch's insistence I should not attend the tryst – the lovers' flight and marriage were not his aim, never had been. What he had sought among a hundred other schemes was just this, that Rob Bell and Adam Fleming should meet, unprotected, in high temper.

I slid headlong down a muddy bank, hit a tree straight on. Blood tickled about my eye. I shook my head and ran. O cunning, cunning man! For it did not matter which died in that meeting, only that one killed the other. Fairfax there to mak siccar, and be witness. And the troopers . . .

I slowed, then stopped amid the woods. I could hear the Kirtle burn now, and went on canny, canny towards the brig.

There were three riders, motionless in the rain, on the far bank. The others would be stationed beyond Kirkconnel, at Palmersgill brig, and most like a couple more at the top end of the Lea. All were there to make siccar that one man would die, the other be arrested, charged, the family unmade, their lands made over . . . How else had Buccleuch risen from the petit laird of Branxholme?

It was good as done.

Perhaps it was the thought of those I loved most, or fury at being so gulled (and having so gulled myself), but instead of turning back, I made my way through the wood and scrubs on this side of the burn, towards Kirkconnel. I went slow and quiet till well past the troopers, then crossed the river at the Howarth ford and ran on fast as possible through willow and beech.

*

I came at last to the bend where the burn turned shallow and wide. Great swathes of laurel lined the bank below. I shuffled down through the trees, pausing and looking before moving on. Finally I gained the nearest laurel, kneeled, pushed the glossy green aside and peered across the burn at the gable of the Kirkconnel kirk, veiled in rain.

There were none by the kirk. No lovers, no troopers, no Fairfax and Bell. All silent, just a reeshle of water spilling from leaf to leaf to the ground, and the wind in the treetops. A shepherd boy dawdled in the drizzle on the far side of the Lea. A bull bragged, then gave up.

Perhaps I was mistaken. Then I thought of the riders up at the brig, less than minute or two off away. A whistle, a gunshot, would fetch them, and their fellows.

Rob Bell had thought to catch the lovers, but they were also bait for the trap into which he himself had come. Doubtless Dowie Fairfax would be just ahint him, whispering encouragement in his ear. But where were they all?

The door at the top of the steps opened and the lovers stepped out.

She was in green, pale and resolute. Adam had her lightly by the arm, she turned to him, looked up into his face. Something was being said, their heads were very close. Even from across the river, I saw how their bodies sought each other, paired in close-rhyme. They stood a moment on the highest step of the stair, looking out over the gravestones. He pointed into the woods, she lifted her hand in what might be protest or assent . . .

Then I saw movement in the laurel below. Then patternless green revealed an arm, a dark head, a long pistol raised to aim. What followed defined five lives, yet would have taken but a minute by the dark timepiece in the Fleming hall.

I screamed, '*Run!*'

The pistol wavered. Helen jerked towards Adam, and in that flinching passed in front of him. The shot boomed, she cried out, then slumped back against her lover, began to sink as the legs went from her, I saw the crimson bloom right about her heart. A truly remarkable shot.

A cry of dismay from among the bushes, a wordless curse. Through leaves I saw a fresh pistol passed by another arm. Bell was now standing up among the bushes, fixed on Helen as she went down.

I thrashed through the bush, reached inside my jerkin, glimpsed a startled face turning my way, a trim jawline beard. Fairfax's hand went to his sword, but tangled among the laurel he could not get it free as I snaked through the tangle. His eyes were dark and wide as he struggled to get his weapon up. I forced myself between two branches, could get no further so punched my arm forward through a gap. The stiletto juddered on a rib. Fairfax's mouth opened. I withdrew, punched again and it went right in. A twirl to make siccar, then he drooped silently among the branches.

Adam was thrashing through the river. Helen lay ahint him on the steps. Rob Bell stood like a stookie, staring at what he had done, then slowly raised his arm holding the fresh pistol as

Adam sought to climb the bank, clutching a branch in one hand, the other gripping his sword.

I squirmed through the laurels and stabbed at the leg before me. The squeal and the bang were simultaneous as Adam rose dripping on the bank.

His sword passed right through Rob Bell. I saw the point emerge through the back of Bell's coat, the useless pistol drop.

'*I cuttit him in pieces sma,*' the ballad insists, twice, the better to make its hearers grue. My friend was scarcely human as he cut and slashed at the fallen man, making siccar and double-siccar. Then he stood above Bell and skewered the point of his blade through the belly into the ground below.

He stood, head lowered, gasping, a sight more pitiable and ugly than the corpse at his feet.

I took his arm. 'You must awa,' I said. 'Troopers are coming to arrest you.'

'Troopers?' He shook his head. Blood, Helen's blood, wet on his cheek, Bell's thick on his hands.

'This was planned. You maun awa, man!'

'But, but . . .' He turned to look back at the green shape unmoving on the steps.

'She's deid, you ken that,' I said. 'For your family's sake, awa!'

Still he hesitated. His hand went to his side. Fresh blood oozed through his fingers, then he nodded.

We stumbled back into the woods. I heard shouts, saw the troopers gallop into the kirkyard. One ran up the steps, leaned over what had been my cousin, my friend, my other self. As he reached down to touch her, she was already passing into story.

We made it to the top end of the wood. A crash of horses, we dropped down as the second group of troopers rushed by. Adam looked at me, uncomprehending.

'I think she would hae come wi' me,' he said.

'I think she would hae,' I said gently. 'Now show me where your horse is.'

We parted under the trees as the rain passed and sun struggled through. I got him onto his horse while he was still dazed and passive.

'Who did this?' he asked, looking down at me.

'Bell and Dowie Fairfax,' I said firmly. 'And they're both deid.'

I told him twice not to go by Carlisle, for they would be looking for him there. He gave me a queer look, then winced, still holding his side. He agreed to go by small ways to the Border, gain and follow the old Wall, get to the east coast and sail from there.

'Then the world is yours,' I said.

He looked at me from eyes like dark piss-holes in the snow, his face all blood, snot and dried tears.

'But the pearl is lost. There'll no be anither.'

'No.'

Soft plops as the last water ran from leaf to leaf to ground. He straightened up in the saddle.

'They will not harm you?'

'This ambush was never for me,' I said. 'I should be able to talk my way out.'

'You aye do.'

He twitched the reins, turned his horse for the Border.

'I trust we'll meet again,' I said. 'But I must tell you . . .'

He looked down at me. We clasped hands.

'I know, Harry,' he said. 'Me and aa', and for aye.'

Then he was gone, and I headed back through the woods towards Nether Albie. There was nowhere else to go, and foreby I was beyond caring.

I nearly made it back. Just climbing the last of the brae when three troopers burst out of the trees and surrounded me. The Captain's second jumped down from his horse.

'Where is Fleming?'

'No idea.'

He put his hand to his sword. The others likewise. This was where the Fates would cut my thread.

'Whaur's he gane? Is it Carlisle?'

A gey long pause. The sun was full-out, now low and yellow across the far hills. It was a bonnie world, right enough.

'Aye.'

The second looked at me, saw what he expected to see, a man surrendered into truth. I vaguely heard someone riding up ahint me. The second turned away from me, put one boot on his stirrup, ready to mount.

'Kill the wee bastard,' he said casually.

The nearest trooper drew his sword. I instinctively stepped back, reached within for my stiletto and I was just raising it when the sword slash came. I put up my right hand against it, and saw fingers fly into the sky and the world turned black and white, and down and out I went.

DONJON

Clearly, I came back from that sword slash, but never again quite the whole man.

I wandered through caverns of Hell with my right arm flaming, my own burning flesh lighting the way. I was dragged, bundled, tormented, cross-examined by demons, some of whom I recognized. I was given cool water, then burned again. I understood well I was dying here, and wanted it done. My mother sought me out and looked me in the eye, the eternal fires burning at her back, and said, *I tellt ye, son, I tellt ye!* In pity I reached out with my good hand, my left, my scribing hand, and gently said, *It is but as you dream, Mither*.

And in the saying, knew it to be so.

The room was small, of cold grey stone. My hand and arm burned still, but it was only a fleshly fire. The man looking at me calmly was but a human demon.

'We cauterized the stumps,' he said.

'Thank you,' I croaked.

Buccleuch almost smiled. He leaned over me where I lay.

'I wanted you alive, that you might know my displeasure.'

'I did what you asked,' I protested. 'My lord, I tellt you the tryst.'

He took my bandaged hand between his.

'Indeed you did. Then you did the one thing I said you must not do. You interfered.'

He squeezed. After a while my scream tailed to a whimper, then gasping, then silence. He watched me with interest.

'Had you not done so, the lassie would still be alive,' he said softly. I said nothing. There never would be anything I could say to that.

'But Rob Bell is dead, as you intended,' I protested. 'The Bells have lost their leader and Earl Angus is weakened.' He kept the steel of his eyes on me. 'And the marriage will not happen, so the Irvines have lost alliance with the Bells.'

'The Irvines are lost to themselves, I fear. Without the money anticipated from the match, they will soon be bankrupt. The Crown will most like hold the lands, which I shall administer. Earl Angus will ruin himself with little assistance from me.' He waved his hand, a minor thing. 'You have not asked about your friend.'

'Did you capture him? Is he alive?'

He gave a queer smile.

'Adam Fleming will not be seen again in this land.'

It could mean one thing or another. The more I pleaded to know my friend's fate, the more inscrutable he became.

'Enough,' he said. He leaned forward, his face inches from mine. 'You disobeyed my clear instruction – I have had men hanged for less. Second, you have killed Dowie Fairfax, who has long been a conduit between me – I mean, the King – and Cecil at the English Court. I have lost my most useful man, and the Auld Bitch will have a fit. I suspect she will want you hung slowly, then your guts burned afore you – aye, the hail hypothec and rigmarole.'

He smiled, and I looked into human Hell on Earth. Thank God we finally die, and that forever.

'What of Jed?'

'Horsburgh? He was killed yestreen, trying to escape.' He shrugged. 'Regrettable, but it happens.'

Jed had seen this coming. There was nothing left. Walter Scott of Buccleuch steepled his fingers and considered me.

'Then again, as you say, matters have worked out not o'er-ill. And I admit to a passing fondness for you. In another place, at another time, we would have had much to talk about. Foreby, though you should by rights be hanged *and* beheaded, it is tricky to kill a man twice.' He looked over his fingers and smiled down at me. 'So what *are* we to do with you, eh?'

'Set me in your service for life, my lord.' It seemed that, despite everything, I was still keen to live. It is a lifelong habit. 'I could be most useful.'

He nodded. 'I do not doubt it. But then again, you have disobeyed me once, and might do so again.' He stretched his arms wide and stood up.

'You mind our discussion about Earl Bothwell? How he was shut alane in the dark below Dragsholm fortress, and furrowed a deep rut all round his pillar as he went insane?' A great dreid rose in me then. 'Here at Crichton Castle we have a fine donjon. An *oubliette*. It will be interesting to see how long your inner resources last, as you contemplate the loss of all you hold dear. That may get you through the first five years.'

'May your balls roast like chestnuts on the Deil's fire! Lord Buccleuch my arse – you are nowt but a jumped-up laird.'

Buccleuch flushed, his hand went to his dagger. Then he paused, nodded and reached for the door.

'Quite so,' he said. 'Death is indeed preferable.'

Then they came, bundled me down steps, opened a mighty door and threw me down into the pit.

How absolute that dark. How alone one is. How complete the silence. Then one hears one's heartbeat and one's thoughts, and both become torment inescapable. There is nothing else but a blanket, a bucket. Without room to lie down, one sits, stands, kneels. From time to time – hours, days? – a clunk, faint grey light, gruel and water are lowered down. One ingests them, then darkness and silence resume.

The sound of your heart. Alone at the mercy of your thoughts. Terror begins to eat you alive, without end. Weeks, months?

Complete darkness. Timeless. Devoured not by fire but by absolute dark and the heartbeat gnawing in your ear. This is Hell indeed.

I can write of this no more, lest it comes to me yet again in the night.

EXILE

The light of day jabbed needles into my eyes. Throughout our interview, they would not stop watering.

'Interesting experience?' Buccleuch asked.

'Ghastly.'

'No doubt, no doubt. Alone in pure dark under the ground. Buried alive.' He paused, looked at me keenly as I wiped my eyes against the light. 'How long would you say you were there?'

'Dinna ken,' I stammered. 'Six months? A year?' It had felt like forever. I mean just that. No night or day or season, just unending dark and one's ceaseless thoughts. It seems we do not need the fires of Hell to torture us.

'Interesting,' he commented. 'It was but a month. I wonder what ten years would feel like.'

He knocked on the door, his man passed him some items, then went away. Walter Scott sat on the stool and offered me a cup. I sniffed it and felt dizzy. It was the pure South. Vineyards

319

under hot sun, distant hills shimmering, poplar trees along the turpid river.

'Drink,' he said.

I sniffed again, and drank. If it killed me, so much the better.

'In idle moments I have been considering your case,' Scott said. 'Good, is it not?'

'It is life itself,' I blurted.

'Yes, each vintage seems better than the last . . .' He slapped his knees. 'It appears Fairfax's death has not been unwelcome in the English Court. It seems he had swindled the Earl of Essex of a small fortune – as who, given half a chance, would not? – and has been reporting to Spain. A man may serve two masters, but three . . . Robert Cecil congratulates me on a job well done. We have agreed Dowie Fairfax was stabbed to death by some insignificant runt in private quarrel. What d'you reckon on that?'

'Very like, my lord. Very like.'

I gulped down wine. It warmed all the way down, and left in the mouth a fulsome dryness that made you desire more. The hand that held the cup, mine own, was unearthly white and shook.

'On the other hand, Jamie Saxt – His Majesty, to you! – is disconsolate. It seems he valued Fairfax – they might have fondled in younger days, who knows? He would like to see the man who killed him die a long and painful death. Moreover, he kens I have this man – you, laddie – locked up in Crichton donjon. So what are we to do with you?'

And then he told me. I would be transferred to a place of execution – Melrose would do nicely – and on the way I would escape.

'Like Jed?' I said.

'No, you really will escape. I will make it convincing. After that, if you are identified and captured, it is none of my affair, and they will certainly hang you. I would suggest you make for Berwick and sail from there to the Continent *and do not return*.'

He was very clear on this. I should not return before Jamie Saxt became King of the Two Nations, and the Borderlands had been put down, the Bells silenced, Earl Angus dead, Johnstone made weak, and Janet Elliot and her husband, and even he himself, gone the way of all flesh. Should I live that long, of course.

Did I agree to his conditions? Damn right I did.

On the bright morning Scott walked me through the lozenge courtyard to the guards who were to take me to Melrose for hanging, he took me by the elbow.

'We will not meet again in the land of the living,' he said mildly. 'Or if we do, I will have you killed. If you talk or write about me or this affair, I will have you killed. You understand me?'

'Without difficulty,' I said.

He smiled. 'It has been, in its way, most interesting,' he said. 'Good to see the low-born rise – but ceiling, laddie! Mind the ceiling!'

We paused some twenty paces from the guards. He reached into his doublet and casually dropped into my pocket something that chinked.

'A wee something for the journey,' he murmured in my ear. 'Gang weel, laddie, as though you were my ain.'

Then he called to the guards, 'Take this trash to the High Sheriff to dispose!' winked at me and was gone.

The overnight lock-up in Peebles was little more than a shed. My manacles were left loose, the high window unbolted.

I dropped down onto the ground in the silent night. I awaited the ambush, the immemorial 'killed while trying to escape'. None came. A thin moon lit my way through the houses and byres to the river. I set myself downstream towards Berwick as my patron had suggested.

Like hell I did. You think me stupid? Buccleuch might change his mind, or be having his fun with me, or it might suit his purposes to have me picked up across the Border. I believed I was beginning to get a hold of his subtle mind: if I survived, it proved I was fit to survive. If I did not, then I was not.

I followed the Tweed upstream through the night, till dawn found me in a hay-barn hard by the lesser-used drove road to the markets of Embra town.

I rested up through the day, kept an eye on the road, and took stock. I had nothing but some ill-fitting, sturdy boots, my old jerkin, a plaid cloak and an antique hat it had amused my

322

lord to clap upon my head. I had become a stoorie-fuit, one of no consequence, a stravaiger best avoided.

When dusk came, I took to the road and headed north. The Hunter moved across the sky, owls and their prey were my only company through those starry hours. I did not allow myself to mourn, or think of anything except my goal. My legs were weak, the night was bitter, but anything, including death, was better than the pit from which I had come.

My secret purse, and much craft and caution, in three days brought me to the city gates at dawn. Though longing tugged my heart, I gave them the by, and passed instead the day sleeping in the woods of Holyrude, below the Seat where in another life two young student friends had scrambled to the top by night and opened their hearts to each other.

The night was moonless, but I knew the way well enough, and dawn found me in the small rain in Port of Leith, reaching into the lining of my jerkin as I walked greasy quays in search of the *Sonsie Quine*, trading into Antwerp.

Captain Jan Wandhaver broke the seal, read the note and glanced up at me. His eyes were sea-blue and clever, mismatched in his brown turnip of a head.

'Mistress Jarvis no longer owns this vessel,' he said.

She had come by a fortnight back, and on the spot sold her share of the boat and wine business to him. A knock-down price, for she was in urgent need. She had sailed with him, hidden in the bilges.

'Do you know where she has gone?'

'After Antwerp?' He shook his head. I believed him. Not because he was necessarily honest, but because she was canny.

'She had marks on her face and was damaged . . . elsewhere.' He glanced at my hand, the blackened stumps. 'She asked me to carry you away if you came. For her I will do this.'

I sailed without regret, for none dear to me remained alive in Scotland. The crew was but four and they spoke little. I spent days on deck, sheltering behind packing cases, eyes gripping the horizon. Nights I bedded down among the cargo, which was mostly fleece and hide, tight-packed, stinking of life and death, being not fully cured.

I went up on deck one morning to find we were sailing upriver past the Isle of Dogs. I complained to Wandhaver and said this was not what I had expected.

'Extra cargo, son,' he said and winked.

We tied up at Southwark. The first couple of days I was fearful of being found out, and skulked and sulked below. On the third evening I could bear my own company no longer and went ashore.

The inn was in a slurry-filled street behind the waterfront. I found a quiet corner, thought to try English beer, willing to forget myself. A crowd of players came in, a couple of the lads still in rouge, with painted, pouting lips. Several I recognized from that gaudie night at Crichton Castle. They brought their swirl of energy, jokes, gossip, flirtation, anxiety and songs. Among them were the senior men, the hefty, imposing one, and the quiet man with lustrous eyes.

He hailed me, waved me to their table. It was just what I needed, to dissolve myself in drink, wit and make-believe. In the hubbub, he leaned close to me.

'So how did it end, the story of your troubled friend?'

'Badly.'

'You surprise me,' he said, dry as unsugared sack. 'Some detail, perhaps?'

Something about him made one want to tell all, like a confession but without any judgement made at the end. His listening was its own absolution.

He bought me Rhenish wine – the beer was pish – and I told him how it had gone since we last met. Then he bought me port and I poured out what was left of my heart. Whatever I said, he soaked it in, then waited. The man was a sponge. His listening minded me of Buccleuch, except I sensed it was not earthly power that this man sought. Nor did he seem especially bent on Heaven.

'Those not already dead,' I concluded, 'will be soon enough. Or scattered, exiled, dispossessed.'

'No ghosts?' A quick sideways keek at me. 'Did you see any ghosts?'

'None.' I explained that in the Borderlands the living were frightening enough.

'Pity,' he said. 'We can do ghosts – always makes them shit their pants.' He leaned back in his chair. His eyes wandered off and I feared I was losing his interest.

'Was your friend's stepfather really trying to kill him?' he enquired casually.

'No. He had been very close to his mother.'

'Of course.'

'His brother, then his father had died – the latter in suspicious circumstance. He didn't want to be heidsman, but he hated to be passed over. He was . . . troubled in mind. And in love.'

The senior man nodded. 'Thought as much.'

Not a sponge, I thought, more a blotting pad. The drink – we were on brandy now – was turning my brain to pigswill.

'I can get you free entrance for tomorrow,' he said. 'We are more reliable on our second afternoon. It's a comedy, of sorts.'

I thanked him, but said we were sailing on the morn's tide. In any case (this I did not say) I preferred to read plays rather than attend them.

'No matter,' he said. 'The next one will be better.'

He smiled to himself, thanked me for my story, and turned back to the company. All were lively, many witty, some musical, a few romantic. I drifted and forgot myself, forgot the past, the deaths of all I held dear, as I was swept forth on a tide of conviviality and drink.

We heard the various bells chime a staggered midnight. The senior men looked to each other. 'Rewrites!' they chorused, then left us to it.

I awoke face down on rancid fleece, with an actor's prompt of *Love's Labours Won* folded in my jerkin. The *Sonsie Quine* was heaving and moments later so was I, hurling beer, wine, port, brandy, venison pie, from the pit of my stomach over the rail into the gurly sea.

When even bile was emptied out, I clung to the rail on shaking legs, vacant, evacuated, searching into the grey for the coastline and my second life to appear.

HAWTHORNDEN

Yestreen I watched an elderly packman come up the drive with his living on his back. He came to the side door and slipped his load. He straightened up, swung wide his arms, looked around, relieved the carry was over. Then his head dropped. He looked lost and dead done before he raised the energy to put on his selling face and chap on the door.

I felt for him then, and now. What a sair fecht it was this morning to climb the four flights from the kitchen to this wee room. The destination achieved, the story near told, I felt at first relief and lightness, and then – now – great weariness.

That man travelled in knives, polishes, trinkets and household gee-gaws, and sold them with snatches of stories and song, and passing display of his injuries and wounds from ancient battles. Need I say more about our brotherhood?

Through near-on three decades I wandered through Europe from one patron to another, from Church to Law to Politics to Business, whatever trade needed a man with a good hand and many languages. I finessed wills, edicts, summaries and histories, corrected translations and checked galley proofs, amended sworn depositions. I have been scholar, private secretary, amanuensis, clerk, librarian.

What can most of us say of our lives but we have worked, been paid and eaten? I have stood a respectful distance from high men and petit scoundrels, ready to receive instruction or give advice (seldom heeded). When I moved through the Low Countries, it was in hope that one evening I would enter a well-run inn, and know at once by the homely ease, a certain smell, a brightness in the air and the glimpse of a yellow bonnet, that Elenora Jarvis had remade the Fortune Rigg.

It never happened. And everywhere I asked as I drifted through the years to Italy (keeping well clear of Rome) for news of a tall, fair son of Borders gentry, most likely a soldier. But Buccleuch was right, Adam Fleming was never seen again. Very likely they caught him within a few miles of Kirkconnel Lea, and his bones lie in some peat bank or bog. Yet they never found his horse, which would have taken more to dispose.

But it was widely reported that on a street in Milan a certain John (Clapper) Bell fell into violent argument with another Scotsman. The struggle was fierce and brief before Bell coughed up his life in the dirt and the other man fled.

It might have been him. Certainly the story still lingers, though as we have learned that does not make it true. Though some folk tales say otherwise, I doubt if Adam ever came back to Scotland. It would have been insanely dangerous, and he had nothing to come back for.

When the Auld Hag finally died, Jamie Saxt united the Crowns, and as Buccleuch and even I had foreseen, that quickly put an end to the old reiving ways. Earl Angus reverted to Catholicism, was exiled to France an ill man, soon died.

Buccleuch was given a free hand. He promptly hanged many of his old comrades of the great raids, including those who had helped him free Kinmont Willie from Carlisle Castle. Dand Fleming was among them, protesting his innocence to the last. (Janet Elliot was not killed or ravished — I think Scott did rather admire her — and ended her days in a Flemish nunnery.) Others were exiled, a few bound themselves to Buccleuch. Most, including the Irvines, lost their lands and their followers. Within five years, none but Buccleuch and the King could raise armed men in any numbers.

Peace of a sort then came to the Borderlands. The peel towers and their balefires at the ready fell into disuse, inhabited only by pigeons. Most of the heidsmen's strongholds were razed, their stones used to build farm cottages and byres. I hear Nether Albie is but a wee farm now, not a stone of the peel tower standing.

I have never known whether to think of Adam Fleming slipping from his horse and dying of his wound in a ditch near the Borderline, or growing old somewhere in Europe, on an army pension perhaps.

I never found out, and now never will. So I am at liberty to picture him as reported by the aged, sottish stableman at the

Fortune Rigg. He claimed — and for the price of a drink, still does — that as a lad he saw Adam Fleming towards the end of the day of the shooting of Fair Helen Irvine, riding the Kielder way into a low red sun, clutching his side like a speared Christ.

I like to think (as some folk tales also say of the Christ) that he survived, went to another country, found work, met and married a good woman, had children and kept his incendiary thoughts to himself. Whatever happened, he was not heard nor seen again on this earth.

In my long lamplit nights, I see him on the roof of his tower, bouncing a tennis ball and acting the daftie. I see him sprushed up to go courting. I mind his breathing presence at my side during our night in the kirk, his hand coming over my arm. My last image of him is not of our hurried, bloody parting in the woods. It is, typically, something I never even saw — a tall figure riding uncertainly into the red sunset, clutching his wound.

GRAVE

Last night as I lay wheezing in the dark, the door scraped, a lamp flickered, and she came to me. She bent over me, her breath sweet, and my fetid garret smelled of river-willow. The ever-shifting whoosh of water and the reeshling of leaves came from her lips as they moved.

She leaned closer, till there was only her eyes looking into me. The lamp flickered, and in the depths of her eyes I saw gold flecks gleam. As what passes for my soul stood still, they began to drift, then swirled by some nameless current they poured into the black hole at the centre, to coalesce a bowl of light that overflowed without end into the dark.

'Fear not,' she whispered in my ear.

It was as though I had been waiting all my life – or at least since my mother breathed her last – for these words, and something amiss in my understanding of *De Rerum Natura* was made right.

Since that final visitation, whatever my approaching end holds, whenever it comes, my heart is whole and lichtsome.

Naught affrichts me, for the incorruptible has kissed me atween the een.

I came back home, of course I did, once all were safely dead.

I met William Drummond at an Embra gathering, recognized him as my dead friend Fowler's nephew, and quoted the opening lines of *The Cypresse Grove* to him. This led to an invitation to come to Hawthornden. Somehow I have never left.

A few months later I stood in the kirkyard as the rain dragged its murky shift across Kirkconnel Lea. I asked the sexton's laddie where the keys might be for the vestry. He shrugged. In any case, the lock looked rusted solid. Or the Maxwell vault below?

'Nae Maxwells aboot here.'

It seemed in my long absence the parish had been amalgamated, and the wee kirk left abandoned ever since. It may have had too much of the Old Faith, or too much death about it. It was much reduced, practical folk needing good stone for building houses and byres.

I asked where Helen Irvine's grave might be.

'The lady in the story, wha died?'

'Aye,' I said. 'That one.'

He stopped among the seeding thistle and long grasses, parted them with his foot.

'They say she bides here.'

I looked down at a grey, unmarked stone, shaped like a coffin for a child.

'There was a heidstane, whiles, like,' the lad said. 'But it was broken aince, and the next carried awa.'

By the remaining Bells, I supposed. Understandable. On the way here I had been shown Blackett House, a decent dwelling hard by their ruined stronghold and peel tower. The survivors must have made their peace with the new disposition.

I looked down at the moss-speckled stone, thinking not of what lay below but the one I had known, strong-willed and helpless as an imprisoned queen looking out at a world that cannot be hers.

An anonymous stone, and ballads and stories inaccurate or untrue – it seemed fitting, for few, if any, had truly known Helen Irvine.

'Ye kenned her?' the lad asked.

'Aye.'

He stared at me, then down at the glove I wear in company to cover my right hand. His eyes widened, he stepped back a pace.

'Are ye her beau, as hackit Bell tae pieces?'

I had to smile at that, and the boy turned and fled.

Alone I climbed the stone steps up to the vestry door. This is where they had emerged, where I had cried warning and she had flinched across her man and so died. The river was loud hard by, and the laurels still spread dark green where the shot had been fired and Bell and Fairfax met their bloody end.

My legs shook so. I sat on the topmost stair, leaned back against the door and looked my fill.

I did not return to Kirkconnel Lea again for some ten years. In the calm, douce order of Hawthornden, my thoughts shied away from it and all I had known there. Then when the leaves began to fall and fly last year, Drummond had one of his private soirées of music and recitation and flyting.

In a late hour, a skinny, intent youth stood to hitch the small pipes under his elbow. The drones locked onto their implacable threnody, summoning Fate and Doom, wind keening through broken walls, empty moor and dank forest, the skull and hourglass we Scots inscribe on our tombs to counter any pious suggestion of the life to come.

Most satisfying. I leaned forward in the shadows, much drink taken, and drank more. Then the chanter cut in, thin and high, and from the first few notes I knew what it must be. The lad opened his mouth and sang, his eyes fixed, like all true singers, on some further place.

> *O gin I were where Helen lies!*
> *Night and day on me she cries;*
> *And I am weary of the skies*
> *Of fair Kirkconnel Lea.*
>
> *Curst be the mind that thought the thought,*
> *Curst be the hand that fired the shot,*
> *When in my airms burd Helen dropt,*
> *Wha died for sake of me . . .*

I wept. Drummond alone noticed, and let me be. I wept at the grave truth of the singing, and at the sentimental guff of the words, with their chastity, noble sacrifice and sighing. *This will not do*. Besides, there was no mention of the others there, nor of the absent ones who made it happen.

I lay awake that night by creusie lamp, my right hand on fire. In the lamplight or with my eyes closed, it made no difference as those faces, scenes, delights and horrors paraded afresh before me, unburied. No brandy, no prayers, no wit and wisdom from Lucretius or Montaigne could silence or honour them.

I asked for leave and a horse, pursed what savings I had from my itinerant life, and went back to Kirkconnel. The old sexton had died, the new one of the Reformed Kirk knew me not. Why should he? We stood among the graves by the old kirk. The grass grew long, the nave had vanished now, only the Maxwell vault and upper vestry chamber remained. And the steps of course, the steps.

I took him to the uninscribed grave and told him what I wanted. He gave me a queer look.

'I dinna like it,' he said. He looked into my face, at my gloved hand. 'Are you he?'

My smile makes some uneasy. I hefted my purse in my good hand.

'I will need a legal undertaking,' I said. 'A signed document, to be executed after my death, which will be soon.'

Like the lad a decade before him, he backed away. I trickled gold onto my palm, and that held him.

'One third on signing,' I said. 'The remainder will come from my executor, once it is done.'

He stopped. Licked his lips.

'Yon's an awfy lot of money for a plot and a stane,' he said.

'It is completely deleerit,' I agreed. 'But it pleases me. Foreby, it will give folk something to talk about for a lang while.'

When I got back to Hawthornden, my right hand no longer burned. The next morn, heart swollen and girning like a pregnant sow, I wrapped up well and sat down in my rime-ridden garret chamber, and began.

And whiles the mason's chisel has chipped away. Round Christ Mass a note came to say it was done. Another grey, small, coffin-shaped stone now lies in the sexton's yard, awaiting my death and internment by Kirkconnel Lea. It is twin-companion to hers, except it is inscribed in the name of the one I loved all my life and could never have:

HIC JACET ADAMUS FLEMENG

I think that will do.

'J'ai seulement fait ici un amas de fleurs étrangères, n'y ayant fourni du mien que le filet à les lier.'

I conclude with Montaigne, then lean forward to wipe my breath from the glass. Clouds slide over the hill, more come into view. The trees above the North Esk have begun their greening, the sycamore's black buds are sticky to the touch. Drummond and his eldest lass walk by the river, deep in conversation as he tries to persuade her to the match he desires. *Plus ça change*, eh? The packman left this morning with food in his belly, hitching on his load again, a man condemned to be his own horse as he struggles down the yew alley to his next call.

Though I had but minor part in the events I have scrieved, those days made and unmade me. The rest has been one long *post scriptum*. My job here is done, and so am I. '*I have gathered a garland of other men's flowers, and nothing is mine but the cord that binds them.*'

When folk cry Helen Irvine *fair*, I think it was not for any by-ordinar beauty of form, face or limb, but on account of something they had glimpsed within her, of which she was but the bearer, and it cost her dear.

As for my friends and foes and loves among the reivers, they too have passed from life to ballad, from flesh to sculpture. No matter how much I have insisted they were but human, they have become golden and outsize, as though their living forms and faces were remade in clay then dipped in layers of bronze.

The feather that once scratched out a mind's wind flutters down, is still.

H.L.

SCOTS GUIDE

aa' *all*

agin *against*

agley *askew*

ahint *behind*

aince *once*

aircock *weathercock*

airt *direction, as of wind*

alane *alone*

amang *among*

anither *another*

ashet *large plate*

atween *between*

awa *away*

awfy *awful/ly, very*

aye *ever and yes*

bairn *child*

birl   *turn, whirl*

bleezin fou   *totally pissed*

bonnie   *pretty, fine*

bougie   *candle*

brig   *bridge*

brither   *brother*

bruck   *rubbish, mess*

bunnet   *bonnet*

by-ordinar   *unusual, extraordinary*

ca' canny   *be cautious, go carefully*

callant   *lad*

canna   *can't*

canny   *careful/ly, shrewd/ly*

carefu'   *carefilled*

chapped   *knocked, strike, as on door*

chanty pot   *chamber pot*

clart   *dirt, muck*

clash   *chatter*

cleuch   *ravine, gorge*

clype on   *inform on*

coory, cooried   *snuggle, embrace*

corrie-fistit   *left-handed*

cott   *cottage, cot*

creusie lamp   *simple oil lamp*

cry   *call, name*

dae   *do*

daftie   *fool, idiot*

daunder   *stroll*

daur   *dare*

the Deil   *the Devil*

deleerit   *crazed*

dene   *vale*

didna, dinna, disna   *didn't, don't, doesn't*

dirl   *pierce*

dominie   *schoolteacher*

doolie   *melancholy*

doos   *doves*

doo-cot   *dovecote*

dowie   *melancholy, miserable*

dreich   *grim, severe*

dumfounert   *dumbfounded*

dwam   *trance, day-dream*

een   *eyes*

Embra   *Edinburgh*

fecht, fechter   *fight, fighter*

feckful, feckfu'   *powerful*

flyting   *formalized contest of insults, ideally in verse*

feir   *friend, trusted companion*

foreby   *as well as, additionally*

forky golach   *earwig*

fou   *drunk*

gey   *very*

gie   *give*

gill   *ravine*

gin   *if, would*

glaur   *mud*

glisk   *quick glance*

gowk   *cuckoo, fool*

greit   *cry tears, grieve*

grue   *shiver*

guddle   *a mess, muddle, also verb*

guid   *good*

haar   *mist*

hail   *whole*

hairm, hairmless   *harm, harmless*

hairst   *harvest*

hame   *home*

hap   *gather, cover*

haud   *hold*

heidsman   *clan or family leader*

heid yin   *boss, leader*

heuch   *quarry, cliff*

Hieland   *Highland*

hirple   *hobble, limp*

hot-trod   *legitimized hot pursuit*

houghmagandie   *sexual shenanigans*

howff   *shelter, haunt*

in-by   *entrance*

isna   *isn't*

jack   *long jacket, usually reinforced*

jalouse   *suspect, intuit*

jouk   *jerk, dodge*

keek   *peep, glance*

ken, kenning, kenned   *know/ing, knew*

knowe   *knoll*

kye   *oxen, cattle*

the Lallans   *Lowlands, incl. Language of*

lang syne   *old times*

lave   *those left, the rest*

laverock   *lark*

lichtsome/ness   *light-hearted/ness*

loup   *leap, jump, bound*

lug   *ear*

makar   *maker, poet*

maun   *must*

morn   *tomorrow, morning, e.g. 'the morn's morn'*

muckle *large*

muir *moor*

nane *none*

neb *nose*

neuk *nook, corner*

no *not*

peel tower *fortified tower with signal-fire*

pend *covered archway or passageway*

quine *female, woman*

rammie *fight, brawl*

reeshle *rustle*

reiver *robber, rustler, especially of livestock*

saft *soft*

sair *sore*

sclaff *scuff, slap, swipe*

scunnered *fed up with, loathing*

shoogling *shaking*

sic *such*

siccar *safe, reliable, certain*

skeely *skilful*

skelly *squint*

skite *dash, hurry*

sleekit *crafty*

sma *small*

smeddum   *spirit*

smoor   *smother*

snell   *sharp, biting, as in wind*

sonsie   *plump, hearty*

sough   *sigh, bearing*

speir   *ask, enquire*

spey-wife   *female fortune-teller*

sprush   *spruce, smart*

stookie   *statue, scarecrow*

stramash   *upheaval, brawl*

stravaig   *wander*

stushie   *disturbance, fracas, fuss*

thegither   *together*

thirl   *subject, bind, enslave*

thocht   *thought*

thole   *endure*

thrapple   *throat*

thrawn   *crooked, contrary*

trod   *road, track*

tummle   *tumult*

twa-three   *a few*

unco   *unusual, exceedingly*

wabbit   *very tired, exhausted*

wanchancy   *unlucky, ill-fated*

wassock *fool, idiot, gawk*

watergaw *rainbow*

wean *child*

whaup *curlew*

wheen *small amount, several*

whilie *short while*

wi' *with*

wynd *alley*

yersel *yourself*

yestreen *yesterday evening*

yowes *ewes*

ACKNOWLEDGEMENTS

I am deeply grateful to John Wallace of Kirtlebridge for first drawing my attention to the Border Ballad 'Fair Helen of Kirkconnel Lea'. His walking tour of the principal sites and peel towers, filling me in on the history and families, made it real. His guidance, sense of personal connection, introductions and enthusiasm have been invaluable. Many thanks also to Alastair Moffat, font of Borders history, especially on the matter of horses. This book draws on his *The Reivers*, also on *The Steel Bonnets* by George MacDonald Fraser.

Andrew Dorward took me to Crichton Castle, corrected my history, and filled me in on aspects of the Scottish Reformation. Reading *The Swerve* by Stephen Greenblatt reawoke me to the extraordinary *On the Nature of Things* (*De Rerum Natura*); Sarah Bakewell's *How to Live: A Life of Montaigne in one question and twenty attempts at an answer* brought me to the *Essays* and into that man's life-enhancing company. In this at least Harry Langton's tastes are mine, though I do not possess an actor's prompt of

Love's Labours Won, which may yet be among Drummond of Hawthornden's papers.

Also a big thank you to the Royal Literary Fund, whose Fellowship at the Office of Lifelong Learning at Edinburgh University has greatly aided the writing of this book.